PRAISE FOR TIFFA
and her captivating novels . . .

"Tiffany Clare writes a swoon-worthy romance filled with rich details and vivid characters. Any readers wishing for a bold and sweeping historical romance need look no further—Tiffany Clare is a treasure of an author!"
— Lisa Kleypas, *New York Times* bestselling author

The Secret Desires of a Governess

"With its irrepressible heroine, deliciously dark and dangerous hero, and suitably atmospheric setting, Clare's latest impeccably written novel cleverly references the classic gothic romances of Victoria Holt and Madeleine Brent, while at the same time incorporating plenty of the steamy passion and lush sensuality found in today's brand of sexy historical romances." —*Booklist*

"With its brooding hero and dark backdrop Clare brings an updated gothic twist to her latest novel. By incorporating the themes and red herrings of a classic Victoria Holt or Daphne du Maurier, she entices readers to keep turning the pages to uncover the mystery and savor the highly sensual romance." —*RT Book Reviews*

"This is an entertaining throwback to the Victoria Holt legendary Gothic tales as Tiffany Clare employs all the elements from the innocent female, to the foreboding castle, to the brooding hero inside a romantic suspense thriller. Abby and Elliot are terrific lead characters while the support cast, especially his son, the villagers, and her family, make for a wonderful Victorian Gothic romance." —*Midwest Book Review*

"*The Secret Desires of a Governess* is excellent reading material for those who like their romance novel with explosive love scenes and a good solid plot." —*Fresh Fiction*

"Hauntingly sensual, *The Secret Desires of a Governess* is a compelling read that will have readers hoping for more." —*Single Titles*

The Seduction of His Wife

"In her second captivating historical romance, Clare turns up the sensual heat with a sizzling, sexy tale of a husband and wife engaged in a seductive battle of wits that proves to be splendidly entertaining." —*Booklist*

"Steamy." —*Publishers Weekly*

"The second chapter of Clare's trilogy is as bold and alluring as this exciting newcomer's first book. Clare takes a 'second chance at love' romance, twisting the theme into a highly sensual tale of passion and suspense. But there's also humor, created by secondary characters, and love to round out a tantalizing read." —*RT Book Reviews* (Top Pick)

"An arousing and amusing Victorian reverse romance!" —*Fresh Fiction*

"An exciting read that captivates the imagination and arouses the senses. Suspense, intrigue, and passion abound in this historical romance." —*Romance Junkies*

"[*The Seduction of His Wife*] will draw you in. . . . You'll find yourself riveted." —*Night Owl Reviews* (Top Pick)

"Tiffany Clare has penned another superb and masterfully crafted romance. *The Seduction of His Wife* has all that I love in a book: humor, suspense, sigh-inducing romance, and fan-your-face, sizzling sex scenes. Ms. Clare's first book, *The Surrender of a Lady*, was a bold and daring story, and her latest book is equally as entertaining. If you've never read a Tiffany Clare book, run to your nearest bookstore. You don't know what you're missing!"   —*Romance Dish*

The Surrender of a Lady

"A unique, unforgettable, sensual love story sweeping from the harems of the east to staid Victorian ballrooms. Watch out for this sizzling new talent to rise to the top."
                                                     —*RT Book Reviews*

"Exotic, bold, and captivating. Tiffany Clare's rich, sensual prose is delightful indulgence!"
        —Alexandra Hawkins, author of *All Night with a Rogue*

"Dazzling, daring, and different! Exotic and erotic! *The Surrender of a Lady* will have you turning the pages until you finish, no matter how late it gets. Tiffany Clare is a brilliant new talent in historical romance."
        —Anna Campbell, author of *Midnight's Wild Passion*

"Tiffany Clare has written an exceptionally exciting and heart-wrenching story of devotion and survival of a young mother, sold into the most despicable of circumstances… Fast-paced, full of suspense, and totally exciting with each turn of the page. A new and refreshing plot has been woven for the reader."   —*Fresh Fiction*

"Emotion-packed . . . a heartrending, very sensual historical romance that will touch your heart."   —*Romance Junkies*

Also by Tiffany Clare

Wicked Nights with a Proper Lady

The Secret Desires of a Governess

The Seduction of His Wife

The Surrender of a Lady

Midnight Temptations with a Forbidden Lord

TIFFANY CLARE

St. Martin's Paperbacks

This is a work of fiction. All of the characters, organizations, and events portrayed in this novel are either products of the author's imagination or are used fictitiously.

MIDNIGHT TEMPTATIONS WITH A FORBIDDEN LORD

Copyright © 2013 by Tiffany Clare.

For information address St. Martin's Press, 175 Fifth Avenue, New York, NY 10010.

ISBN: 978-1-250-00803-9

Printed in the United States of America

St. Martin's Paperbacks edition / May 2013

St. Martin's Paperbacks are published by St. Martin's Press, 175 Fifth Avenue, New York, NY 10010.

10 9 8 7 6 5 4 3 2 1

For Scott . . .

Chapter 1

London

If anyone were to guess what wickedness was going through Lady Charlotte Lindsey's mind, they'd usher her away from the ball and lock her in a room where she could cause no trouble to anyone, including herself. Thank goodness her thoughts were her own. Because the very moment society's biggest rogue strode into the ballroom, her plan moved from imagination to reality.

She hadn't thought she'd ever be given the opportunity

to take her future into her own hands; she had only hoped for the possibility.

The Marquess of Castleigh was tall and handsome with hair nearly as black as the evening sky and cut longer than fashionable. It was long enough that she wanted to run her fingers through it to see if it was as silky as it looked.

No, that didn't seem right. She did not *want to do any such thing.*

She tried to focus on her task and not on how his presence was throwing her off balance. Though they'd never been formally introduced, she knew precisely who he was. It helped that she read all the rags that described the exploits of the ton's deviants with regularity. For once, they'd done his appearance justice.

She had to force her gaze away from him to see who he had arrived with. His companions had reputations nearly as depraved as his, but she wasn't interested in any of them. She returned her attention to the marquess.

When she and Ariel had come up with a list of *potentials* to aid in her ruin, the marquess had been at the top for a number of reasons: he liked nothing more than biting his thumb at society; he had yet to reach the age of thirty so he wasn't likely to offer marriage; and—although she realized the point was shallow—he was devastatingly handsome. Perhaps the most sinfully attractive man she'd ever laid eyes upon. She would try not to allow that to unsettle her plan.

When she'd made up her list of roués, pulled from her three-year collection of *The Mayfair Chronicles,* the gossip surrounding the marquess was less . . . damning than that printed about the others. While some gentlemen were said to "make some misses puffy, rounded, and unmarriageable, if not forced to retire permanently to the country, or devastate the reputations of whole families by way of their charades," she thought the Marquess of Castleigh more interested in poking fun at society than in causing real injury to a lady's standing. And while she sought ruin, she didn't want to be hurt in the process of said ruin.

And how convenient for her was it that he was attending the duchess's ball this evening?

Of the three gentlemen to step into the room—the fourth in their set was the Dowager Countess of Fallon—Castleigh was by far the most arresting with his strong, sleek form and striking blue eyes that were accentuated by a fan of thick lashes and dark sculpted brows. Charlotte was convinced that his smile could melt a woman from the inside out in under a minute. Perhaps less, since she was halfway besotted although she'd laid eyes upon him only a few moments ago. She shook her head and tore her gaze away from his face to inspect the rest of him.

Aside from the heavily starched white cravat that was elaborately knotted at his throat, he wore black from head to toe. She doubted many men could pull off such a bold look. But he did it superbly.

With a flick of her wrist, Charlotte opened her fan and leaned closer to her dearest friend, Ariel, to whisper, "Look who has arrived."

Ariel's eyes widened, not with reservation but with anticipation of the events that were about to unfold.

"Oh, my." Ariel laughed behind her fan. "Mother will be having conniptions when she sets eyes upon *them*."

Ariel's mother was the biggest gossip in society and hated the slightest impropriety. If Lady Hargrove ever learned of the lengths to which Charlotte would go to stop her marriage to Mr. Warren—a man of her father's choosing—Charlotte would be sent to the country and hidden away until her wedding day.

Charlotte's focus returned to the young men vying for her and Ariel's attention. She gave Mr. Ellis, the youngest son of an earl and third in line for the title, a demure flutter of her lashes as he released her dance card with a shy smile. His hair was dark, his nose overly large, and his height admirable, but he was her age and probably only attending the ball because his mother had bid him to do so. He was also too kindhearted to be of help in stopping her marriage to Mr. Warren.

Mr. Torrance, a man of strong form and decidedly masculine features, stood next to Ariel. He had been by her friend's side since the season started. Though he was not titled and prattled on far too often in downright embarrassing verse, his feelings for Ariel seemed genuine. More importantly, both gentlemen were fine companions for enduring a dull ball.

Yet, how could she consider this a tedious affair when four well-known society degenerates had just joined the party? And, as luck would have it, the one she was interested in seemed to be heading directly toward her.

Charlotte clutched Ariel's wrist, trying to convey a silent message that this was her chance to change the course of the life her father had thoughtlessly mapped out for her. She was sure many young ladies would love to marry a man in line to inherit a title as blue and lucrative as that of the Earl of Fallon. They might even be willing to endure a solitary life—she'd heard Mr. Warren tell her father that she'd reside in the country after they were wed while he remained in London. It hurt that her father wanted to pair her with such a cruel, unloving man.

Needless to say, she and Mr. Warren had not started

off on the right foot. They were two completely opposing personalities; they did not share one hobby between them, and more importantly, she had a strong impulse to push him out of the carriage every time he took her through Hyde Park. Mr. Warren was high-handed, unkind, and she couldn't recall a single occasion where they'd had a decent conversation without one of them insulting the other. She'd rather meet some horrible end than be forced to marry him.

Hence the necessity of her plan.

She pasted on her most playful smile and lowered her fan marginally in coy invitation. Not only was the marquess headed in her direction, but his target seemed to be her and not the punch table she stood next to.

Ariel, her best friend since the age of five, understood precisely what Charlotte intended. Her friend nudged her forward with her shoulder. Not so hard that anyone would notice, just enough for Charlotte to take the hint that she needed to take action, not stand around fluttering her lashes like an infatuated fool.

Why should she give up the life she'd always thought to have because her father wanted a political alliance? Worse yet, her father well knew that she and Mr. Warren did not enjoy each other's company. She might have a great deal of respect for her father, but he'd gone too far this time.

It was now or never.

It was simple, really: the Marquess of Castleigh was a means to an end.

As though she needed a sign that she was taking the right step, the orchestra started a quadrille, which would be suitable for introducing herself and last long enough for her to make a good impression on the man. She hoped.

It was true that she was known for her outrageous boldness, but this move was monumental and had the potential to drastically change the course of her life. All for the better, she had to believe.

The marquess was quite focused on her, as if he had but one plan. She stepped forward with her heart in her throat, boldly threaded her arm through his, and turned them in the direction of the dance floor. This was pure insanity.

He stood quite a few inches taller than her, and he matched her gait smoothly as they walked into the throng of dancers and took their places.

"Good evening, my lord." She tried to find the words to introduce herself but the moment she looked into his icy blue eyes, she was suddenly speechless and her mouth as dry as the Saharan Desert. Goodness, he certainly was handsome, devastatingly so.

He quirked one brow and gave her a sinful smile that turned all her thoughts and intentions to mush.

With difficulty, she tore her gaze away from his once again and tried to suppress any vestige of nervousness that remained. It wasn't working. She felt a fine sheen of sweat on the palms of her hands inside her gloves and at her temple. The hair on her arms exposed to the air stood on end.

"I hope you don't mind that I've borrowed you for this dance." Her voice sounded whispery and pathetic to her own ears. This wasn't going as planned.

"Not at all, my lady." The timbre of the marquess's voice was as decadent as strawberries dipped in chocolate. "Shall we make introductions ourselves, or should we wait to be formally introduced despite our risqué partnering in this dance?"

A nervous laugh escaped her lips on hearing his teasing tone. She felt she was botching their first meeting, but couldn't seem to pull her wits together long enough to fix it.

"I do suppose we can skip formalities." She glanced at him from beneath her lashes, bewildered by her visceral reaction to his presence. She was never shy and nervous. What was it about the marquess that affected her in that way?

"A lady after my own heart." He bowed and she curtsied hesitantly as they took their positions amid the circle of dancers. Her stomach fluttered, causing her to miss the first steps into the dance. He would think her a buffoon before long if she didn't focus on her plan.

With a deep breath, she gathered what remaining courage she had and pulled on his arm, bidding him to lean closer to her ear. "Were you headed directly for me, or did I prevent you from reaching the punch table?"

She had to know whether he'd been the one to seek her out, that it wasn't her imagination.

His hand spanned over the small of her back as they walked forward. He kept a respectable distance so he wasn't touching her directly, but she could swear she felt the heat of his hand through her dress. They took their opposing partners' arms, turned in the center, and then met again on the other side.

"Perhaps I intercepted you before you could search out a family member." He looked around the room, as though wondering if she'd be stolen away by a concerned parent or chaperone.

Searching the sea of faces, she looked for her cousin who acted as her chaperone. Charlotte wasn't going against Genny's wishes by dancing with the marquess. Genny had only told her not to leave the room unattended. And she hadn't left the room . . .

Yet.

"My cousin attended the ball with me." Why was she telling him that?

"Ah," he said, unable to say more when their formation changed again. Perhaps this type of dance wasn't the best way to introduce herself to him after all.

They moved forward with the other dancers, switching partners to spin around the center of the circle. Each time the marquess's arm snaked around hers, Charlotte's heart jolted with a shock of excitement.

"Allow me to present myself." They were still paired and turning arm in arm in their own private circle. "Tristan Bradley, the Marquess of Castleigh." He dipped his head with his introduction.

She gave him a slow smile, knowing her dimples were showing and hating that she couldn't better school her features in his presence. "I know precisely who you are, my lord."

They stopped on the outskirts of their circle as they waited their turn to join in the dance again.

"Does my reputation precede me even among the young misses moving in society for the first time?"

"I doubt there is anyone in the room who doesn't know of you." She inched close enough to him for her shoulder to press against his chest. He was very firm and didn't seem to mind their proximity. However, she thought it odd that no one had noticed her dancing with the marquess.

"I'm always happy to be singled out."

"Perhaps I shouldn't have been so bold as to dance with you?"

His hand stroked the length of her arm as their positions changed. "I couldn't agree with that. I suggest you dance the night away to your heart's content."

He had both her hands so she ducked her head again. "My name is Charlotte Lindsey. My father is the Earl of Ponsley."

"It is a pleasure to make your acquaintance, Lady Charlotte." With a gentle squeeze of her hand he continued to lead her through the dance.

When she partnered with him again on the other side of the circle, he placed his hand firmly over the small of her back in what could not be mistaken as simple positioning for their dance. This time she knew it was not her imagination; she felt the warmth of his hand through every layer of silk and linen and even through the boning in her corset. His fingers ran the length of the buttons that disappeared under the bow tied at the base of her back, and she felt herself sway a little closer to him. She was *not* the swooning type, but the very idea of this man carrying her away stole all the breath from her lungs.

She had a moment of clarity when she recalled the reason she was dancing with the marquess, and put a few inches between them. She simply wanted him to regard her favorably so she could ask for his assistance in her ruin. And if she was to accomplish that, she must remain in control of her errant thoughts. She would not be swayed from her goal, despite being unsettled so easily by this particular man.

Perhaps she should look over the other names on her list again? She rejected the idea just as quickly as it had come to her. No one else would do now. And why was that?

"Now that introductions are out of the way, may I request a favor?" she asked, feeling brave and bold again.

"I aim only to please you." As they turned, he reached up quickly and pushed one of her wayward curls back from her forehead.

Each touch made her falter. He was a step ahead of her in the game they played, and it was supposed to be the other way around.

"I don't think anyone is as shocked as they should be that you stole a dance from me not three minutes into your arrival." She pouted her bottom lip in a show of disappointment. "Will you take another dance with me?"

He laughed; the sound was deep, reverberating through the length of her body. Admittedly, her knees weakened for the briefest of moments, but her resolve to succeed in her goal made her back stiffen and her arms grow rigid.

"So your only desire is for our names to be printed side by side in the gossip sheets?" He hitched her closer so that she was nearly pressed against the solid warmth of his body. They might not be touching, but his heat surrounded her like a much-needed blanket on a cold winter's night. When she took in a deep breath, her chest surged against his unintentionally. This time it was he who seemed shocked by her boldness, for his hand briefly tightened around hers.

"Well, not necessarily with *you*." She winked at him and spread her fingers over his shoulder, feeling the latent strength and muscle beneath. "I suppose *any* of your friends would do for what I have in mind."

She glanced over toward the outskirts of the dance floor at one of his friends who was conversing with her cousin.

She missed a step and the marquess had to right her direction. How could her cousin possibly know that man? Genny looked irritated and a flush colored her cheeks as she spoke to the marquess's friend. If there was one thing

Charlotte knew well it was that Genny never did something so simple as converse; she lectured, and all the while the man standing with her merely smiled.

The marquess's hand tightened around hers again, drawing her attention away from her cousin. "You're far too young to understand the game you're playing."

His smile slipped for a moment and the intensity in his eyes felt dangerous and had her breath stilling in her lungs as she studied him.

"I wouldn't call this a game."

A game implied unmitigated amusement. This was more like a mission, or better yet a goal and a desire so deep she couldn't imagine not accomplishing her ruin by the time the summer season ended.

"Then why did you seem so insistent that we dance?"

"I'm merely experiencing all that life has to offer." Though she wasn't so sure about that sentiment, courting the marquess was not about self-indulgence—all right, that wasn't quite true, either, because she was sure the marquess would be far more amusing and a lot more fun to spend time with than Mr. Warren.

"You're young. What makes you rush life along when it happens regardless?"

"Am I a mere child in your eyes?" She suddenly felt gauche.

Perhaps this task wouldn't be as easy as she had originally thought. Maybe he wasn't interested in debutantes, but women more experienced with intimacy? Now that she thought about it, she couldn't remember a single debutante being tied to his name.

"Definitely *not* a child." There was an assurance in his words that settled her flagging nerves. "But I am curious to know what secrets you harbor, my lady."

"If we ladies weren't mysterious, men might grow bored with us."

"That's simply not possible."

The marquess turned her suddenly, his leg going between hers as they neared the edge of the dance floor and approached her cousin. The position was intimate and telling, but his direction baffling. If he wanted to act daring and shock her with bold behavior, why not whisk her out of the room altogether?

She tightened her hold on his hand and pressed the front of her body against his before they parted on another turn. She would not give him the opportunity to think her inexperienced. She must be brazen, and she could not waver in the path she'd decided on for even a moment. The simple truth was: the Marquess of Castleigh would play his part. And she'd find a way to endear him before she could change her mind and before he could think better of his actions.

She needed to act quickly because she had only two choices and each would lead her down very different paths. She could face ruination with the marquess or marry a man she loathed.

Chapter 2

Is there a man more wicked than the Marquess of C——? There's not a scandal that goes by during the season without his name mentioned as the cause. His lordship has a tendency to find trouble wherever he goes but always manages to avoid condemnation for his acts. Perhaps it is his charm and fine form that so easily trick society into seeing an angel where the devil really stands.

—*The Mayfair Chronicles*, May 1846

Since when did a debutante seek him out two months into the season? There was trickery at play here, and Tristan didn't like to be made a fool. He hated to admit it, but Lady Charlotte's boldness did far more than simply unsettle him.

It might be better to cut his losses, find his friends, leave this debutante party far behind him, and pretend he'd never introduced himself to the formidable young lady in his arms. But if he did that, she'd seek out another, and that was unacceptable to him even though he didn't quite know what game she played.

Tristan looked over the crush of guests in search of the friends he'd arrived with. Leo stood conversing with a plainly attired woman on the other side of the dance floor. Tristan did not recognize her. His friend Jezebel, who also happened to be the woman responsible for his attendance at the duchess's ball tonight, was nowhere in sight. She was probably in the gaming room gambling away the last bit of her pin money, with Hayden not far behind trying to preserve what little of Jez's reputation remained intact.

They'd come with one purpose in mind: to win the favor of the Ponsley chit and stop her marriage to Mr. Warren. Warren was in line to obtain Jez's fortune now that her husband was dead, and Jez assured them that the successor to the Fallon title was no kinder than her late husband had been—a cruel man and an abuser of women and those less fortunate.

Revenge was fine and dandy, but Tristan had a very personal reason to involve himself in Jez's charade. It just so happened that he had a vendetta against Warren, one that was older than the Fallon fortune feud.

This was his opportunity for retribution.

Yet, since Lady Charlotte had approached him, the business at hand seemed suddenly . . . unfavorable. Especially since the young lady had sought him out the moment he'd entered the ballroom. So what was her game? He was torn about what decision was the right one to make. Stay and find out her next move or leave well enough alone and forget the whole Warren business? The latter was unlikely to happen, so he needed to figure out what he was going to do with the chit on his arm whether she unsettled him or not.

When the next dance started, he didn't stop twirling

her around the floor to seek out her family, as most gentlemen would inevitably do. Though many might argue whether he was a gentleman. He was known among the ladies as the biggest player society had produced of late, and rightly so since he filled that particular role with relish, liking that he could sample new fare as he pleased.

Focused on Lady Charlotte, he took in her youthful appearance. Having had plenty of experience with the fairer sex, he guessed her to be less than twenty and far too knowledgeable about the male sex for someone of her age.

Her complexion was fair, and he detected a hint of maquillage dusted over her cheekbones. Her eyes shone the darkest blue of the Adriatic Sea, and were highlighted by bountiful dark lashes and finely shaped brows in her oval-shaped face. Tight ringlets fell on either side of her temples, the color a rich chestnut with a strong hint of red that suggested she spent a great deal of time outdoors. Her complexion was nicely set off against the emerald gown that swept off her shoulders front and back. Her wealth was displayed in the extravagant necklace about her throat; the acorn-sized emerald fell enticingly between her breasts.

She was taller than most ladies of his acquaintance and slender in form. A pretty woman to be sure, and if handsome looks were enough to attract him to someone, he'd steal her out of the ballroom right this instant.

Rubbing along with someone required a deeper, non-aesthetic connection, no matter how enjoyable rubbing along might be. Besides, a successful seduction took time and he was a very patient man. And by all accounts, it appeared that Lady Charlotte wanted and expected to be seduced by him. And while he preferred women to be direct, her boldness almost worried him.

"Your cousin looks positively irate," he mused aloud.

Lady Charlotte's relation stood on the edge of the dance floor, staring at Leo with her hands clenched at her sides. She was of average height, wore her dark hair in a simple bun, and dressed like the matrons in the room who were thirty years her senior, a pristine image of virtue.

"She's also my chaperone." Charlotte looked over his shoulder to better see them. "Is she conversing with Lord Barrington?"

"You know us so well," he said drolly. It shouldn't surprise him that she knew of Leo since she had already singled Tristan out in a room half filled with men far more eligible and less likely to cause a scandal.

He didn't miss the spark of mischief that lit her eyes when she focused on his face again. "Everyone knows him, my lord."

While women often threw themselves in his direction for an enjoyable affair—and he had no qualms about that—debutantes either shied away from him, or were cloistered by overprotective mamas. He wasn't sure how he felt about the reversal in their roles, but he felt she should be better shielded from men like him, hence his reason for not leaving her side; he'd not leave her open for the advances of another rogue.

While he might have promised Jez that he would sway Lady Charlotte away from an alliance with Mr. Warren, he questioned the chit's odd willingness to throw so much caution to the wind. True, she was only making his task easier, but it made him pause for the first time in his life and question his role in this. It was oddly disconcerting to be held accountable for his own actions.

Twirling her about in the next set—a couple's dance instead of a group dance—he rested his hand just above the bow at the base of her back and held her firmly against his body. He told himself the daring position was to test her courage in whatever game she played and not to draw her attention away from Barrington.

Where was his calm equilibrium when he needed it most? One thing he was certain of: Lady Charlotte would never look upon Leo as though he could be her salvation; in fact, he'd ensure she never again spared his friend another thought. He'd found her first and had no intention of relinquishing her to any other gentleman in the room.

The one thing Charlotte hadn't clearly thought out in this scheme was how she would actually stage her ruin. And though she was unsure of what exactly complete ruin entailed on her part, she knew she needed the marquess to succeed. The worse the reputation of her partner in crime, the harder she would fall. She did not want to be redeemed by a hasty marriage with Mr. Warren.

One had to wonder how many young ladies had contemplated their own ruin because of an undesirable match set up by their father or mother. A small pang of regret for what she was doing made her falter. The marquess tightened his hold as he steadied her.

"Has someone flavored the punch with alcohol?" he asked.

She gave a weak laugh. Had it been, she was sure her resolve wouldn't waver in the slightest. "How embarrassing to have to admit this, but I'm feeling a little overexerted."

She glanced down as though shocked she'd admitted such a thing. A lady should never reveal such weakness when partnered with a man like the marquess. Would he realize why she'd mentioned fatigue?

Conveniently, a breeze filtered through the doors that opened to the garden, bringing with it the intoxicating scent of peonies and lilacs. The marquess spun her away from the dark balcony and toward the punch table.

"Let's get you freshened up, shall we?"

"I—I . . ." She scrambled for an excuse; something to draw him toward the darkness just beyond the French doors that were so close. "I have already partaken of that bland concoction they call refreshment. Perhaps the evening air will do me good."

"And bring our acquaintance to such an abrupt conclusion?"

"It's only a little air," she shot back, more than miffed that her plan was slowly unraveling. Did he not understand her intent or was he simply avoiding putting her in a compromising position?

And then he laughed as though he understood the precise reason for her annoyance. "Introduce me to this cousin of yours. She seems to be having a heated conversation with Barrington that I fully intend to interrupt."

He wanted to meet her cousin? Did he have designs on her? Yes, Genny was pretty, but she always dressed like a spinster who had no hope of ever finding a husband. Genny was like a chameleon, always blending into the background. And though Charlotte had offered to lend her dresses—they could easily hem them for the evening—her cousin had refused, preferring her plain clothes so she could remain unnoticed.

"Ah," the marquess said, looking over Charlotte's shoulder, "it seems she's found a dance partner in Barrington."

Charlotte whipped her head around, searching for Genny. Dancing? Her cousin did *not* dance. Not once since the season started had she done so; not even when Charlotte's dance instructor came to the house did Genny indicate she could or even liked to dance.

As the marquess led Charlotte off the dance floor, Lord Barrington boldly took Genny's hand and pushed her into a fast-paced mazurka. Charlotte stood on the edge, her mouth slightly ajar. She barely noticed that the marquess's arm threaded through hers to guide her in another direction.

"Hmm," Lord Castleigh said. "What is your cousin's name?"

"Genevieve Camden." She pushed a curl back from her temple in frustration. She wasn't sure how she felt to see that all eyes were on Genny now and not on her while she was on the arm of the Marquess of Castleigh. How could she get the gossipmongers whispering about her if they paid her no mind? The evening was turning into a disaster.

"I never forget a face, so I'm not sure how it is I'm not recalling this magnificent woman who's caught Leo's eye."

"I doubt they know each other."

And what made Genny so *magnificent*? Lord Castleigh was supposed to be enamored with *her,* not her cousin. Charlotte should not be envious because her cousin seemed to attract the attention of two roués, both of whom were handsome and titled . . . and perfect for carrying out Charlotte's plan. Actually, she should be jealous. If her cousin attracted rakes so easily, there would be no one left on Charlotte's list—which admittedly had been shortened considerably, with names crossed off for one reason or another, leaving only four potentials.

She looked at her dance partner and unwilling abductor—why couldn't he have whisked her off into complete privacy? Staring at his knowing expression, and his kind eyes, she realized there were no longer four potentials on her list. Just one.

Her goal felt so close yet so far. But failure was not an option.

With a sweet smile and her attention solely focused on the marquess, she said, "I think I will partake in a refreshment, my lord."

"Excellent." He turned them toward the banquet table with its assortment of punches and tiered trays of fruit, cheese, bite-sized pastries, and other desserts.

"The lemonade or the red punch?" he offered.

"It's probably best we have the lemonade. The punch tastes like sweetened water."

"How about . . ." The marquess reached toward the back where flutes of champagne were lined up in two neat rows. Procuring the fizzing liquid, he handed her one.

"I shouldn't—" she started to say but stopped. Why shouldn't she? If she was going to go down the path she'd chosen, she might as well enjoy it to the fullest. "Thank you. I've never had champagne before."

"All the more reason to try it." He tilted his head with a sly grin playing on his lips and tapped their glasses lightly together.

"How correct you are." She mirrored his move, then put the glass to her lips. Papa could not abide drink of any sort. How wicked she felt. And she'd never have dreamed of doing this a few short minutes ago. Perhaps the marquess *was* a bad influence.

The aroma of the champagne was pleasant, and she didn't wait for him to drink before taking her first sip. The flavor that exploded on her tongue was marvelous. Sweet yet dry and bursting with bubbles that tickled all the way down her throat.

The marquess stared at her as though no one else in the room existed. This was exactly what she wanted—his complete and undivided attention.

Oddly enough, no one noticed them, not even Lady Hargrove, so she took advantage of the temporary privacy by tipping her glass against her lips and draining the contents of the glass.

A hiccough came immediately afterward, surprising a giggle out of her—or maybe it was the bubbles that made her giddy. No, she thought, looking at the marquess's intent gaze; it was the man before her that made her feel so oddly out of sorts.

"Another, my lady?" The marquess didn't seem surprised by her gluttonous display.

She held the glass between two hands and shook her head. "Oh, definitely not." She wasn't sure if the drink had made her light-headed or if swallowing it all in one breath had done that.

She felt rather fantastic.

"I take it you are no longer parched?" he teased.

"Not for champagne." She pressed her fingers to her mouth. It might be normal for her to say things others might not, but innuendo was something she was careful with.

The marquess stepped closer and plucked the glass from her hands to give it to a passing footman. "That I can promise another time."

She had to look away from the intensity of his gaze. It would be so easy to fall into those depths and commit to some very dangerous and sultry things. What she needed was a change in topic. "Why haven't I seen you at any engagements before now, my lord?"

"Had I known this year wouldn't be all bland affairs and dull company, I'd have come out sooner."

"Will you be at the Carletons' tomorrow evening?"

He seemed to think on that for a moment. "It will be a good event to attend if you are among the company."

"I will be there. My cousin knows the Carletons well, and they extended an invitation to my whole family." Her father did not like the Carletons, but he could not outright refuse an invite from people as socially connected as they were. "Though only Genny and I will be attending."

"I look forward to another night in your company." The marquess paused to look at something over her shoulder, and his smile became devilish. "Your cousin will be joining us momentarily."

Charlotte turned, shoulders back, and watched her cousin approach with the earl following closely behind her. Her cousin's face was slightly pinched, her color high, and she looked far from happy to have engaged in a dance with Lord Barrington.

Charlotte needed to figure out how to diffuse this situation so she wouldn't have to say good-bye to the marquess quite yet. Without a doubt, her cousin would object to Charlotte's escort.

"We are needed elsewhere." Genny slid her arm through Charlotte's. Would her cousin drag her away if she refused to go with her?

Charlotte stood firm and made it clear that she would not move. "Cousin, you are being discourteous." Genny seemed stunned that Charlotte had openly reprimanded her. "Let me introduce you to the Marquess of Castleigh."

If such a thing were possible, her cousin appeared to become even more irate. Although Charlotte hardly cared that introducing a lord of Castleigh's rank wasn't something a debutante, especially one of lower standing, should ever do.

The marquess bowed to her cousin and took Genny's hand. "It's a pleasure to make the acquaintance of the two most beautiful women at the ball. And to have you both to myself."

"I know precisely who the Marquess of Castleigh is." Genny said this to Charlotte, as though the marquess wasn't standing before them. "You'll do well to know, cousin, that his type is better suited to those found in a den of iniquity as opposed to a respectable ball." She tugged at Charlotte's arm, quite insistent that she should come with her. "Lady Carleton wanted to discuss the seating arrangements for her upcoming dinner party."

"Firmly rebuffed, I daresay," the marquess said, laughter and amusement thick in his voice despite the rudeness he'd just been subjected to.

What in the world had come over her cousin?

"Why should I have any say on her seating plans? You're being incredibly rude, cousin. Apologize for your brash words at once."

The way Genny acted was embarrassing. And the fact that her cousin treated Charlotte as if she were a girl still attached to apron strings stung a great deal more than she wanted to admit. The worst part was that Genny was treating her like a child in front of the marquess.

"I am positive that Lord Castleigh and Lord Barrington are not in the least offended. After all, I only speak the truth. Don't I, gentlemen?" Genny looked to both lords for support.

"How could I ever forget that you had such a sharp bite, Miss Camden?" the earl finally said.

So they did know each other. Charlotte stood taller, suddenly curious. How did she not know that her cousin was so well connected? Aside from the Carletons being close friends of Genny's, it seemed she also knew the Earl of Barrington. Whatever the reason for Genny's sudden bad mood, it did not excuse poor behavior.

"Perhaps if more names were to fill your dance card, you'd understand what fine gentlemen these are—but that's right, *you* don't have a dance card, do you?" Charlotte jerked her gaze away from Genny, her cheeks heated.

That had come out far harsher than she had intended, but she was growing irrationally annoyed that her plan was failing at every turn. Maybe she'd chosen the wrong man to aid her in her ruin? Maybe she would have to go back to *the list* and pick another name. But she didn't really wish to pick anyone else. Not now that she'd met the marquess.

"Take another turn around the room with me, Miss Camden," Lord Barrington suggested to her cousin. His tone brooked no refusal.

"The attendees might think you intend something of a permanent nature where I'm concerned, Barrington." Genny raised an inquisitive brow.

"No dancing, I promise. Just a few words shared between friends of old."

Charlotte liked this plan a great deal, so she slid away from Genny to draw closer to the marquess. Lord Barrington didn't seem likely to take no for an answer, and if he were to steal her cousin away, Charlotte would . . . she would what? Convince the marquess to take her to the balcony where they would ensconce themselves in a hidden alcove? Maybe she should just ask the marquess for his help? No, she couldn't do that, not when he might refuse.

"And leave Charlotte in the clutches of your friend?" Genny said.

Charlotte opened her mouth to defend herself and the

marquess, but Lord Barrington addressed his friend before she could speak.

"Keep company with Lady Charlotte while I take Miss Camden around the room. We'll be but a moment."

The earl didn't wait for an answer before stealing Genny away.

"I had no idea my cousin and Lord Barrington were so well acquainted." She watched the earl and her cousin, slightly baffled by the connection. Where would Genny have met such a distinguished member of the ton?

"If ever there was a woman to fear, she'd be that woman." The marquess chuckled as he straightened the cuff of his jacket. "I suppose we'll wait right here."

She glanced at him, surprised by his willingness to do exactly as Genny demanded. "Do you generally do what you are told to do?"

"No, but I do not wish to cross swords with your cousin. I fear she'd dance circles around me and have me disarmed before I could raise any sort of defense."

And wasn't that the truth.

A night that had suddenly been in her favor was quickly turning to disappointment. Here she stood with the Marquess of Castleigh, society's biggest rogue, and he trembled in fear at the thought of sparring with Genny.

Charlotte flicked her fan open and thought out her next move. If the marquess attended dinner at the Carletons' tomorrow evening, she'd find a way to get him alone, with her cousin far removed from the picture.

Tristan sat next to Hayden and across from Leo and Jez in the carriage. They'd left the duchess's ball after Jez had thought it necessary to yell obscenities at Mr. Torrance and disturb everyone in the games room. The impudent man had insulted her, called her insensitive, and then he went on to question how she could enjoy a night out when her husband wasn't yet cold in his grave. She'd given him many reasons that had ladies running out of the room with their hands over their ears, and gentlemen tsking at her and removing those women too stunned to leave of their own accord. He wished he'd been in the games room to defend Jez.

It didn't matter to Tristan that their group had been forced to leave the ball after only being there for a mere hour. The lady they intended to finagle away from Mr. Warren had left fifteen minutes prior to them, and the rest of the company at the ball was overly dull. Tristan rested his head on the back of the seat and stretched his legs out, his right shin pressed against Jez's skirts.

The Ponsley chit had trouble written all over her. He'd have to handle her with kid gloves so he didn't well and truly ruin her. He didn't think it was his imagination that she was determined to have him ruin her good name. There was a moment as they danced when he'd sensed her desire to sequester him in the darkness of the gardens.

He was too practiced with the fairer sex to fall for such a ruse, and instead he had maneuvered her in another, much safer direction. While he was considered a man of loose morals, he did not simply indulge at the first presented opportunity, especially where women were concerned. Women should be seduced over time so that they were savored to the fullest.

It was also odd that a debutante would specifically seek him out, and he had to know why Lady Charlotte had done so. Was she already engaged to Mr. Warren and perhaps enlightened to the man's true character? Not possible, since a debutante wouldn't be privy to the same information he was.

Jez had given Tristan the impression that their nuptials hadn't been announced and wouldn't be for some time. Perhaps the young lady just liked to live dangerously. His own name was printed often enough in the scandal sheets for doing precisely that . . . Still, he was determined to know what deviousness Lady Charlotte had planned and why.

Turning his head to the side, he noted that Hayden's expression was dour, concerned even. Leo's gaze seemed contemplative as he stared out at the passing scenery, which Tristan thought had more to do with one devil-tongued chaperone than Jez's current predicament.

"The night is still young, and midnight not yet rung." Jez leaned her head back on the leather seat, mimicking his position. Despite her request to keep going tonight, her eyes were at half-mast from exhaustion. "Whatever will we do to occupy ourselves?"

"Anything you like," Tristan said, not sure why he had agreed to any such commitment when Jez clearly needed to sleep.

Maybe she didn't want to be alone tonight? Or maybe she needed the comfort and support of her friends a while longer. Though she did not grieve for her dead husband— the man had been a vile prick—she obviously lamented the loss of the richly afforded life she'd been accustomed to.

Leo's focus returned to them. "I have a bottle of rum in my study that hasn't been cracked open yet."

"You'll be attending the Carletons' tomorrow and you think it wise to drink a bottle of rum so late in the evening? You'll be three sheets to the wind when you wake up in the morning." Hayden's tone was stern, though his anger seemed directed at Jez and not Leo or Tristan.

"You're turning into your father," Tristan pointed out as the carriage rolled to a stop in front of Leo's town-house—where they usually congregated when they weren't causing mischief about Town.

"You're simply angry that I lost my temper with that cad, Mr. Torrance," Jez said defensively.

"Angry? Simply angry? You've bloody well lost your mind to do what you did tonight, Jez." Hayden remained calm as he lectured Jez, but his gloved hand squeezed the black jade eagle head atop his cane. "You're your own worst enemy; you cannot be so brash and unpredictable without your husband's name to protect you."

"Come now," Tristan interjected. "She'll be excused for any wrongdoing or minor blowouts since her husband has *just* died. Everyone will think that she is grieving."

Hayden glared back at Tristan as he shoved his hat on his head. "I wish that were the truth. I'll bid you all a good night. Unlike you lot, I have obligations in the morn-ing." Pointing the top end of his cane in Jez's direction, he added, "Don't forget our appointment in the morning. Unless you don't care that your husband's fortune may soon be forever out of reach."

Jez rolled her eyes, pushed the carriage door open, and grabbed Hayden's sleeve to drag him down the steps be-hind her.

"Stop being so dramatic and join us for one toast. We must celebrate my newfound freedom." Jez pouted out her bottom lip. "Don't be mad, darling, I've had a dread-ful week."

Hayden removed his hat again and scratched the back

of his blond-topped head. "One drink, Jez. Then I have to be off."

Jez gave them all a winning smile and she seemed much more her radiant self for a moment.

Hayden stayed for three shots and left, and then Tristan, Jez, and Leo sang bawdy songs for God knew how long— until the rum ran out, he thought.

The better plan would have been to call it a night as Hayden had originally suggested. Tristan wasn't sure how he made it home, but he woke in a bath of sunlight, his half-clothed body tangled in the sheets, and his head feeling as if it were squeezed in a vise.

Chapter 3

Those fortunate enough to receive an invitation for the revered Lady C——'s evening soirees often find themselves embroiled in the gossip of the season. My fingers tingle in anticipation of the scandals to arise from such a motley crew . . .
— *The Mayfair Chronicles,* May 1846

It was unfortunate that Mr. Warren thought it necessary to visit her at all. She'd been daydreaming about her previous evening's adventure when the maid had come to tell her that he awaited her in the parlor.

Gathering every ounce of courage she had, Charlotte sat at the vanity, leaned close to the mirror, and pinched her cheeks to bring some color to them. She smoothed out her skirts—she hadn't had time to change out of her checked walking dress—and spritzed water over her hair to flatten the flyaway strands.

Why she cared about her appearance at all she couldn't say. Only, she didn't want Mr. Warren to make some snide remark about her looking unkempt when she would one day be a countess in a prestigious household.

Genny was waiting for her when she opened her bedchamber door, and Charlotte released a sigh of relief that she wouldn't have to go downstairs and face him alone. Her cousin hadn't had time to change out of her walking dress, either, so hopefully Mr. Warren wouldn't comment on her being inappropriately attired as he'd done in the past.

"Did you know he planned to visit us today?" she asked her cousin.

"I think he came because he was not present at the duchess's ball last night."

She'd nearly forgotten he was supposed to be there. Perhaps it was better that he came this afternoon rather than finding her in the arms of the marquess last night. What would he think if he learned that she intended to attract the attention of a certain marquess?

She thought she could tolerate fifteen minutes with the odious Mr. Warren considering everything wonderful that had happened the previous night.

"Let us get on with it then." She motioned toward the staircase and they started walking in the direction of the parlor.

"He's not so dreadful as you make him out to be." Genny defended him far too often.

One of Charlotte's brows rose in disbelief. "You don't seriously believe that, do you? He's always arguing with me and pointing out my flaws. I'm sure if we married he'd see more reason to criticize me."

"He's come into the Fallon estate quite unexpectedly, so he has a lot on his mind. Be kind to him, Charlotte. He'll come around when things settle in his life."

Why did her cousin side with him at all? Was it because she'd never found a husband and had been a companion for family members since her last failed season? It was understandable that her cousin didn't want the same thing for Charlotte, but unfortunately that was not how Charlotte felt—she quite liked the idea of being free, of making her own decisions.

"I'll call for tea and sandwiches," Genny said. "That'll give you a moment of privacy. Endear yourself to him, Charlotte. I know you can if you put your mind to it."

She didn't want to endear herself to *that* man in any way—she wanted him very much out of her life. Charlotte reached for her cousin's hand before she could make arrangements with the kitchen. "You'll sit with me before long, won't you?"

"Yes, once the tea is prepared." At Charlotte's distressed expression, Genny added, "The parlor door will remain open while I make arrangements, of course." And before Charlotte could grab her cousin again, Genny was heading away from her and toward the kitchens.

She took a deep breath and mentally prepared herself for the battle of words sure to come the moment she stepped into the parlor, and slid the door fully open. She had no qualms about the rest of the household hearing their conversation; maybe they'd understand just how vile a man he truly was and try to convince her father that their match wasn't worth the trouble it was sure to cause in the end.

"Mr. Warren. How kind of you to stop by." She dipped her head as she greeted him. The polite action necessitated by her cousin's parting words that she try and be civil. "Genny is instructing the kitchen to prepare tea and sandwiches. She'll join us momentarily."

"We're to announce our engagement soon, so it won't do for me to not pay you a visit."

Mr. Warren stood next to the mantel, his dark, imposing frame overly pressed and too primly perfect. She wished she could roll him down a hill so that he was rumpled and not as well put together—something he'd probably never been in his whole life. He was taller than her by at least four inches and Charlotte had always been tall for a lady.

There was nothing spectacular about his appearance to set him apart from anyone else of her acquaintance. Perhaps she'd find him handsome if he weren't such an ass. His hair was a thick wave of brown that looked smeared in soot it was so dark. And though he wasn't yet an earl, and had probably never expected to be one, Genny had told her on many occasions that she thought him dashing.

Maybe *Genny* should marry him.

His lips were on the thin side, his teeth were brilliantly white, and he had a full smile she did not trust.

The thought of their engagement still made her face screw up in displeasure; she simply couldn't help the reaction since it was so distasteful to her.

"And here I thought you wanted to see me."

"Don't be absurd." His expression seemed almost appalled at the very idea of enjoying her company.

Why should she try to be civil when Mr. Warren didn't seem to have a civil bone in his body?

"You know how important it is to keep up appearances," he said. "What should anyone of worth think if I hadn't called on you once before the announcement is made in the papers?"

"You're right."

"Yes, I always am. You needn't question my judgment about anything."

Pompous ass.

"I constantly question your reason for this farce you insist on calling courting."

"I only visit you at your father's insistence."

"How kind of you to think of my feelings."

"Kindness has nothing to do with it. And feelings are solely a woman's prerogative, and have nothing to do with the better sex." He tapped his fingers almost impatiently along the mantel. "You'll learn your place and to save your feelings for any children we have."

Was she so terrible a person to warrant such cruel treatment from him? She'd never really met anyone who disliked her on first meeting her.

He pulled out his watch and looked at the time. He must be in a hurry, which was fine by her.

"Do you have somewhere else you need to be, Mr. Warren? Don't let me keep you from any engagements."

"I'll stay the allotted fifteen minutes for tea."

What a shame he wasn't in a rush to leave.

She motioned toward the settees in the room. "Would you like to sit with me for a spell?"

He took the seat opposite hers and stared at her oddly.

Charlotte had to fold her hands in her lap lest she fidget under his inspection.

"Were you out walking?"

Charlotte looked down at her dress. "Genny and I shopped along Bond Street."

"I always thought high society fashion and the necessity for fripperies excessive. I suppose there is nothing to be done about it if we're to keep up appearances."

"How very practical of you."

Why did Mr. Warren entertain the idea of marrying her when he so obviously disdained her? Genny arrived before long and Charlotte suffered through the next fifteen minutes of bland conversation, thinking the whole time about the duchess's ball and a very different man from the one sitting across from her. Any life would be better than a life where she'd be forever known as Fallon's wife. She'd find a way to stop the wedding and hopefully soon so she wouldn't ever again have to sit the allotted fifteen minutes for tea with him.

While this might be Charlotte's third Carleton event of the season, she realized for the first time that the marquess hadn't actually attended any of the previous gatherings. She refused to think that he was unable to secure an invitation for the dinner party tonight. She was positive that she had captivated him just as much as he had intrigued her; he'd find a way.

Her gaze strayed to the entrance where guests came into the grandly appointed parlor. Would the marquess wander through shortly with his refined air and dashing image?

Why was she obsessing over a man she barely knew? Maybe the fascination lay solely in what she might uncover about his character?

Not in all her life had she ever been so attuned to one person. Aside from the fact that the marquess's dangerous reputation interested her, she wondered if all rogues had a clever way with words and actions that attracted the innocent so easily. What a ninny she was. Of course they did; that was how they garnered the status of rogue in the first place.

Ariel nudged her elbow lightly into Charlotte's side.

"I'm so sorry." Charlotte placed her hand on Lady Hargrove's gloved forearm as she returned her focus to those she stood with. "What was it you asked?"

She really was allocating too many of her thoughts to the marquess. She should not be the one wholly consumed by him. It should be the other way around if she was to convince him to aid her in her ruin.

"Dearest, you are rather distracted this evening." Concern weighed heavily on the older woman's brows. "Perhaps your laces are drawn too tightly."

Charlotte glanced down at her dress with a sigh; it was senseless to argue with Ariel's mother. The fashion this year was to cinch one's waist to but a handspan. She'd succeeded in doing just that and had gone to great trouble to pick a perfectly demure yet sophisticated blush-rose silk gown that swept off her shoulders and belled out around her elbows. It was ruched over the front bodice with a fine lace overlay. Extra material gathered at both her hips and draped behind her in a train that hit the floor and flourished outward.

This was no simple evening dress by any means, but one meant to entice and to present the wearer in such a way as to appear larger than life. She would not chance Castleigh looking at any other woman present.

Charlotte clasped her folded fan tightly. Lady Hargrove was exactly the type of mother you cringed at the thought of being your own. She treated everyone as inferior, including her own daughter, and often said things that demeaned another's character. But her husband was well connected, even if they weren't as well set financially as some of the other members of the ton.

Because Ariel was her best friend—they'd attended the same boarding school for young ladies—Charlotte allowed the countess to address her as if she were a second daughter under her tutelage, with no sense of how to move in society without the older woman's intrusive guidance.

Charlotte offered a smile. "I must apologize for my inattentiveness. Rest assured I will take advantage of the ladies' resting room once dinner has concluded."

And when she knew whether or not Castleigh attended this evening. Because if he did join the dinner party, the only place she planned to hie off to was somewhere secluded to better acquaint herself with him. She had come to a decision last night when she'd gone to bed: she wouldn't simply deceive the marquess—he didn't seem easy to fool—she would make an ally of him.

"Excellent, dear, I wouldn't want you feeling faint."

Ariel's lips twitched; she was used to her mother's caustic remarks.

Charlotte had to look away from her friend, lest she laugh at the absurdity of the conversation.

Lady Hargrove then asked, "What do you know of Lord Barrington?"

Charlotte's head whipped in the countess's direction. Goodness, word traveled fast. The earl had run into them while they were on their shopping excursion earlier in the day.

"He greeted us at the jeweler's. He seemed most agreeable."

And he hadn't even tried to hide his interest in her cousin Genny. She'd never tell Lady Hargrove that bit of information.

"It was all about Town this afternoon," Ariel said, filling her in, "that he purchased your cousin a hair comb!"

More ladies joined them, suddenly eager for any gossip that might be stirring.

"No, no." Charlotte waved their assumptions away. While she might not mind her reputation suffering for encouraging the attentions of a rogue, she did not want the same for her cousin. "You should call her over and let her explain." Because she didn't really know what to say and didn't want to dig a hole her cousin couldn't easily step out of.

Tristan watched the women converse in the center of the room. Barrington had already joined the tittering crowd of ladies at the hostess's insistence. On entering the house, Tristan stood with Lord Carleton to discuss business matters, but it didn't appear as though Carleton had business in mind and instead nattered on about everyone at the dinner tonight.

It shouldn't surprise Tristan that the first woman he noticed was Lady Charlotte. She was a vision in pink, with her hair curled and cascaded in spirals down her bared shoulders and upper back. The cinch of her waist only further emphasized the becoming width of her hips. Fripperies and fashions aside, it was her impish smile that drew his attention. And that laugh she had that was like a siren drawing in a flock of hapless seamen . . .

He was going to have to start calling her trouble. Did she not realize she was biting off far more than she could chew where he was concerned?

Carleton cleared his throat, not unoblivious to where his gaze was affixed. "My wife gets it in her head to matchmake a few chosen members of the ton every season."

"Is that so," he said.

Did the countess plan to set him up with someone? Or was she more interested in seeing Leo settled into a nice marriage? Marriages were a typical result of the Carletons' infamous summer parties, but they were always mired in some sort of scandal. He would be quite happy to escape any of her machinations.

Lord Carleton rubbed his hand over his short-cropped gray beard and gave the ladies in attendance an assessing look. "I would never have guessed that she would include you with this lot of women."

That was what Tristan had been thinking. There were three debutantes, four widows with daughters in their midtwenties and nearly close to being unmarriageable spinsters, chaperones of varying ages and forms, and two henpecking mothers. Aside from Lady Charlotte, Tristan really wanted nothing to do with the lot of women attending the Carleton dinner party tonight.

"Perhaps the match is for Leo?" he suggested. "Lady Carleton was a close friend of Leo's stepmother. She'd want to see him well settled and all that rubbish."

Carleton slapped him on the shoulder and gave it a fatherly squeeze. "True enough, but you are a son to her, too."

True, since Lady Carleton had never had children of her own she had in a sense taken him under her wing. She'd been a strong female presence in his youth, right up until his parents had died in a terrible storm at sea when he was sixteen. After that, he'd tried desperately to find his own way in life and had distanced himself from the Carletons in his youthful anger. He'd eventually come around. But there had been a strain in their relationship after he'd grown up and become the man he now was.

The Carletons had been close friends with both Tristan's and Leo's parents. They all owned sugar plantations that occupied a large portion of Barbados—three adjoining properties that made many men envious. The three older

men had fought hard together to make sure slavery had
been stamped out and abolished in the West Indies in
their heyday. It was a legacy that had been hard to live up
to. Tristan had never made any significant contribution to
society other than to sire a bastard, which the world had
far too many of already. Thank God for girls because
Ronnie could never be heir to his title. The boy, Rowan,
he'd adopted as his own, not that anyone knew the child
wasn't his.

Regardless, he would always be a shadow of the man
his father was, so he focused on what he loved most aside
from Ronnie and Rowan: women.

And that brought him right back to Lady Charlotte. He
grinned at her from where he stood. He saw that she took
notice of him because her color rose and her fan flicked
open to waft cool air on her pink cheeks.

The dinner bell rang, breaking the spell that had ensnared them. Hopefully they would be sitting next to each
other. If not, he'd steal a moment of her time afterward.
The doors between the parlor and the dining room slid
open and everyone filed into the room to find their names
on the table. One didn't sit by rank in the Carleton household; that would be utterly boring and predictable.

He shouldn't be surprised to find his place card next to
Miss Camden's, but he was nevertheless disappointed
not to be seated next to the woman he'd finagled an invitation to see again.

Miss Camden seemed amused by the seating arrangement, for she said: "Lady Luck is on my side this evening.
Lord Castleigh to my left, as he should be," then more
quietly added, "Though it would be equally satisfying to
put you in that position, Lord Barrington."

Tristan smiled and could barely contain the chuckle

building in his chest. When Leo didn't take her bait, Tristan did. "I'd enjoy playing your devil anytime, Miss Camden."

And because he knew Lady Charlotte was watching their exchange from across the table—where she sat with an elderly man that looked as though he'd fall over at any moment—Tristan gave her a wink and motioned disappointedly to the seat next to him that was still empty.

Sitting next to Miss Camden afforded him the opportunity to learn a few things about Lady Charlotte; things she might not otherwise share with him since she seemed bent on luring him into her little game of seduction. Lady Charlotte glanced at him, then at her cousin as the soup dishes were set out in front of them.

He didn't let his eyes stray from hers too often as he conversed with the dinner guests on either side of him. He talked about nothing of importance, at least not anything remarkable enough to remember as he stared across the table at the one woman he was more than eager to learn all about.

By the third course, Lady Charlotte seemed flustered by his constant attention. And so the dance between them began.

Chapter 4

None other than Mr. T—— has spent an inordinate amount of time with Lady H—— and her daughter. Could there be two weddings imminent this season with the inseparable Ladies C—— and A——?
  —*The Mayfair Chronicles*, May 1846

It was just Charlotte's luck to be sitting next to Lord Chester—a man who couldn't be a day under eighty—a man she wasn't sure could even chew his food properly. Perhaps he had to gum it to death just to get it down. The worst part about having to sit next to him was that she had to shout so he could hear her over the conversation going on around them.

Lord Chester was a kind old man, and he could tell a good war tale better than any of her father's friends, but he tended to talk with food in his mouth and his bad eye was very eerie with the way it *saw* her but didn't really *see* her. She was sure it was glass, but she would not ask such a vulgar question to prove her guess true or false.

Because Lady Hargrove sat on the other side of Lord

Chester, Charlotte pretended great interest in her dinner and let the other woman do most of the talking.

It was difficult to eat, however, with the marquess watching her so closely from across the table. A shame they hadn't been able to sit closer; she would have liked to talk to him instead of being forced to stare at him like a lovesick puppy. Not that she was infatuated with him, but it must look like that to the other guests since her gaze so obviously kept straying in his direction.

He hadn't said a word to her since his arrival. True, he'd appeared only fifteen minutes before dinner was served and had been discussing something privately with Lord Carleton, but that didn't mean he couldn't offer up a "Good day."

It was unsettling the way he stared at her, however, as though she were the only woman in the room. She took a sip of her water, hoping it would clear the nervous lump in her throat. It didn't.

What gave him the right to unnerve her from across the dinner table? If he didn't approach her after the last course and explain why he'd come to the Carleton party but hadn't bothered to seek her out, she would have to corner him and find out for herself.

The spark of mischief in his eyes told her that he was clearly up to something. What the something was, she couldn't guess. But it was a look she often wore when she'd decided upon a specific goal. And wasn't that the crux of her unsettlement right there? He was using a tactic she had perfected when she wanted something from someone. She didn't like the tables turned in this instance. She wanted complete control in the game she was to play with the marquess.

Thank goodness she'd decided to just explain what she

wanted from him. Which was more than necessary considering that what they were doing now felt oddly like courting . . . No, that was too innocent a word for the tension building between them. She knew very well that she was in the midst of her very first seduction. So who was the seducer? She or the marquess?

"What's that, deary?" Lord Chester practically shouted; his one catlike hazel eye focused on her.

She hadn't even been the one to say anything, but she answered him regardless, a bit too loudly. "I've never had a better mint sauce on lamb."

The whole table heard her for they looked in her direction. There were a few sympathetic glances offered her way. Charlotte gave a weak smile and ducked her head. Dinner couldn't end fast enough. They were already on the third course. How many more were to be served?

"You don't like steamed clams, eh? Good that we're a bit far from the coast to make it a regularity with the meal."

Charlotte barely held back her laughter. Tears burned the back of her eyes as she turned away from Lord Chester with a smile on her face. She didn't have the heart to correct him.

"So true, my lord." She cut into her lamb.

When she glanced across the table, the marquess's gaze snared hers. He returned her smile, but there was an intense desire burning so close to the surface that it had her breath catching in her lungs and her fork stilling halfway to her mouth.

She realized right then that she needn't worry about finding the marquess after dinner. He would be the one to seek her company, judging by the way he was staring at her. She licked a bit of mint sauce from her lips, then dabbed at her mouth with her napkin.

The marquess's gaze seemed darker and so much more dangerous than before, as if he were a great tiger stalking closer to his prey. Only she didn't feel hunted, she felt empowered by that all-consuming gaze because she had a leg up in the game she had devised.

She put her fork down, quite sated with food, and leaned back against her chair. She ran her fingers over the pearls about her neck and pretended not to notice the marquess's gaze fixed upon her.

She was a she-devil, and she had no inkling that she was playing with fire. Tristan liked this new side to the Ponsley chit. Had he ever met a debutante so sure of herself? He'd certainly never been acquainted with anyone quite like Lady Charlotte. She was bold and daring, willing to toss her hand in and let the odds fall to her favor because she was so self-confident. Those were some of Jez's traits, and part of the reason they got on so famously. Only, he wasn't as intrigued by Jez as he was by Lady Charlotte . . .

"Miss Camden," he said, helping his companion slide out of her chair as dinner concluded. "It's been a great pleasure chatting with you over dinner." He leaned in close. "Do leash that braggart on the other side of you. He gets away with far too much as it is."

Miss Camden gave him a measuring look and quirked her brow. "I can't say for sure if our conversation has been enlightening or frightening."

"A little of both, I daresay." With a parting wink, he turned in search of his quarry, knowing the men would not stay at the table but adjourn to the study after finger desserts were served in the parlor with the ladies.

Lady Charlotte found him before he made it three

steps from the dinner parlor. The friend she was always with was in tow; he was positive she was the daughter of the gossip, Lady Hargrove. She was pretty, he supposed, with her cherub-round face and loose blonde curls that highlighted the porcelain tone of her skin. Her eyes were blue and bright, her brows and lashes an unfortunate shade of white on her fair skin.

"Allow me to introduce you both," Lady Charlotte said.

His attention was immediately riveted to Lady Charlotte's wry smile as she turned her focus on her friend.

"Ariel, this is the Marquess of Castleigh, not that you hadn't figured it out." She turned to him, her smile still devilish. "Lord Castleigh, this is my dearest friend, Miss Ariel Evans."

"The pleasure is all mine," he said with a bow to both ladies. "Did you find dinner as satisfying as I did?" The question was directed to Lady Charlotte but he looked at Ariel, including her in their conversation.

"It wasn't quite fulfilling and left me hungry for more."

The spark of trouble in Lady Charlotte's eyes unsettled him. What kind of *more* did she refer to?

"Can I interest you in a game of chess?" Charlotte suggested.

"Why don't I accompany you?" Lady Ariel said far too innocently.

He wasn't given a choice in the matter as Lady Ariel practically ushered them away from the parlor and toward the doors to another room far removed from everyone else's company. The room was rather private and would allow them to talk freely.

The Carletons' house was grander than any other in the row of houses this side of Mayfair. Perhaps because it was a corner house much like Hayden's at the opposite end of the street. The parlor they'd been in earlier was the first room off the foyer. The marble floors they traversed met a rich oak hardwood floor that led a path to the other rooms on the main floor. He was intimate with the layout since he'd been here many times as a child.

There were five rooms on the main level. The parlor and dining room, the library and study, and an intimate sitting room that couldn't house more than half a dozen people. That was where Lady Carleton took her tea in the morning since the windows faced both the street and the back garden. And that seemed to be where Lady Charlotte was leading their small party. He followed without comment.

Lady Charlotte was the first to enter the sitting room; she made herself comfortable on a damask chair. Tristan motioned inside the room, allowing Ariel to precede him. The young lady busied herself with the bookshelf recessed into the wall, browsing over the spines with her forefinger. Tristan shut the door behind them and found himself a seat across from Lady Charlotte.

One of the young ladies must have been in here already, because sure enough, there was a chessboard set up and ready to go. She really did intend a game of chess. He nearly laughed.

"You surprise me, Lady Charlotte."

She reached forward for one of the white pawns and moved it up two spaces on the board. "Your play, my lord."

"Are you referring to the chess game or something else entirely?" he asked.

"You haven't figured out my purpose?" She nibbled on her bottom lip, the action belying her certainty of the situation they now found themselves in. "I thought you better practiced in such games."

Tristan scooted forward on the seat and leaned closer to her so that he'd not have to shout across the table and have her friend hearing every word of their conversation. "The only question I have is what do you gain by attracting my attention and favor?"

He moved a pawn forward, baring his king.

"We come back to women being mysterious creatures, Lord Castleigh. We must have some secrets to intrigue the other sex." Lady Charlotte tapped her finger against her dampened lip in thought and focused on the board. When her eyes met his again, she said, "How would we get on in the world without our feminine wiles?"

When she reached in to move her next piece, he took hold of her wrist, trapping her hand above the board. He felt her pulse at the tips of his fingers; her skin was soft, delicate . . . tempting. "You can burn yourself playing with fire."

She sat on the edge of her seat and stared back at him, daring him to say or do more. God, he wanted to do something she wouldn't expect, like kiss those full lips and press her back into the chair as he took possession of her mouth. Anything to make her speechless even for a moment because she was far too brazen for a debutante; for the first time in his life, he couldn't quite figure out this particular woman's purpose.

And worse, he wanted to figure her out.

"But I'm the one wielding all the matches so you needn't be worried about the flames just yet," she said.

Narrowing his eyes, he released her reluctantly. Lady Charlotte might be young, but she was no fool.

After they had both had a few turns, she moved her rook behind her pawn.

"Let us speak plainly, Lady Charlotte."

"By all means, though I was under the impression that we were already doing so." She motioned toward their game, indicating he should make his next move.

"I'm not a man easily taken advantage of. Nor will I be fooled into marriage . . ."

He moved his bishop to block his king.

"It's not marriage I'm after."

"What makes you think I'm willing to play along with someone so untried? You can't possibly understand the consequences in this amusement you've devised."

"Then I should give you a proposition you simply cannot refuse."

She played another move, giving him time to line up his queen in a position of power. "What makes you think you can offer me something that will trump sound judgment?"

Which was a lie, she could tempt him to hell and back, he was sure, but the chit was too smart for her own good and played a game of intrigue better than any experienced widow he'd had the pleasure of knowing.

There was the matter concerning Mr. Warren that he fully intended to sort out with her help, but showing all his cards in their first real conversation wouldn't do. He was enjoying it far too much. It was better to have an intelligent lady with whom to spend your time than one who knew only how to flatter her opponent to death.

He liked a freethinking woman and wondered what she'd be like in ten years' time, even five years from now. There was no doubt in his mind that she'd be able to twist her meanings and words enough to have him second-guessing her more than he did now.

"Perhaps I have nothing you want just yet. But you have followed me away from the party to share a moment of privacy with me, even though we are occupied over a game of chess and not indulging in more delectable pursuits." She leaned in closer; the soft scent of lilacs tickled his nose and drew him like a bee to nectar. "I'm sure you haven't failed to notice that the only thing standing in the way of my complete ruin is my friend's presence."

She looked in the direction of said friend. Tristan turned his head, spying Lady Ariel with an open book in her lap and a glint in her sharp gaze that was equally as dangerous as Lady Charlotte's. Had he ever met two women who were better matched?

"Life is not a game of chance, my lady." He took her knight with his queen.

She covered a bored yawn with her gloved hand. "It most certainly is. I have no intention of living blandly through the motions of life. I will enjoy everything it has to offer to the fullest."

"By courting danger, you risk the freedom to experience everything life has to offer. Most women wait till they're married for this type of . . . extracurricular activity."

"And I'm not most women, my lord."

Her bishop took his pawn, and he saw then how the board was lined up in her favor and smiled. When was the last time he'd lost a game of chess? Never, he was sure.

"Indeed, you are not." He claimed her knight knowing it would not be enough to save the game. "Check."

"It wouldn't do to compare me with your past conquests, either." She moved her queen. "Check—"

Tristan's gaze swung to the door. Miss Camden came in with a furious look on her face, her hands on her hips as her gaze scanned the room.

Tristan's eyes narrowed on seeing Leo come in directly

behind the chaperone. Well, wasn't that interesting. Did Lady Charlotte know her cousin would come looking for her so soon after their escape from the main parlor? He didn't think so since Lady Ariel watched over them with an eagle's eye.

With the conversation enlightening but hardly leading to the answers he'd hoped to uncover—he frowned down at the board—their game had ended far too quickly. It was time for them to return to the rest of the company.

Miss Camden looked her cousin over with a critical eye and carefully studied the folds in her dress to make sure everything was in order. He could not contain his bitter smile. Miss Camden might think she knew men like him, but she would be wrong in her assessment. There was no arguing over his reputation, which was well deserved considering his past, but he saw now that she would judge him no differently than the rest of society had. It was a shame that so many people were shortsighted, but he supposed their misconceptions revolved around his children.

"Lord Castleigh," Miss Camden said. "You can't simply abscond with my cousin as the mood takes you. Had you asked for her company, I would have been willing to escort you both from the parlor to a more private setting."

Tristan made eye contact with Leo for a moment before his friend's gaze landed on the chaperone again. He only half listened to what the ladies said as he tried to figure out his friend's involvement with the chaperone. Was Leo giving him an escape route? That was the plan they'd discussed briefly at the duchess's ball, wasn't it? Divide and conquer two of the ladies present?

Lady Charlotte looked at the chessboard, then looked at him with a grin that was far too knowing; she'd trounced him in more aspects than one. His only excuse was that he was distracted by their conversation, so much so that the game hadn't even come to mind as he tried to puzzle together the young lady before him.

"Pooh," she said. "We'll have to arrange to play another game now that I've angered Genny. And I was winning."

She stood, and he followed suit. Would they escape the chaperone without being scolded for their boldness? When was the last time anyone had scolded him?

Lady Charlotte turned toward the door without so much as glancing at her cousin again. "Do escort me back to the rest of the company, my lord."

He followed her out into the hallway. Once they were in the corridor, the door clicked shut after Lady Ariel, leaving Miss Camden and Leo behind. Tristan turned, an amused grin tilting up his lips. What a rascal Leo was.

"What do you suppose they're up to?" Lady Ariel asked, eyes wide.

"Catching up," Tristan said, in defense of his friend, whom he knew did not deserve the same disreputable reputation as he.

"They are better acquainted than I ever imagined," Lady Charlotte said.

"They go back a number of years." Tristan took each of the ladies' arms and walked toward the rest of the company. "Your cousin has been absent from society for a long time."

"How do you know she was absent?" Charlotte's brows lowered questioningly.

"A lucky guess, and you have just confirmed that suspicion."

On entering the parlor, they went largely unnoticed by the other guests. The only exception was Lady Hargrove, who came up and snatched her daughter off Tristan's arm, whisking the young lady across the room so fast that he still felt her warmth on his arm as he nodded to her from across the room.

"I'm afraid Lady Hargrove is hard to win over."

Tristan looked at the one lady still on his arm. "I believe I have more fodder on her than anyone else in the ton."

Lady Charlotte's eyes widened, not with surprise but with interest.

"Has anyone ever told you that you are the very definition of trouble?" He stood near the doorway a while longer with her, knowing he could not monopolize her company with so many eyes and ears present.

"My father says I'm a perfect angel, and Grandmamma dotes upon me. Mind you, I am the only grandchild in the family."

"I believe it. How you came to be so cunning is a story for another day."

"Will we see each other again, my lord?"

"Sooner than you can imagine. I have every intention of learning all your secrets, but we must part company for the night. We wouldn't want too many whispers speculating about our alliance."

"Will you be visiting the Carleton estate this summer?"

"I'm not one to plan summer escapes. My poor sister wouldn't be able to handle my children for an extended period of time in the hotter months."

Lady Charlotte stood more rigid in his hold, her gaze perplexed. "Children?"

"Uncouth of me not to mention them sooner. They occupy my thoughts since they've just come down from my estate up north."

Why had he mentioned them at all? He was supposed

to win the young lady over to his favor. Now he was liable to frighten her off with the mention of children. This was different, though; he was out of his realm of expertise with this particular woman. He had always preferred a more experienced lady.

"No, I don't mind knowing. You just seem so young to have children." She swallowed visibly. "How many do you have?"

The pitch in her voice said he'd done precisely what he didn't want to do—scare her off. "A boy and a girl."

"Their mother?"

"Are you worried that 'philanderer' can be added to my description?" She slipped her arm away from his.

He looked at the confused expression in Lady Charlotte's eyes and wanted to promise her that he'd never hurt her like Warren had hurt his sister.

He was not winning her over this evening. And he wasn't generally unsuccessful at garnering the attentions of the fairer sex. He blamed the task at hand. Jez had said to charm and win the girl from Mr. Warren. Which he had every intention of doing, because the blighter would not be given the chance to get his hands on another young woman worth more than that man would ever amount to.

There was no disgust displayed in Lady Charlotte's features, probably because she had no idea that his children were from the wrong side of the sheets.

"I am not married," he assured her, which also meant his children were not born of a wife.

Damn it.

He needed to call it quits for the evening. It would have been better for her to hear that particular truth through the rumor mill; it unsettled him to see disappointment in her expression.

"I see," was all she said.

He needed to fix this.

"My lady. I didn't mean to cause you any distress and it would have been better had I not said anything." He bowed so he didn't have to look into her eyes a moment longer. He did not want to see disappointment there. "While I must call it a night, I do hope we chance upon each other in the near future. My evening was all the better for having spent it in your company."

"You're an interesting man, Lord Castleigh." She ducked her head as he took her hand and kissed the back of her knuckles. "I do look forward to conversing with you again—hopefully the setting will be more private next time and with fewer interruptions."

"You're more daring than any woman I've ever had the pleasure to meet."

"So I've on occasion been told." She leaned in closer, her smile playing on her lips again. "Though I'm sure my tongue is liable to get me into trouble sooner rather than later."

"I wouldn't mind in the least if you caused a stir. I only ask that I can witness it firsthand."

His hand slipped away from hers. He wanted to feel every contour beneath her thin gloves, but he could not linger in her company for much longer. The chaperone would be back soon enough, and the guests around him would likely take note of his interest in the young woman.

Would that be such a bad thing? Couldn't he woo Lady Charlotte for all to witness?

No. He'd have to be careful, otherwise her father was likely to call him out and demand retribution—and not in the form of a proper courtship if he wanted Warren for a son-in-law. He was sure her father's definition of fair compensation for engaging his daughter's heart would be Tristan's head on a platter.

He'd have to strategize his next move very carefully. And it couldn't happen tonight so he bid Lady Charlotte adieu and said his thank-you and good-night to the host and hostess.

Chapter 5

*Nary a soul is to be found out of doors and easily ob-
served when the heavens decide to open up. Rain
makes for dull gossip on most occasions. That's not to
say that secret meetings behind closed doors haven't
been noticed. Very recently the Duke of A——— was
seen leaving his residence in the cover of night . . .
and was not seen at any of his usual haunts or gaming
hells. So where precisely did he disappear to?*
                                        —The Mayfair Chronicles, May 1846

"Papa, it's time to wake up," his son shouted.

Rowan was jumping on his bed, bidding him rather
loudly to meet the day when really Tristan could use a
few more hours of sleep. He couldn't remain abed,
though, with the mattress bouncing and jostling his body
every which way. Tristan cracked one eye open. Sun
shone around his room, making it impossibly bright.

"Has the rooster even greeted the day yet?" he asked.

His golden-haired child Ronnie giggled. "Papa, it's
after eight."

He let out a heavy sigh and draped his arm over his eyes to block the light until his sight was better adjusted. "I need to have heavier drapes installed so you cannot open them to the morning before I've had a decent cup of coffee to wake me."

"But you always tell us how clever we are, Father. We'd find a way to open them," Ronnie said matter-of-factly.

He reached out and grabbed Rowan around the waist since he was still bouncing about. He hauled him down onto the bed and tickled his stomach until he could say nothing through the gales of laughter that robbed him of breath.

"But then you would sleep till lunch." Ronnie brought over his robe.

Letting Rowan up, he pulled his robe on and slid his legs over the side of the bed. Ronnie sat next to him, Rowan on his other side.

"Aunty Bea wants you to come down to breakfast," his daughter said.

Tristan patted her plump cheek. Ronnie was such a serious child, and not inclined to games and fun like her brother. However, three years separated them so perhaps his daughter thought it childish to play the games that her brother loved.

"Bea's probably set a plate of kippers aside just for me."

Ronnie and Rowan laughed in unison. A revolted shiver ran the length of Tristan's body; he hated fish of any kind, yet his sister insisted on making him eat the slimy stuff because it was good for his digestion or some rot. He didn't believe her for one second; she was probably poisoning him slowly, enjoying the fact that she could torture him while she insisted something he despised so thoroughly was good for him.

Cinching the robe around his waist with one final yawn to greet the day, he stood and let his children lead him to the breakfast room.

Bea was sorting through his correspondence, something she should do for a household of her own, but not a possibility since she'd been forced to drop out of society when she started increasing. His sister used to be dressed in the height of fashion, but now she hid behind bland colors—a checked gray day dress this morning—avoiding gowns that draped off the shoulders as was the recent fashion and preferring long shawls even when the weather was warm.

"Anything good?" he asked when she didn't acknowledge his presence.

His sister looked up from the stack of parchment with a smile on her face, one hand shuffling through the papers, the other clasped around the locket he'd gifted to her on the day her son was born.

"Unless you consider cards at Lord Hauxley's on the third of June noteworthy, I'm afraid it's mostly the usual."

He came forward and kissed his sister on the cheek before taking a seat across from her. Her chestnut-colored hair twisted becomingly at her temples and was tied into a bun at her nape, simple and unnoticeable. It saddened him that his sister couldn't find a husband and have a family of her own.

Ronnie and Rowan filled their plates from the long table while a footman came around and poured Tristan a cup of coffee.

"There was a note from Lady Carleton," his sister said as she placed the rim of her teacup to her lips and watched him.

He raised an eyebrow in silent query.

"She wanted to send an early invitation to her house party at the end of June. She knows how you are often unavailable come summer."

He hadn't been invited to a Carleton summer party for more years than he could remember. Not that he cared, but it was an event that Bea had cherished the summer before their parents' untimely death, and it had been the place where she'd fallen in love for the first and only time in her life.

"I'll not leave you alone with the children. You've only just arrived in London, and I plan on spoiling them rotten before we head north for the hotter weather."

"You're trying to change the topic." Her sister slid a few of the envelopes from the top of the stack until she came to the one she was looking for. She fished out the ivory parchment with a monogrammed C decorating the flap.

"You should go," she said. "I don't mind staying here."

"You've only just arrived." He dropped a sugar cube in his coffee and gave it a frustrated stir. The Carleton party would be a perfect excuse to get closer to Lady Charlotte, but his family always came first. He would not neglect them for a mere infatuation. Not even for his promise to Jez.

"I've not seen you for months."

"You're impossible, brother."

"And you, sister, are relentless and often overbearing."

"Where would you be without me to keep you in line?"

"You're in a mood this morning." He gave her a quizzical glance, trying to figure out what game she'd devised, and why she would care so much that he go to this particular house party. "Besides, it really should be you attending these country house parties, balls, and soirees. I say, they're all a bunch of rot with far too much postulating."

His sister looked at Rowan and then Ronnie pointedly. "They were on occasion fun, but I don't miss it in the least."

He took a long sip of his coffee, savoring the strong brew Cook had made. She'd put a dash of cinnamon in it this time, and he quite liked the hint of spice.

When he opened his eyes again, he drolly looked at his sister. He couldn't care too much about her invisibility among the ton or she'd be offended. "It's not right that you hide yourself away in the country to care for the children."

"It's my choice," Bea said, stacking up the envelopes violently and turning her gaze away from his.

He would not fight with his sister. Not over this. "And I've always supported whatever choice you wanted to make."

Rowan sat next to him, his plate filled with eggs, toast, and little potato wedges that Cook prepared in a fryer. Tristan stole one from his son's plate.

Rowan pouted his bottom lip. "Papa, why did you do that? Aunty Bea has a plate of stinky fish for you—"

Tristan raised his forefinger to his lips to shush his son too late. Now his sister was on to the mischief he'd already caused this morning.

"Tristan!" Bea admonished. "If you tell them what you dislike, I'll never be able to get them to eat certain foods again."

"It's probably better they don't eat the herring."

"I'll eat it, Aunty Bea," Ronnie said, and took her seat next to Bea, pointedly taking a kipper and placing it at the side of her plate.

Bea gave her a hug around the shoulders and let her eat her meal. He wanted to bet a shilling that his daughter would cry off and say she was too full to eat it come the end of breakfast time. He did nothing of the sort and smiled to himself instead.

"You know it's about time you married," Bea said.

They were back to this, were they?

"I haven't found a woman that I like enough for such a task."

"Task? You make it sound like an exercise."

"It most certainly is. You have lived with me your entire life. You know I'm very particular about a lot of things." His sister had brought this up the last time they'd spent family time together over the Easter holiday. "You are awfully insistent that I do this."

"You should still find a wife. *You* can have more children before you're too old. I wouldn't mind looking after them as I have Ronnie and Rowan."

Ronnie let out a cry of excitement and bounced in his chair. "I want a little sister, Papa. Can I have one? Please? I've always wanted one."

"And why shouldn't it be a brother?" Rowan said between mouthfuls. "You are already bossy enough. I need someone to stand up for me."

"I wouldn't have to be bossy if you did what I told you to do."

"Papa," Rowan protested.

"Children." Tristan's command was firm but gentle. "There is no sense fighting over this. When the time comes, we'll discuss it as a family. Now finish your breakfast. The faster your lessons are completed, the sooner we can go to the park."

They both ate with added gusto. Tristan picked up his coffee, drained the contents, and made his way over to the breakfast platters. Perhaps his sister was sad she couldn't have another child now that she had retreated from society. The members of the haute ton thought Bea was unfit for marriage because of her questionable parentage. No one knew about the boy being hers, though.

Tristan was approaching his thirtieth birthday, and his sister was right in saying that he should settle down and marry. Perhaps Lady Charlotte could fill the role of wife? He nearly laughed out loud at the idea, but managed to hold it back as he spooned a few potatoes onto his plate. Lady Charlotte would sooner run to the next degenerate for aid in her ruin than consider the idea of marriage to him.

Sitting back down at the table, he looked across at his sister who was explaining how to properly hold the knife and fork to Rowan.

He could never marry someone who didn't accept his family exactly as they were. He wouldn't make any other arrangements, his children would always be around, legitimate or not. His sister, too, because he loved her just as fiercely as he loved Rowan and Ronnie. Could Lady Charlotte accept his life as it was?

Oddly enough, he mulled over the idea a while longer: marriage to the young lady might be a perfect solution for them both . . .

Charlotte tucked the letter she'd penned into her bodice, not sure what she would do with it. Goodness, she wasn't sure why she had written a letter to the marquess, but she felt she needed to prove her continued interest in him after last night's disastrous end. She was afraid she hadn't hidden her shock well enough. But in all fairness, how was she supposed to react after his bold announcement that he had children?

Children.

And the fact that they did not have a mother could only mean one thing . . .

She would not think about *that* right now.

Steeling herself, she gingerly walked down the stairs of her townhouse, holding her dress up so she didn't trip. Genny was directly behind her. They were set to *enjoy* the afternoon air with Mr. Warren. And though her stomach protested the very idea of spending a beautiful afternoon with this particular man, she put on her best fake smile and greeted him cordially with a tilt of her chin.

"Good day to you, Mr. Warren. I'm so pleased the weather has turned around in favor of our carriage ride through the park."

"You are as bright as the sun, my lady." Even a compliment from him managed to sound like an insult.

With her back to him as he handed her up into the carriage, her smile pinched into a look of disgust. Why did Mr. Warren want to marry her if he was going to come into his own wealth when he took the Fallon title? Her cousin was right. Her fifty thousand pounds wouldn't matter once the earldom was his. So why not take a more biddable wife?

All she could come up with was that there must be a political alliance between Mr. Warren and her father. Did they plan to join forces in Parliament? It didn't matter right now; what mattered was putting on a pleasant expression as they rode through the park.

The ivory-colored carriage was open, with a small leather seat that sat no more than one person in the back and a bench in the front that was fit for only two. She would have to bump legs with Mr. Warren for the next half hour.

His grays were hitched up to the carriage, their manes braided and heads held high. How cruel to make a horse stand in such an unnatural position. This display of wealth and brutality was yet another reason for her to despise him.

With her cousin sitting behind, and she in the front, Mr. Warren came around the other side and stepped up into the carriage using the axle of the wheel.

"Since the rain has subsided and the day has warmed brilliantly, I shall take you ladies for ices after our ride."

"That would be so kind of you, Mr. Warren. I've not had an ice this season; it'll remind me of my youth." She had to turn away from him to roll her eyes.

Genny grasped the back of Charlotte's seat, leaned forward to point out someone on the path, and jabbed her in the back. Charlotte flinched and glared at her cousin. Genny pointed an admonishing finger at her.

True, Charlotte was being mean, but that couldn't be helped. A better use of her time would be to find out what Warren's plans were so she could better avoid him over the coming week. "What are your plans this evening, Mr. Warren?"

"Nothing terribly exciting. I have some personal business to attend to."

"You won't be present at the opera then?"

They were going to be seated in the Carleton box tonight. She hadn't been to the opera since they'd settled in Town for the season.

Mr. Warren flicked the horses' reins, putting them at a trot. "I've never been a fan of stage dramas."

"What *do* you like?" she said under her breath.

He heard her—not that she was trying to be unheard—and gave her a dissatisfied glare before returning his gaze to the road ahead.

He turned his grays down the path that led into the park. It wasn't as busy as normal, probably because the mud from the earlier rain dirtied the walking paths. If the sun stayed out, and the day continued in this fashion, she'd have to drag her cousin out here later for a decent stroll. Without Mr. Warren to interfere.

"Life isn't about amusements. It's about hard work," Mr. Warren said firmly.

This had to be a new record for their interactions; disagreement had sparked in less than five minutes of being in each other's company. Why did Mr. Warren want to marry her when he obviously disliked her? It was a question she was dying to ask, and she might have done so had her cousin not been seated directly behind her. She'd have to wait for another opportunity to ask him precisely what she wanted, consequences be damned.

"I can't imagine a life without amusement," she said, hoping he interpreted her precise meaning: she would dislike marriage and a life with him.

"You're young yet."

Charlotte huffed out a breath and faced the road. The man was impossible. He cut her down at every opportunity. Shouldn't he extend some of his respect and kindness to her if he was such a good friend of her father's?

The lace shawl slipped from her shoulders, and a draft brushed against her upper back. She looked over the side of the carriage, saw the tall wheels kicking up dirt. If she dropped the shawl, it would muddy and catch up in the wheel. Was the slip of material around her shoulders enough to stop the carriage and end their drive through the park?

Genny tucked the shawl back over her shoulders and gave Charlotte's arm a reassuring squeeze. Had her cousin read her thoughts?

Conversation at a standstill, her cousin spoke: "I'm glad the weather let up for our afternoon ride, Mr. Warren."

"Yes, I couldn't be more pleased. The grays haven't been out nearly enough since I purchased them."

"It would be far kinder to let them run in the country. The cemented and cobbled roads must be hard on them," Charlotte felt the need to point out.

"Never fear, Lady Charlotte, they are well cared for."

"I wasn't suggesting otherwise. It just saddens me that their heads are pulled up so high, and they are forced to walk on such hard ground. It must be a great strain on their bodies to walk so unnaturally just so one can be fashionable. All those fripperies you so dislike are fully on display in this instance."

There was a tic at the side of his jaw where he clenched it. She swore she heard the grinding of his teeth for a moment before he let up and gave her a forced smile. "We will have to agree to disagree, Lady Charlotte."

"Indeed," she said with a tight smile on her face. She wanted to stamp her feet like a three-year-old. The man was infuriating, snobbish, and unpleasant. "About those ices, Mr. Warren? I find I am rather parched now that the day has warmed."

"My thoughts exactly," he said, and turned his horses back on the path toward Berkley Street. "Gunter's should be busy with the sudden increase in the temperature."

"Especially since it seems no one is strolling about the

park today," Genny said before Charlotte could interject with another caustic remark. "I'm sure the foot traffic and riders in the park will increase once the last puddles of rain dry up."

"I don't doubt it for a moment, Miss Camden," he said.

Arriving at Gunter's, they saw it was as they'd predicted—a full house. People spilled out onto the lawn in the park across from the shop since all the chairs and tables set up outdoors were filled.

As Mr. Warren came around to help her and her cousin from the carriage, Genny grabbed her sleeve and drew her close to whisper, "Do keep a civil tongue."

Charlotte faced her cousin. "I have tried for civility, but the man is determined to disagree and argue with me at every turn. He dislikes me as much as I do him, Genny. I don't understand why he's agreed to marriage in the first place. Surely he can tell my father to find another husband for me as he would be terrible at it."

Her cousin let out a frustrated groan, and then put on her brightest smile. Mr. Warren put his hand up for Charlotte to take. There were far too many witnesses for her to ignore his gesture and jump down on her own, so she braced herself against having to touch Mr. Warren at all and gave him her gloved hand without really returning his hold. Even touching him made her skin crawl and her lip curl in distaste.

"How kind of you, Mr. Warren."

His hand spanned her waist and hip, surprising a small squeal from her. Every bone in her body stiffened the moment he touched her. When she raised her head to stare at him, she didn't fail to notice the many patrons sitting on the close-clipped lawn where the carriage was stopped, watching everything that transpired between them.

The blighter. The intimate touch had been intentional. With a satisfied grin, he stepped around her to aid her cousin next, not offering the same display of ownership that he had with Charlotte.

She fumed. She thought of a thousand things to say, but they could never pass her lips, no matter how desperate she was to call him a cad or a scoundrel and share her opinion with the world around her that Mr. Warren was not a man worthy of any lady's company. "Loathe" wasn't a strong enough word for what she felt as she forced her smile back on her lips and widened her eyes so they were bright and beguiling and not pinched in anger.

She would play this game of *courting* a while longer.

"Thank you, Mr. Warren," Genny said for them both.

Mr. Warren took Charlotte's arm and led her safely across the wide, busy road where carriages and men on horses clipped along at a quick pace and urchins and passersby strolled away from the mud-strewn road, men near the curb and women toward the shops.

By taking her arm, Mr. Warren made his claim on her clear to all those who were present. This was very different from a simple ride in his carriage, though. True, that too reeked of courtship, but his actions today made it seem as though she approved because she could not defy him publicly. And Gunter's being one of the few places a lady could visit without a chaperone in public with a man who was not her relation didn't help matters. The gossips would be busy saying her name tonight. She had no desire to read her name in the rags next to his; she had envisioned another man's name with hers.

She held her shoulders back and blocked out the faces of everyone around her, ignoring the small voice in her head that demanded she yank out of his hold. No one would know of her shame for allowing Mr. Warren to take her arm. No one.

"Lady Charlotte," someone called.

She released a sigh of relief on seeing Mr. Torrance greet them just inside the entrance of the tea and ice shop. He was a welcome sight, flowery prose and all—if he wanted to wax poetic as he often did.

"Mr. Torrance. How fantastic to find you enjoying ices, too." Charlotte smiled at him, hoping she looked grateful for his company and not desperate for a companion other than the one on her arm.

Mr. Torrance took her hand and kissed the back of her knuckles gallantly without actually touching his lips to her gloved hand. Charlotte didn't fail to see the look of disgust that curled Mr. Warren's lip. Good, she hoped he was so put out that he couldn't bring himself to touch her again.

Reluctant to quit Mr. Torrance's company now that it was obvious Mr. Warren would like nothing more than to order their ices and be rid of the man, she lingered. This was a grand payback for the way in which he practically claimed her as his own in front of the many noteworthy people sitting across the street in the park.

"The weather seems to have brought everyone of good name to this fine establishment," she noted to Mr. Torrance.

"And who are you here with?" Genny asked.

"My sister, Miss Camden." He nodded toward the park. His sister, a thin, shorter woman wearing a white-sprigged walking dress with a pink ribbon sash about her waist and a winning smile, waved back at them.

Before Charlotte could offer to have a longer conversation over ices, Mr. Warren said, "A pleasure to see you, Mr. Torrance. But we must bid our adieus, as we are for the counter. Perhaps another time we can arrange a picnic party."

Mr. Torrance backed up with a bright smile. "I didn't mean to interrupt. I simply had to say good day." Mr. Torrance tipped his tall hat at both her and Genny. "I will see you ladies soon enough."

Most certainly they would since he seemed to follow Ariel about in the evenings.

"Good day, Mr. Torrance. It was really lovely to see you," Charlotte said just as he turned and made his way back across the street, dodging carriages and horses alike to return to his sister's side.

Mr. Warren pulled her forward before she was ready to take a step and she stumbled into his side. He didn't apologize for his rough handling, just carried on as though he didn't notice her body colliding into his.

When they reached the polished mahogany counter, he ordered a lime ice for her—did he do so because he knew she secretly hated the tart flavor?—and a bergamot water ice for himself.

"Miss Camden, which is your preference?" he asked, and Charlotte wanted to stamp her heeled shoe on his foot for not asking her what she liked, as well. What point was he trying to prove?

Charlotte hoped that Genny could see the fiery rage clear in her gaze; surely it was obvious that he was intentionally treating her as inferior. There was no denying that Mr. Warren was high-handed only when it came to her.

"I think I might like the muscadine ice." Her cousin truly did love her. Muscadine—which was grapelike in flavor—was Charlotte's favorite ice flavor, and she knew that Genny didn't care for ices at all.

"Excellent choice, madam."

Their order was confirmed and the man behind the counter told them that he would find them in the park once the ices were ready. Charlotte found herself free of Mr. Warren's arm as he dug into his vest pocket to retrieve a few coins to pay for their treat.

Charlotte didn't waste the opportunity of being free of him and quickly threaded her arm through Genny's. Just because she was set to marry him in the fall didn't mean he had the right to act as though he had any say over her actions now. Goodness, she certainly hoped he didn't mean to dictate every part of her life when they—

She stopped that thought.

She would stop their marriage. And if the Marquess of Castleigh could be won to her favor, she'd have no trouble at all ending the engagement before summer concluded.

"Wherever shall we find a seat?" Charlotte asked, hoping they would stand in the crowd only long enough to eat their ices before he took her and Genny home.

Gunter's was positively overflowing and there wasn't a seat to be found. That was why patrons sat out on the lawn across from the ice shop. They'd have to do the same, though she supposed they could eat in the carriage.

"We'll sit on the grass." Mr. Warren turned and glanced at both their dresses. Charlotte wore sunny yellow muslin; Genny had opted, as she often did, for navy blue. "The ground seems to have dried out so it shouldn't damage your dresses any."

Finding a stretch of grass in the sun, Mr. Warren told them both to wait a moment so he could retrieve a blanket from his carriage. It was the first gentlemanly behavior he'd shown her all day—perhaps it was for Genny's benefit.

The moment he left, Charlotte started in on her cousin. "Did you see what he did? He made my decision without consulting me. As though he already has control over what I do, what I say, and how I should act. The man thrives on putting me down and making sure I'm at my wit's end." Charlotte pressed her back against an elm tree and suppressed the urge to cross her arms over her chest and sulk her complete and utter annoyance.

"When it's decided that you'll marry before you have had the opportunity to really get to know someone, it creates hurdles you must triumph over. You're a smart woman, Charlotte. I know you can sway Mr. Warren to your favor as you do your hundred beaux at every event."

"Mr. Warren does not want to be charmed."

"Perhaps not, but he is often cross with you because you constantly challenge his authority."

Her cousin paused, eyeing the crowd around them. Did she see someone of interest? Charlotte glanced over the faces, seeing many acquaintances, and hesitated . . .

Was that the marquess?

Chapter 6

Gunter's offers the best grounds for fodder on various members of the ton. You merely need to order one of the shop's specialties, find a nice seat under the shade of a tall tree on the park lawn, and watch everyone around. A significant glance—sometimes even a passing caress—may be witnessed. And what salaciousness was revealed to me on this unusually hot May afternoon.

A greeting between a young lady freshly introduced to society and a rake with too many years' experience to count; a humble patron of virtue soon to be exposed as a charlatan; a man of decency engaged in an illicit affair that will do more damage than he can anticipate to the woman he pleasures. Are your ears burning for me to reveal what I've only started to uncover? Soon, dear readers, soon you'll learn everything I know.

—The Mayfair Chronicles, May 1846

The marquess was here and Charlotte was positive her cousin hadn't seen him for she would have made some scathing remark about his character. She felt suddenly light-headed as the blood pounded heavily through her veins, and breathing became difficult as her heart skipped at a frantic, excited pace. Never had she felt so attuned to another person.

The first genuine smile of the day tilted up her lips. She would not reveal his presence to Genny. The letter she had addressed to him and hidden in her bodice before they'd left the house burned against her breast. She had been right to bring the letter with her, instead of having her maid deliver it directly into his hands.

The marquess was with another woman and two children. Could those be the very ones he'd mentioned to her? The girl had blonde hair braided on either side of her round face. A straw hat with periwinkle ribbons blew gently in the breeze; she looked to be about ten, but it was difficult to ascertain at this distance. The boy was dark-haired, and his back was to her so all she could tell was that he was younger than the girl, and his hair was dark and unruly like his father's. There was no doubt in her mind that both children were likely as striking as their father.

Charlotte tapped her finger to her chin as she scrutinized the woman. Who was she? Definitely a relation—they shared many of the same features, from their dark hair and light eyes to their slender forms.

She could only make out the marquess's profile when he turned to address one of the children and the woman he sat with. To Charlotte, he looked more relaxed—different, almost—when surrounded by his family. More so than when he was charming half a dozen ladies in any given drawing room. It was almost as though he allowed himself to be less refined. More of his true self and not the profligate lord society expected of him. How she could make that out from across the park, she had no idea.

Now she had to find a way to give him the letter, and she must do so before Mr. Warren came back with the blanket.

Charlotte's eyes flitted from patron to patron, hoping to see someone familiar. And wouldn't luck have it that Lady Hargrove stood not ten feet away from the marquess. A most perfect opportunity had just presented itself and she'd not waste what could be her only chance to see the marquess today.

"Oh, look, Genny." Charlotte stood on her toes and nodded her head in the direction of Lady Hargrove. She was conversing with Mr. Torrance. "I must offer a hallo. It would be rude not to do so."

"Very true." Genny sighed. "We definitely need to pay our respects to Lady Hargrove. I'll wait here for Mr. Warren. It wouldn't do for him to think we'd wandered off without him."

"I promise to be quick." She fluttered her lashes at her cousin. "I really wouldn't want Mr. Warren to feel put out."

"That gleam in your eyes says otherwise."

There was no censure in her cousin's comment, only a hint of laughter. Maybe she, too, was sick to death of the less than civil exchanges between Charlotte and Mr. Warren.

She kissed her cousin's cheek. "I won't be overlong."

Charlotte felt a strong skip in her heart to have this opportunity. Weaving her way through the guests, she curtsied to Lady Hargrove when she was close enough to converse with the older woman.

"Good day to you, my lady." She nodded to Mr. Torrance. "And a pleasure to see you again so soon."

"Dearest." Lady Hargrove placed a hand on each of Charlotte's arms and gave them a gentle squeeze as she pulled her in for a brief hug. "What brings you to Gunter's? Tea or ices?"

"Ices, of course. Mr. Warren is treating us."

Lady Hargrove glanced over Charlotte's shoulder to see where her companion was. "How nice. I see him retrieving a blanket. It'll be a lovely picnic with the weather finally cooperating today."

Charlotte turned and noted that he was indeed carrying a small blanket toward Genny. She had but a few moments before she knew he would become suspicious and search her out. And she wanted no additional eyes on her as she completed her errand.

"You could join us for a spell," Charlotte offered, knowing they would refuse.

"I mustn't, dear. I'm headed home to retrieve Ariel from her piano lesson, then over to the confectionary to order some chocolate desserts for our dinner party next week."

"Well, I wish you a successful afternoon, then." She ducked her head, knowing it was now time to hand over the letter to the marquess. "Mr. Torrance. Lady Hargrove, I wish you both a wonderful day."

"You, too, my lady," Mr. Torrance said with a tip of his hat.

"I will see you tonight, child," Lady Hargrove said with an affectionate squeeze of her hand.

Charlotte lifted her skirts slightly so she could turn easily, and made her way toward the marquess. Glancing across the lawn, she saw that Mr. Warren had just made it back to her cousin's side, saying something cordial that made Genny smile. Why was he so nice to everyone but her?

On reaching the area where the marquess sat with his family, she said, "Good day, my lord."

He turned to gaze up at her. His expression was soft as he stood to greet her properly.

"I simply had to stop and say hallo when I noticed you from the corner of my eye. I was just conversing with Lady Hargrove."

She tucked her hand into the top of her bodice and pulled out the folded letter she'd had the sense to tuck away. The marquess noted the action, for his eyes dropped to her bosom and then back to gaze upon her face with a knowing smile that was so deliciously wicked she wanted to reciprocate with some sort of naughty behavior. Their setting and the children stopped her from doing anything rash.

Too low for anyone but her to hear, he said, "You play a dangerous game."

She looked at him through her lashes, her expression demure and inviting. "It's the small things in life that keep me happy."

He took her hand, pressed his lips against her knuckles, and palmed the letter from her hold.

"You should return to your cousin before she sees that you have found me."

"I am safe for a moment more while they set up the blanket." She nibbled at her bottom lip and finally met his fiery gaze. She wasn't sure what else to say, and wished she could converse with him for the rest of the afternoon instead of stodgy Mr. Warren. Another time perhaps.

"I love a woman who eschews the rules of society."

She felt her cheeks pinken under his regard. "Rules are made to be broken, my lord. But you are right, I must return to my party."

He looked over her shoulder, watching out for her even now. It was obvious the marquess didn't want Charlotte to be discovered, which surprised her considering his reputation.

"I'll bid you adieu," he said.

She fingered the lace edge of her sleeve, regretting that her interlude with him was so short. "What a shame it is that we can't have a few more moments without anyone noticing. I do hope to see you soon, my lord."

"Likewise."

"I look forward to your correspondence," she said as she turned away from him.

She hoped that he would turn and sit facing his family before Genny could take note of his presence. However, her cousin didn't turn to look for her until Charlotte was nearly upon them. Mr. Warren held out his hand for her to take, so he could assist in seating her.

"Thank you, Mr. Warren." Her sudden civility had him halting and eyeing her quizzically; in fact, he seemed momentarily taken aback.

Before he could comment, his gaze strayed behind her. "Our ices have arrived."

Mr. Warren took each glass from the shopkeeper and handed one to Charlotte and one to Genny. Once he had his in hand, he sat across from Charlotte, resting his back against the tree trunk, stretching his legs out in repose. Charlotte had never seen him so relaxed since they had been introduced a month ago. Perhaps he was warming to her just as Genny said he would. She nearly snorted at the ridiculous thought.

"I've been looking forward to indulging in ices since you suggested it," Charlotte said.

Genny looked at her with distrust gleaming in her eyes.

Had Charlotte sounded far too chipper? She was in high spirits. Her plan was finally set in motion now that her letter was delivered to the marquess.

"I have been looking forward to this, too," Genny said. "But now I wonder if we could switch ices. I'm craving something a little more tart."

There were no words to express how appreciative Charlotte was. "I'd be delighted." As they switched glasses, Charlotte smiled sweetly at Mr. Warren. "This is a nice change from our usual routine."

"I'll be sure to offer more variety in the future, Lady Charlotte."

"I had hoped you would join us at the opera, Mr. Warren," Genny said.

Charlotte couldn't care less about Mr. Warren's attendance and wondered briefly if the marquess would be there.

"We will be seated with the Carletons," Charlotte added, hoping he disliked them as much as her father seemed to.

"I have already said that I dislike opera."

Perfect, she thought with another genuine smile, because she had given the marquess her itinerary for the coming week.

"That's a pity. I do love the stage in any shape or form." If she married him, she had a suspicion that he'd ban such frivolous activities. "Will we see you at any engagements this week?"

"None, I'm afraid. I need to attend to business matters." His gaze veered off and seemed to be caught by someone in the crowd behind her.

Charlotte wanted to turn and see what had so thoroughly snagged his attention, but she couldn't do so without being obvious. Was he looking at the marquess? She'd purposely put her back to his party so she wasn't tempted to look over at his group. Would Mr. Warren have heard that she'd danced with the marquess at the duchess's grand ball?

"Such a shame we won't see more of you, Mr. Warren," Genny said. She, too, noticed that his gaze was focused elsewhere.

When he returned his attention to Charlotte, his eyes pierced right through her. There was a flash of . . .

Longing?

No, it couldn't be.

Whatever it was, it was not directed at her, for the brief vulnerability vanished and he was back to his usual annoying self. "We'll have our usual ride through the park this week. We must keep up appearances."

"You are intentionally short to me." She couldn't stop the words from coming any more than she could stop her hand from fisting the spoon in her hand.

"Charlotte!" Her cousin gasped.

She stared at her cousin, ready to retaliate against her, but blinked her eyes, took in a sharp breath, and pasted a smile on her face. At least she held back from flinging the contents of her glass all over Mr. Warren's smug expression. Why did he enjoy goading her so much? What had she ever done to him to incite such disdain, such dislike? Charlotte was well loved by everyone she knew—except him, of course.

"I'll not pretend to like you, Mr. Warren. My father seems intent on our match. I can only assume it's for political reasons. Whatever reason you have for agreeing to it, I wish you would simply cease. It would save us both a lot of trouble."

"My lady," he said, rubbing the side of his face with his hand. "I didn't mean to give you that impression. This is hardly an appropriate conversation to be having, so let us leave now and start off on a better note the next time we see each other."

He stood, took Genny's hand and lifted her to her feet, and held his other hand out to Charlotte. There was an air of concession about him. His shoulders weren't held back as rigidly as they normally were, and there was a kindness in his expression that wasn't usually present— although she did not trust it.

Nor would she stoop so low as to take his hand for assistance. He leaned over at her refusal and took her elbow regardless.

He whispered in her ear, "It'll do you well to remember that I hold all the cards in this courtship. Do not displease me or make a buffoon out of me again."

She yanked her elbow away and glared at him. "You would do well to remember that my will cannot be trampled by your bad temper."

She bustled past him and headed toward the carriage, forcing her cousin to catch up while Mr. Warren went about collecting their things and having someone take their ice glasses away.

Before she could climb into the carriage by herself, Mr. Warren set his hands about her waist and lifted her inside. She turned to further reprimand him on his conduct, but he was already walking around the back of the carriage to find his way to his own seat.

She glanced at the crowd around them. The only person to note their leaving seemed to be the marquess. His brows were drawn low and one fist curled around his stylish cane so hard his knuckles had turned white. He watched her leave as his children helped the young woman he sat with fold their blanket.

Was he so attuned to her now that he worried for her welfare? Had he seen all that had transpired between her and Mr. Warren? She hoped he had. It would do him well to be pushed into helping her. Her gaze snapped away from the marquess's as the horses jolted forward with a quick command from Mr. Warren.

"I'm sorry you saw him here. I should have waited till he left before packing up our picnic items." Bea cupped her hand around Tristan's arm as she spoke quietly enough that Ronnie and Rowan and others around them couldn't hear what she said. "Let it alone, Tristan. You'll accomplish nothing if you confront him here."

"He'll pay for what he's done to this family, Bea." He tapped his cane on the lawn in annoyance. "Destroying his good standing will be the only thing worth accomplishing this season."

Warren's carriage jolted forward, carrying Lady Charlotte. Their gazes snapped as she left Berkley Square and then he was forced to return his attention to his family. He fingered the small letter in his hand and slid it into his vest pocket. He was eager to read the contents, impatient to see what secrets Lady Charlotte revealed on the pages.

"Forget about him. He's not worth the grief."

He was still watching the carriage from the corner of his eye—not a smart idea as half the ton was scrutinizing him as he mingled in polite society with his children in tow.

He turned his back on his foe and the intriguing lady he wanted to learn so much more about, and helped his family gather up the items from their picnic. Warren would pay for his misdeeds. And it would be sweet revenge to win over the lady set to be *that* man's wife.

Chapter 7

Mr. T—— was out and about in the company of a fe-
male relation. A lady not often in society, not since
her engagement with that scoundrel Lord M—— was
called off last summer. Friendly and ebullient as ever,
the poor creature was still shunned by all but one
man lurking in the shadows watching her. Dare I say
it almost looked to be Lord M—— himself?
      —The Mayfair Chronicles, May 1846

Tristan locked himself in his study and looked at the parchment he'd taken from Lady Charlotte's palm. Had she known he was going to be out with his family? Or was it happenstance that had them meeting in so public a setting? She hadn't seemed put out by his children's presence. He should care less about that, but for some reason her opinion of him mattered since he'd revealed the truth to her.

He slid an opener beneath the wax seal fashioned in the form of an ibis. The intoxicating scent of rose water that had been dabbed on the letter wafted up to his nose as he unfolded the parchment. It started: "Dear letter holder." Smart on Lady Charlotte's part. Should the letter contain any information that might compromise her, she'd not be easily identified.

I really don't know what has propelled me to pen such a letter as this, but it must be done because I feel as though I have not swayed you completely to my favor. Since our very first meeting, I knew that we could benefit from each other's company. Though you might think otherwise, I believe that we are kindred spirits with a similar attitude toward society as a whole. I do not wish to be a mere subject, a marionette for others to master, but instead I aspire to be a woman who cannot be controlled by those who consider themselves superior to all others.

Tristan put the letter down. How was it that someone so young could be so aware of the machinations of society? Intrigued didn't come close to describing what he felt. He read on:

I attend a few more events before the annual Carleton house party is upon us. However, I do not expect your presence since you are rarely seen attending social functions during the season. I've taken note of you because I believe you can help me accomplish something that will forever guarantee my independence from society. Are you asking yourself why you should help me at all? Well, the scandal will be simply decadent, and I think you will be unable to resist such temptation.

But really, I might as well get down to the essence: I know that you stand on the opposing side of my father where politics are concerned; and while I don't pretend to understand all that happens in such matters, I do know that my father will lose sway if his daughter is not brought to heel. Even though my father dotes upon me, he has made a grave decision, against my wishes, to marry me to a man I loathe.

I will not trap you in a marriage neither of us wants, but I do think you are the key to my freedom from the bonds that will smother me over time. I am sure we can see eye to eye in this matter, and I look forward to your response. I attend the opera tonight, should you wish to make an appearance.

Tristan tapped his finger against the pages as he set them down on his desk. There was nothing damning in the letter. Should it end up in the wrong hands, the words would mean nothing. Stuffing the missive back in the envelope, he placed it inside the top drawer of his desk and leaned back in his chair to contemplate everything Lady Charlotte had just revealed.

She was right. Her father would lose face should another man make claim to his daughter. In fact, Tristan was sure that the old man's alliance with Mr. Warren—who held the majority of sway in parliamentary matters—might very well be lost.

A knock came at his study door.

"Enter," he called out.

Bea poked her head inside. As usual her lips were pursed in a tight line.

"You're a welcome sight, Bea." He stood and motioned to a chair across from his wide mahogany desk.

"I just wanted to see if you were all right." Bea sat,

curling her feet under her, as she was wont to do. "You seemed so enraged earlier that I thought it wise to check up on you."

Tristan raised one brow. "Enraged? It wasn't so bad as that."

"You cannot act foolish where that man is concerned."

"When am I ever foolish?"

"I'll counter your question with another: are you planning something questionable?" Her earnestness had him smiling.

"You know me better than that, Bea. Have I not been a bloody pillar for you all these years?"

"You've done more for me than I deserved."

Tristan drummed his fingers on the edge of his desk, annoyed. "Nonsense. You are my sister, questionable parentage or not."

"I can never have the same status as you, Tristan. My name was ruined when our parents died."

He did not share a mother with Bea, though they'd been raised to believe they were blood related and of equal status.

"That doesn't give anyone the right to mistreat you, Bea."

His sister looked away from him and toward the window. "You know I lost a lot of faith in myself when those letters were found."

He nodded, even though she wasn't looking at him. He, too, had lost a lot of faith in everything he thought he knew. Why did it always seem that when you thought your life was figured out, something would propel you in an unexpected and unanticipated direction?

"It's been a long time since I thought about any of this." His sister was contemplative, not seeing what was out the window, but looking at the past in her memories. Hopefully she was not reliving it as they discussed said past.

It hadn't been a good time in either of their lives. It had taken them both a number of years to get their lives back on track after their parents' deaths. Tristan finally had the estate in order, and Bea had seen her first season and had made a worthy match. Then it had all been taken away with the exposure of a few damning letters.

He hated to think what would have happened had he not been old enough to deal with the repercussions.

There was no use fretting over something that didn't matter anymore. The past could not be changed. And giving the children a decent life was all that mattered to him and Bea now.

Bea gave him a questioning tilt of her head as she assessed him. "What did the girl give you at Gunter's?"

Tristan grinned. "Saw that, did you? And I thought I was being so sly in greeting her."

"I've raised the two most mischievous children God has ever gifted the planet with, and you didn't think I would notice that something was passed between you two? Was it a letter?"

"What she gave me, my darling sister, was ammunition against a mutual foe."

Bea raised one eyebrow and waited patiently to be enlightened.

"She's to marry Mr. Warren before the year is out." He held out his hand when his sister opened her mouth to ask how he knew. "Let me finish. The source is Jez. He mentioned his intention to marry the Ponsley girl at the reading of the will."

"Of course." Bea sat back heavily in the chair and stared

down at her entwined fingers. "He's to inherit everything that was hers, is he not?"

"Unfortunately, yes." Tristan rested his elbows on the edge of his desk and steepled his fingers. "I can't stop it from happening, nor can Jez. The will handicaps her gravely. Everything, including most of her inheritance, is entailed in the estate."

"Will he toss her out so cruelly?" His sister looked away again, though he thought maybe she was fighting tears she didn't want him to see. "I guess he will, considering her less than scrupulous behavior these past few years."

"How right you are." He stood, walked around the desk, and squeezed his sister's shoulder affectionately. "I can't stop him from taking the seat but I can make his life very difficult."

Bea looked up at him, her eyes watery, but not one tear fell on her porcelain skin. "And would it be for your sake or for mine?"

"He has a debt owed to us both."

"I've moved on from the past, Tristan." She removed his hold from her shoulder and took his hand in hers. "You need to let go of what cannot be changed. I like how things are."

"You've grown used to how things are, Bea. There is a difference." He clasped her hand once more before releasing her. "I will never forget or forgive. Life would be so much different for you had he manned up and taken you as his wife. Instead . . ."

Instead the cad had left his sister pregnant and completely shunned by society.

Bea stood with a sigh, a look of calm about her. "I wouldn't change my life back for the world, you know.

Rowan is the best thing to have happened to me. And I would make the same mistake a thousand times over just to see his sweet, loving face smiling up at me."

"Yes, but to truly celebrate your independence and the life you love, you should be able to call him son."

She fisted her hand over her chest, grasping a locket that held pictures of their family. "I know in my heart that he is mine."

Tristan put his hands in his pockets and watched Bea head for the door. "You are too kindhearted and gentle a soul, sister. Warren does not deserve your forgiveness."

"And why not? I've moved on, and managed to build a decent life for myself."

Though she had a point, it didn't mean Warren wouldn't pay dearly for the undue suffering he'd caused Bea, whether Bea acknowledged the other man's mistakes or not. Whether she forgave him or not.

Bea didn't argue or agree with him, but she did give him a sad smile before she left the study to attend to her duties for the rest of the day.

Sitting back down at his desk, he pulled out a pen and dipped it in ink. He must return a letter to Lady Charlotte without delay. It simply wouldn't do for her to find someone else to create the scandal of the season. Tristan would send away any man that tried to step in his path. Lady Charlotte was his and his alone.

Examining why that was so might prove interesting but would have to wait for another time. The one certainty he had was that once he won Lady Charlotte's affections, he would stare Warren in the eye and dare him to challenge him. Had his sister revealed the whole truth of her ruin at the time her name was put through the wringer, Tristan would have challenged Warren then, but

as it was, too much time had passed, and now an end
needed to be found so he could move on.

> *My dearest lady,*
>   *There was no end to my delight upon opening*
> *your missive. And the enticement to create a social*
> *flurry spoke of a kindred spirit indeed. Intrigue me*
> *further—the Zoological Society, one in the after-*
> *noon. I will find you.*
>
> *Yours*

He gazed down at the letter in his hands. There was
nothing of significance that would indicate the author of
the letter or its recipient. Tristan would have his valet deliver it personally to Lady Charlotte's maid. Folding the
letter, he tucked it into a plain envelope, heated wax over
the back flap, and used the flat end of his seal to press it
down. He tucked the letter in his breast pocket and headed
toward his room.

Next, he needed to pay Hayden a visit and see what his
friend had found out about Jez's fortune. Jez was unlikely
to marry again after the violence her husband had subjected her to. It was only fair that she be given a chance to
live the independent life she craved and needed most.

Not that her receiving compensation for the horren-
dous marriage she had lived through would keep him
from seeking to ruin the one man he reviled above all.

Charlotte hadn't been to the Zoological Society since she
was in apron strings. It felt wonderful and exhilarating
and oddly nostalgic. How she'd convinced Genny to attend with her was a wonder. Her cousin had looked at her
oddly when she requested that they visit a place reserved

for family entertainment. But she didn't care what her cousin might think because they'd have fun regardless.

The best part of it was that she'd managed to convince Ariel and her mother to attend, and, of course, Mr. Torrance and his sister had joined them. Charlotte hoped that because they were a large group, she would be able to sneak away from their company unnoticed.

Her heart skipped in her chest and her fingers shook with anticipation as they made their way from one cage to the next. She barely took note of all the animals; she was too eager to meet with the marquess and wondered when he would show himself to her.

Comments went around about the fowl that came from Canada and China in the same pen with a small pond. Directly across from them there were various species of geese. Next on their walk were the pelicans from the Americas—such a majestic bird with its odd, long beak that nearly touched the ground and a large pouch to hold fish in its mouth. The birds made loud squawking and coughing noises.

"Goodness, if I ever met a bird like that on the seaside, I'd probably run away terrified," Lady Hargrove commented as the great white bird's wings opened and flapped futilely and it made an odd growling noise.

Genny covered her ears. "What a dreadful sound it makes."

"Indeed, madam," Mr. Torrance said. "I don't think the bird cares to impress us in the least. He'd rather steal fish from a fisherman's net than amuse anyone visiting the zoo. He's merely making his displeasure known."

"I think the bird rather handsome," Ariel said. "I can't imagine they would be threatened in the wild, since they are so large."

"It's possible," Charlotte said. "But I prefer the birds from the jungles around the world. The hyacinth macaw is a favorite of mine, actually."

Everyone took her hint and moved along to the wired cages that housed a number of brightly colored parrots. They varied in size and color. Everyone oohed and aahed over the beautiful birds. When she came to the one she admired most, she put her hands against the wiring, wishing the bird would come closer. She clucked her tongue, trying to draw its attention, but the bird stared somewhere else, its head tilted inquisitively as it chawed loudly enough to make her ears ring. The blue of the bird was so vivid, so beautiful that she stood there staring at it for a spell.

Because her party had wandered off, she said to the bird, "You are far more majestic than any other bird here."

"I wouldn't get too close, Lady Charlotte. That bird is liable to take your thumb before you can blink," a low, delectable voice said close to her ear.

Her heart slammed against her chest and an excitement she couldn't possibly contain or explain overcame her. Instead of releasing the fence, her fingers curled tighter around the heavy wire.

She didn't turn around because she knew who stood behind her, and she didn't want to draw the notice of anyone from her party.

Finally able to think coherently, she dropped her hand away from the wire fence and took a step back . . . closer to him. Her skirts pushed forward when they pressed up against the man behind her. She closed her eyes to savor their proximity, and she swore there was a whole minute that she was unable to draw a single breath.

Why did he have this effect on her? Why couldn't she remain cool and distant in her dealings with him? Why did she want him to press close enough that they were touching? She reminded herself that she barely knew this man. Though that hadn't stopped her from constantly thinking about him since their first meeting.

"Be at the monkey house in fifteen minutes, my lady. I will find you," he promised. The back of his hand brushed a tantalizing line over her shoulder and down the length of her back to her hip.

She nodded and gave him a breathless, "I'll be there." She daren't turn and reveal that she was talking with anyone. The marquess was her secret alone; she hadn't even told Ariel yet that she was meeting the man in so public a setting and with so many potential witnesses, but she had every confidence that the marquess would keep his presence hidden from the rest of her party.

She'd been counting down the minutes till she saw him today, and now she'd have to wait a while longer. But how could she spend much time with him when her cousin was close at hand? Panic rose for a moment and she feared that the next encounter she would have with the marquess would be just as fleeting as the private words they'd just shared.

There was no denying that she wanted more. And what more with this man entailed she was all too eager to discover.

What was wrong with her? She took a few steps back from the cage and turned to follow her party farther into the park. She knew a flush covered her cheeks and was happy that she'd put on her powder this morning, so it would conceal the color on her face.

"The animals are exquisite," Lady Hargrove said. "I don't think I've been here since you and Ariel were eight years old."

"Has it been so long?" Ariel mused.

Falling back a few steps, Genny chuckled next to Charlotte.

"What's so amusing?" Charlotte asked.

They were coming upon the camel house. Next were the elephants if she was reading the map correctly, and then the monkeys. And the marquess.

"I don't know why," Genny said, "but I find the camel to be such an odd and funny creature."

"Do you realize you are giggling?" Charlotte was amused by her cousin's good spirits.

"I can't help it. The way they stand and stare at everyone, chewing whatever it is they chew. It's like they are cutting you, glaring at you as though you are inferior, yet they are the ones in the pen."

Charlotte shook her head, laughing as they neared the brown beasts.

Lady Hargrove held a monocle to her eye to read the sign set up outside the camels' arid enclosure. And sure enough, a tall humpbacked creature stood near the fence glaring disdainfully down at them as though they were unamusing pests. Charlotte leaned on her parasol as though it were a cane and stared at the stubborn-looking animal.

"He's thinking rather ferociously," Charlotte said.

Lady Hargrove held a handkerchief in front of her nose, made a sound as though she were short of breath, and stepped away from the camel, which had moved ominously close to inspect them. "Dirty beasts," she murmured. "Ariel, dearest, read the sign to me."

Ariel, apparently not bothered by the smell, stood closer to the sign and read the information about the animal out loud. "It's called a dromedary camel, and hails all the way from the African and Arabian countries."

The camel, not shy of their presence in the least, reached for the feather in the top of Ariel's hat. Charlotte stepped forward quickly and yanked her friend back so hard that they both nearly fell to the ground.

"Easy there," a man said, catching them both and helping them back on their feet as they giggled. They whipped around at the newcomer's voice.

Mr. Torrance moved forward to assist them.

"We're well enough now," Charlotte said to him, still laughing.

"My apologies for not acting sooner." Mr. Torrance's demeanor was cross and he directed his displeasure at the newcomer. His sister threaded her arm through Mr. Torrance's and smiled brightly to make up for her brother's sour mood.

Charlotte focused on their rescuer again. A gentleman, most assuredly. He was neatly put together, wearing a light brown suit with a cream-colored vest. His dark brown beard was trimmed short and he had a strong, commanding presence. His smile was kindhearted and welcoming.

Ariel looked at the gentleman with an expression of awe. "I can't thank you enough. Surely it wouldn't be too forward to ask the name of our rescuer?"

"Lord Jack Greyson at your service." His voice was deep, provocative even, his hazel eyes arresting and a perfect blend of both green and brown.

Lady Hargrove said in a squeaky voice, "The president of the Zoological Society?"

"The very one," he responded with a tip of his hat in Lady Hargrove's direction. "How do you do, my lady?"

Lady Hargrove flicked her fan open and studied the man standing across from them. "Very well. Thank you for your assistance."

"I just happened to be making my rounds this afternoon. Charlie takes offense at birds of any type. He was merely trying to pluck it away from the young lady's head." He still spoke directly to Lady Hargrove, as though waiting for the rest of the introductions to be made.

"It's a pleasure to make your acquaintance, Lord Greyson," Genny said. "I am Miss Camden. This is my cousin, Lady Charlotte, and her friend with the feathers atop her hat is Lady Hargrove's daughter, Lady Ariel."

"A pleasure," he said to Genny.

"The camel has a name?" Genny asked, clearly entertained by the situation as she giggled again.

"All the animals do, madam."

"I think we'll stand back from the camels from now on," Ariel said, a wry grin on her face as she studied the animal that wanted to snack on her finely made hat. "Though I find them oddly beautiful."

The brown beast then spat a wad of something dark and gooey at their feet. The two younger women gasped as they jumped away from the disturbing mass of slop.

"Never fear," Lord Greyson said. "It's merely his dislike of your hat that has him agitated and showing his leadership skills. Really, it's a defense mechanism when they are unsure of a situation."

"You're very informed," Mr. Torrance pointed out.

"I should hope so, kind sir, otherwise I wouldn't be fit for this position. I'll bid you all adieu. Please enjoy the rest of the exhibits." With another tip of his hat in their general direction, Lord Greyson headed off. His stride was quick, but he nodded to many of the guests and offered a polite hallo as he went on his way.

"What an odd man," Ariel whispered in her ear.

"He was, wasn't he?" Charlotte had to agree. "Here one moment to save the day and your hat, and gone just as quickly."

"I think I've had all I can take of the camel house." Genny couldn't keep the amusement from her voice, drawing all eyes to her. "Let's see if the elephants are more hospitable and accepting of our company."

"So long as they don't take it upon themselves to shower us with water, I'll be quite happy to move on," Miss Torrance said with a grin.

Genny turned around and headed deeper into the animal park, forcing them all to follow. Ariel looked behind them once more before capturing Charlotte's arm with hers and following their group.

The elephants were tranquil and standing on the far side of the pond within their enclosure. Charlotte was glad their group didn't stop there long, because the delay at the camel pen had brought her meeting with the marquess closer. She was anxious to reach the monkey house. Surely he agreed to the terms outlined in her letter. If he hadn't, why would he decide to meet her at all?

Dark clouds started to roll in overhead and their parasols wouldn't protect them if rain were to come down in sheets.

"We may be in for quite a storm," Ariel said.

"I think you're right." The wind started to pick up and Charlotte had to put her parasol away or risk losing it to a strong gust of wind. This couldn't be happening. She had to meet the marquess. "Perhaps there is a shelter up ahead where we can step inside," she called out to the others in her group.

"We might as well try and find somewhere to wait out the storm," Lady Hargrove said, and Mr. Torrance ran ahead to look for shelter before they could say anything further.

Within minutes, they were at the monkey house, and Charlotte pulled her friend aside as she looked around, hoping to spot the marquess. Should she tell Ariel why she'd wanted to come here of all places today? The rain still hadn't begun, but it didn't look far off.

"I failed to mention something important about today."

Her friend looked at her quizzically.

"The marquess said he would meet me here. I sent him a letter, asking for his aid in my ruin."

Ariel's mouth dropped open in surprise. "How could you not tell me!"

"I wasn't sure how today would turn out, or if he would come."

"What did you say in the letter?"

"I explained my circumstances and he responded with a request to meet me here today."

Ariel looked around them, too. "I don't see him."

"He's already approached me, so I'm sure he is near."

"When?"

"When we were at the aviary," she said in a whisper, so no one could hear her. She wasn't sure how she felt about sharing all her secrets with Ariel anymore. Shouldn't she keep some to herself?

"You sly devil, Charlotte. I can't believe I didn't take notice of his presence."

"It was fleeting. No more than greetings were exchanged. That and the request that I meet him here five minutes ago."

She pulled Ariel over to the first cage in the row and looked at the creatures climbing around on the trees. They were the same monkeys she'd once seen in a circus; their bodies were black and their faces and chests ivory-colored. The bronze sign labeled them as capuchin monkeys.

"Perhaps he has already gone." She hated to voice her fears, but she couldn't help herself.

"He'll come. He's already gone to the trouble to approach you once, he'll not resist doing so again," Ariel said.

"How can you be so sure?"

Her friend grinned at her. "Because I saw him behind a tree just before he disappeared into the crowd."

Charlotte's breath hitched and she froze to the spot, not wanting to give away that she was looking for someone. Fat drops of rain hit her hands and face. And though she should care that her maquillage would run, she didn't want to seek shelter from the rain just yet.

Ariel looked up at the sky. "I don't think we can wait here much longer." She chewed on her lower lip contemplatively.

"We can't leave yet."

Suddenly, an umbrella was shielding her and Ariel. "No, we can't have you leaving just yet."

"Good afternoon, Lord Castleigh," Ariel said with a beaming smile on her face.

Had she known he was coming up behind them? Oh, she would pay for this later.

"How did you think to bring an umbrella along with you today?" Charlotte asked, still not ready to turn around and face the marquess.

"Bea thinks of everything for our day excursions." He reached around her and handed another umbrella to Ariel, who took it without hesitation, opening it up as she walked a few steps away from them without being asked.

"We have temporary privacy," he whispered in her ear.

She slowly turned, her skirts brushing against his legs as she did so.

"Why did you want to meet?"

"To clear up a few things. It's much easier to do so in person than on paper."

"Was my request not clear?"

"Very. This is also a lot safer than missives, which can be traced back to the sender. You should take care to protect your good name, my lady."

"Is that not the opposite of my purpose in courting your favor?" she countered.

"Yet, if we should be caught out too soon, it will be the end of your little game."

She narrowed her gaze. "How can you be so sure?"

"That's how these politically aligned marriages work, my dear. You do something your father disapproves of and I can promise you he will move up your wedding date."

She pursed her lips. The bitter taste of anger flooded her. "I despise Mr. Warren. And I will stop at nothing to end the engagement."

"Have you thought of what that would mean for you in the long run?"

"I would be an independent woman."

"To do what, my lady? Continue attending your balls and soirees without censure from the rest of the ton?"

The rain was starting to fall harder and plopping against the top of his umbrella at a steady staccato.

"You make me out to be a fool." She took a step away from him, and rain hit the back rim of her hat. "I know what social ruin would mean for me, but I have a way to live quietly in another town, even on the Continent should I wish it."

He thought about this for a moment, narrowing his gaze on her and taking a step closer so she was under the umbrella with him again. "How many years before you come into your inheritance?"

It annoyed her that he had figured her out so easily. "Less than three years."

"And how will you keep yourself until that time?"

Of course he would ask about the one problem she hadn't solved yet.

The marquess whistled out a breath and shook his head. "Just as I thought. You haven't figured it out."

"Perhaps we could make an arrangement."

His eyes snapped back to hers, anger evident. "It's beneath you to whore yourself out."

Her mouth dropped open again. "I didn't mean that!" she hissed back.

The anger seemed to leach away from him. "Aside from your father loosing favor in the House of Lords, what benefit will I gain from an alliance with you?"

"You are different than I imagined."

"Only because you put too much stock in gossip."

Why were they arguing about this? "Are you angry with me? If you dislike my approach in this, then I will find another to help me. I thought—"

"That I would help you because I responded to your letter? You're right about one thing: I will not let you find someone else for your charade. I think I've become a humanitarian since we met." He put his forefinger under her chin and tilted her head up toward his, stepping closer still. "You're liable to find more trouble than you've bargained for, and I would hate to see such a lovely woman destroyed by her own lack of sense."

She ignored the insult. "What do you propose?" she

whispered, hating that she wanted him to lean his head closer so she could feel his breath on her, so she was close enough that they could kiss.

"You could marry me." When her mouth dropped open, he released her and stood tall again. Had he wanted to kiss her? "Though I don't think that's quite what you had in mind."

"The only thing that could persuade me to marry is true love."

He shook his head at her again. "You are more naïve than I thought. No one in this day and age marries for love."

"I'm starting to dislike you at a rather alarming rate."

"Hopefully not as much as your Mr. Warren."

"He's not my anything." She looked away from him, frustrated that she couldn't keep her emotions in check.

"No, I suppose he's not. But he will be if we can't come up with another plan for you."

"Can't you simply court me in public?"

"And have your father rush your nuptials? It won't work."

He made a valid point. She really hadn't thought this through. Ariel would have to help her come up with the best ways of ensuring she didn't have to marry Mr. Warren.

"I introduced myself to you hoping that we might be found in a compromising situation," she admitted.

"I knew what you were about, my lady. Besides, that's far too risky. Your father would have my head in a duel if I ruined you. I like my head right where it is, on my neck, Lady Charlotte."

That earned him another smile. How was it that the marquess found humor in just about any situation? "Why do you want to help me?"

"Because, despite my better judgment, I have grown to like you these past few days."

She pinched her lips together to keep from smiling, but was unsuccessful.

"I think you are laughing at me, my lady."

"I might be." She turned back to the monkeys and saw two of them huddled together grooming each other as they sat atop a wooden platform. "There has to be a way to make this work," she thought aloud.

"Tell me why you dislike the thought of marrying Mr. Warren so much."

"We agree to disagree about many things." She tilted her head to the side so she could see him from under the rim of her hat. "We are ill suited and a union between us would make us both miserable."

"Perhaps it's not you that needs ruining but Mr. Warren."

She gave him a droll look. "That man is as proper as they come."

He raised one brow. "So you've been led to believe."

"What do you know that I don't?" She loved gossip as much as the next young lady.

That devilish smile of his was back in place. "Let me see what I can come up with, my lady. But for now, I think we should part ways before the rain comes down any harder."

It was falling at a steady pace, and the rest of their party had probably taken shelter. Charlotte turned to her friend and beckoned her over. Ariel lowered the umbrella as she drew nearer.

"Thank you," Ariel said to the marquess as she handed back his folded, dripping umbrella.

"There is a covered gazebo just past this set of cages. I'd lend you an umbrella, but it might look suspicious."

"As though we met someone on the way?" Charlotte smiled up at him. "We'll be fine—it's only a little water."

"We'll race as though the devil is at our heels, Lord Castleigh," Ariel added. "Mother will have conniptions."

"Good day, my lord," Charlotte said as she took her friend's hand and did just as Ariel suggested and ran for the gazebo.

"I have so much to tell you, Ariel."

"We'll have to wait till tonight to discuss this. What should we say when we catch up to everyone?"

"Only that we didn't see which way they went. We've been gone ten minutes, and we were together the whole time. No one will question us; they'll all be busy complaining about the rain."

Chapter 8

Where doth the Dowager Countess of F—— hide?
She's been absent from society since the duchess's
grand ball. Not a squeak has come from her direction,
though I hear rumors that the earl's old valet has left
the country with an immediacy that makes you won-
der what secrets the F—— household hides.

Shame should be her greatest reason for retreating
into the shadows, but many would be content to think
that she's seen the error of her ways and wishes to
mend the damage she's done to her name for far too
many years to count. I certainly don't think this to be
the case, though stranger things have happened.
— *The Mayfair Chronicles,* June 1846

When Tristan arrived at Jez's townhouse, the butler
showed him to her drawing room. He was to escort her to
Hayden's tonight, so why wasn't she dressed yet? He sat
in the folds of a green brocade high-backed armchair,
stretched his legs out, and crossed them at the ankles. Impatient to be playing a game of cards, he tapped his cane

on the hardwood floor, the staccato beat loud in the all too quiet house.

Come to think of it, he didn't hear anything but the ticking of the mantel clock. He sat forward in the chair, tuning his ear to the corridor. There wasn't a servant to be heard.

Jez glided into the room five minutes later, in complete dishabille. She wore her Chinese-style scarlet dressing gown decorated with golden dragons. Her hair was a mass of loose red curls around her shoulders. He stood as she entered, a frown forming on his face.

"Have you forgotten about our night out, love?"

She looked paler than usual and there were dark circles under her eyes that looked to be caused by illness. She seemed to sway listlessly where she stood. He rushed forward, caught her elbow, and guided her toward the sofa. She *was* unwell.

"Thank you," she said, her voice cracking as though she were parched and hadn't had a drop of water all day. "I haven't been sleeping and I think the insomnia has finally caught up with me and has made me ill."

Steadying her with one arm while his other supported her around the waist, he settled her carefully on the sofa. "I can see you're ill. And I'm not generally one to point out any faults in the fairer sex. You look dreadful, Jez. Are you taking something to help you sleep?"

She gave him a weak smile. "You know me; if a glass or two of wine can't settle me for the night, I'm not one to imbibe something stronger—no matter how much it's needed." She waved away his concern and collapsed back against the sofa as though her current state were normal. "I'll be sitting the next few nights out."

"You've always had trouble with sleep; are you sure you haven't just eaten something off?"

"If anything it's my soul purging the evil of my late husband."

He shook his head. She was always so dramatic. "Would you like me to call in your maid?"

She shook her head. "I'll be fine. The stairs are a little taxing right now, but manageable."

"Then I'll take you back up to bed straightaway, and I won't hear otherwise."

He didn't give her a moment to protest as he lifted her up into his arms. It didn't seem as though she had the energy to argue with him, however, for she wrapped her arms around his shoulders and rested her temple against his collarbone with a sigh.

When he passed through the drawing room door, the butler stood to attention; it seemed the man was awaiting his instruction. "Please go up ahead of me and get the doors. Your mistress needs to stay abed for at least one night to help cure what ails her."

"Right away, my lord."

When they entered her private chambers, he had the butler toss back her coverlet so he could settle her onto the mattress.

She rubbed the side of his face while he was still leaning over her. "Thank you," she whispered.

"Should I call for someone?"

She reached for his sleeve and held it tight, shaking her head all the while. "No. I'm sorry I didn't send you a note to save you the trip here."

He sat on the edge of her mattress. "I'll stay if you want." And he would; cards could be saved for another night. "I don't like seeing you like this, Jez."

"Even the strong have moments of weakness, my friend."

Jez was like a little sister to him, despite the fact that only a few months separated them in age, he being older by three months.

"I'll be better in a few days." She yawned, garbling the last of her words.

"I'll be by to check on you in the morning."

"I just need to sleep. I promise you I'll be in top form before the week is through."

"You had better be, or I'll have Bea over here to nurse you back to health, and she comes with two little imps that like nothing more than jumping on any cushioned surface and terrorizing the help."

That brought a smile to Jez's wan face, which made him feel a little better about leaving her alone for the night. And he was only leaving because she had insisted.

He brushed his lips against her cheek, and wished her a good night. He was sure she was asleep before he closed her bedchamber door behind him.

The butler walked him down to the door, all too eager to show him out. Something felt wrong. Before leaving, he turned to the old man. "Call on me if she worsens."

"Will do, my lord." The man bowed cordially.

"Have someone bring broth up to her." She should eat something since she didn't look as though she'd eaten for days. Hopefully the butler would pass the message on to the cook.

"Of course, my lord," he said with a nod and closed the door behind Tristan.

Was the butler anxious to be rid of him? He'd never been ushered out of Jez's house so fast. He stood on the front porch a moment, wondering what the best course of action would be. He could demand entrance into her home again and stay at her bedside to ensure she slept through the night, or leave her to her privacy and visit her on the morrow.

Jez valued her privacy above all things, so he was left with only one option: to check on her first thing in the morning. Maybe he should bring his sister along. In his experience, women opened up better to their own sex. He couldn't blame them. There were a few things he would never talk about to anyone but another man, so why shouldn't the same be true for a woman?

Hayden lived only a dozen townhouses down from Jez's so he walked the rest of the way. The night brought cooler weather, and fog started to settle heavily on the streets, making visibility difficult. After he took the front steps of Hayden's townhouse two at a time, the footman opened the door before Tristan could raise his hand to the knocker.

"Good evening, my lord." The door was opened wide so Tristan could be admitted. He removed his hat and gloves, and handed them to the footman. "You'll find His Grace in his study."

"Has Leo arrived yet?" He handed off his cane once the footman hung his hat.

"Lord Barrington has been here for a quarter hour."

"Thank you, Carson."

He strolled down the long hallway that led to Hayden's study and doubled as a vast library with a large collection of rare books—a pastime of Hayden's father that had passed from son to son for six generations.

On entering, Leo greeted Tristan with a nod. "About time you arrived," he said.

"I stopped by Jez's. We were going to come together but she has taken ill." Both men were silent. Did they already know? "Am I missing something?" he asked.

"Nothing," Hayden said, and turned back to the sideboard where he was pouring out three glasses of whisky. "There goes my partner for whist. I suppose we could sit down and play an old man's game."

"Cribbage?" Leo suggested.

Hayden shrugged as he looked at them.

"Short a hand as we are, I think we can pass on the card game tonight. We'll try again next week," Leo said, and headed toward the sofa and chairs that circled a cozy spot by the fireplace.

Leo swirled his glass under his nose and inhaled the aroma. "Now *that* is nicely aged."

Hayden took a sip of his drink and nodded his agreement as he set a tumbler in front of Tristan. "I had a few bottles brought down from my last trip over the border. Those Scots know how to make fine spirits."

Tristan took his usual seat at the corner of the sofa and put his feet up on a footstool. He tasted his drink and agreed with Leo's assessment when the liquor washed over his tongue and down his throat. It was smooth and delicious.

"You're headed to the Carleton estate for part of the summer, aren't you?" Hayden asked Leo.

Leo grunted and put his head back on the chair. "It's not for a couple of weeks yet." He looked at Tristan, and said, "Did you ever receive an invitation? I don't remember you saying so."

"Unfortunately I won't be able to attend. My summers are devoted to Ronnie and Rowan." Which they all knew, but maybe Leo thought Tristan's outlook might have changed now that the Ponsley chit was participating in the summer fun.

"You could take a break from the family for once," Hayden pointed out, as he sat back in the sofa, crossing his ankle over his knee.

"I'm well aware of that, but I choose not to. They'll be off to school for the year before long, leaving me to life in London. I doubt I'll miss anything at the Carletons'."

Leo looked at him oddly. "It is usually the best party of the season."

Tristan shrugged. "I've been once, and look where that landed me."

"Ah, yes," Hayden said. "But what else could you expect from a married woman whose husband wasn't even in attendance?"

He'd not have put it past Ronnie's mother to have passed the child off as her late husband's had he died sooner. Instead, after an idyllic few weeks at the Carleton residence with him, his paramour had been forced into seclusion, and some nine months later, a babe was dropped on his doorstep with a note stating the child's name.

"It's not important," Tristan said. "What's far more interesting is the matter with the chaperone and Leo."

Leo raised a brow, seemingly not put out by the prying observation. Tristan knew that Miss Camden was not up for discussion, but since they were dissecting Tristan's life, turnabout was fair play.

"A chaperone?" Hayden said, bemused.

"Miss Camden and I go back a number of years. In fact, we met at one of the earlier Carleton parties." Leo swirled his glass around on the arm of the chair.

"She's either a puritan, and you won't forgive yourself for not getting her petticoats above her—"

Leo was up from his reposed position on the chair and

grabbing Tristan by the cravat before he could finish his sentence. Leo lifted him right from his seat and glared at him.

How very, very interesting.

There was no way to make a man angry faster than to insult a woman he revered above all others.

"You'll refrain from making assumptions with that forked tongue of yours," Leo snapped at him.

Hayden stood, ready to intervene. "Must we resort to fisticuffs in the study? Take it out to the street if you want to act like a pair of ruffians."

Tristan wrapped his hand around Leo's wrist and pried his friend's hand loose from his cravat. "You're predictable and foolish. If I can so easily make out your feelings toward her, how are you going to hide them from everyone else attending the Carletons'?"

The veins stood out on Leo's neck, but he took a calming breath and reined in his rage. "There is nothing between Miss Camden and me. I'm merely ensuring that she doesn't find herself in an unfavorable position. The Carletons' parties are notorious for the scandals that brew behind the estate walls."

Hayden sat again and put his feet up on the footstool. "Yet Tristan makes a valid point. Since the Ponsley girl will be in attendance, what exactly do you have planned for Lady Charlotte?"

"Nothing," Leo responded as he released Tristan. He pulled his coat down, and fixed his sleeves, still glaring. "I'm paying my respects to the Carletons, keeping Miss Camden out of harm's way and probably the girl in the process. I will also be visiting my estate while in Hertfordshire."

"You should learn how to tell a lie," Tristan said,

straightening his cravat, never letting his eyes stray far from Leo since his friend was still angry.

Leo shrugged. "I'm sorry we'll miss you."

"I'm sure you are," Tristan said.

He took his seat again and drank his glass of whisky as he listened to Hayden and Leo discuss Jez's will before going on to upcoming parliament matters.

A certain troublesome chit consumed Tristan's thoughts during their conversation. Would she be attending the most notorious house party of the season with her father's approval? That seemed odd only because Ponsley and Carleton stood on opposing sides in political dealings. Could it be because the Carletons were influential?

The rest of their evening proceeded without incident. They stayed for two drinks, ate a few small plates of sandwiches, and bade Hayden a good evening.

Tristan walked with Leo since the night was warm and neither lived far. The fog continued to blanket the city.

"Why are you really attending the Carleton party?" Tristan asked.

Leo gave him a long look. "I have my reasons. But for now, they are my reasons alone."

"You may be a changed man by the time you return."

Leo shrugged noncommittally.

"You should see Jez soon. She wasn't herself when I was there earlier."

"You said she was ill."

"There was something more. Something she wasn't telling me." Should he tell his friend that the butler had been anxious to be rid of Tristan? Perhaps he was over-reacting. Leo would have to form his own opinion when he paid Jez a visit.

"She's had a great shock since her husband's death.

Her life has spiraled in a direction she never wished for," Leo said.

"True, but a life without her husband should be the start of something fresh."

"One would think so. But I agree, she is acting odd."

"I understand she's distraught over the sordid business regarding the title and her income now that neither will be in her possession for long. But you should judge for yourself when you visit her next."

"I had already planned on seeing her tomorrow." Leo rubbed the side of his face where a day's worth of beard was growing in. "You'll have to keep an eye on her while I'm away. I don't trust Warren."

That made two of them, and he didn't doubt for a second that Hayden felt the same way.

"Should something happen, I'll send word. But Warren won't get anywhere near her, that I can promise."

Leo slapped Tristan on the back of the shoulder and turned to walk up the stairs to his townhouse. His staff was ever vigilant, and his valet opened the door before he could turn the handle up.

Tristan shoved one hand in his pocket, and the other clicked the cane against the cement with every step he took down the street. It was only half past eleven, but the streets were bustling with partygoers, and the night air warm and welcoming. There wasn't a breeze to be had and the fog had settled in, taking hold of the city, reducing visibility the closer he got to his townhouse. Before long he was home. The maidservant came to him wide-eyed as his footman took his hat and cane and helped him with his jacket.

"My lord." She curtsied, bobbing her head respectfully. "There be a visitor for you in the kitchen."

"Who is it?"

"She won't say, just says she's got to see you upon your return."

"Go on to bed, Sarah. I'll make sure our visitor is taken care of."

She curtsied and nodded again before heading to the back of the house where the servants' quarters were. After dismissing his footman, he headed toward the kitchen, eager to know who could be paying him a visit so late in the evening. The brazier was going, and the amber light from the coals pressed out between the cracks of the door, which he opened slowly, still unsure who his midnight visitor might be.

She was cloaked and had a hood pulled over her head to hide her identity, and she was perched precariously on the edge of a wooden chair. He crossed his arms over his chest and pressed his shoulder against the door frame as though he were holding it up.

"I'm told you're here to see me."

She stood rather suddenly. Her hands reached up to the hood of her cloak and pushed the material back. Of all the women it might be—because he did have many acquaintances, not just paramours—he wasn't expecting to see her face.

His eyes widened in surprise, then narrowed. What was she up to? Surely this was some sort of trickery. They'd seen each other a few days ago, and though neither of them had penned another letter, he was still thinking of ways to assist her.

Lady Charlotte's bottom lip was wet where she'd likely been nibbling on it.

"And to what do I owe the pleasure of your visit?"

"I hadn't heard anything from you. I worried that you'd changed your mind."

"You've not been far from my thoughts since last we met." Which was the truth. He'd not stopped thinking about her, trying to find another way—aside from marriage—to help her out of her conundrum.

She sucked in her lower lip. "I—I was afraid to send another note."

"That is no more dangerous than you showing up here in the flesh, my lady."

She glanced down at her entwined hands as though she were embarrassed by her actions. Had she been thinking about him, too, these past few days?

"I wanted to see you before I left for the country," she whispered.

"You don't leave for another week. And even then you will only be gone for a few weeks, Lady Charlotte."

She reached for his arm, pulled him farther into the kitchen, and pushed the kitchen door shut. She released a breath of relief once they were cossetted in the relative privacy of the room. Now what? Good Lord, he'd never been baffled by the presence of a beautiful woman in all his life. But there was no denying that Lady Charlotte befuddled him.

"You should have sent a note. Your presence here is . . . dangerous."

He didn't want her taking any chances with her reputation—not till they had a firm plan in place. He reached for her arm, needing to touch her and assure himself that she was really here. A strong urge to take her in his arms and promise her that everything would work out nearly overtook him.

He took a step away from her as her gaze met his. Strike that. He wanted more than to comfort her. She needed to leave before he did something irrational like kiss that pout away from her lips.

"If you're trying to frighten me off it won't work," she said.

"How else am I supposed to act when you show up at my house in the middle of the night? The only thing I want to do right now is to kiss those delectable lips of yours, Lady Charlotte."

"Oh—I see." She took a step back, her bravado faltering only for a moment. "I thought we shared a common goal?"

That brought a grin to his lips. "We do."

He walked toward her, widening his arms, taking in her form, covered by that dreadful figure-shielding cloak. She took another step backward.

"What are you doing?"

Her voice was husky, and without an ounce of trepidation. He knew without question that she wanted to taste his lips just as much as he wanted to drink her in.

"If you want to ensure your marriage to Mr. Warren never happens, we can solve that problem right now." The promise in his own voice halted his forward momentum for a second. Oh, the wicked things he wanted to do to her.

"How—how do you suppose we'll end my engagement?"

"Take your cloak off and find out," he offered, moving toward his quarry.

She stood her ground and released the frog at her throat to let the black velvet pool on the ground. The dress beneath was midnight blue, sweeping off both shoulders, and ruched in a vee shape down the front of the bodice. Her breasts were high, and her waist so small he wanted to wrap his hands around her. What a sweet enticement she was. A banquet for the eyes, and a feast that would only end once his hands and mouth devoured every bit of her naked flesh.

"You plan to seduce me here, then? Is that your bright idea?" She pointed her finger at his chest, halting him midstep. "Because there are so many people here to witness that I'm in a compromising position. Well, let me tell you how I see it, Lord Castleigh: you are no more than a very sad excuse for a rogue, one who could probably take lessons in a proper seduction from me."

He put his fingers beneath her chin and angled her face so she had to look directly into his eyes. His hold was gentle, and she could easily pull away at any time if she so wished. She evidently did not for she stood still.

Her eyes were dark pools of molten lava, even though he knew them to be a true sea blue. Something was happening between them, and he was helpless to stop himself from exploring exactly what that something was, even though he knew he should release her and take a step back.

She sucked in her bottom lip, the tip of her tongue visible as she wet it. When she exhaled, he was done for. He stole her breath the next moment as their mouths meshed together and their tongues tangled, lost in a passion he never expected from a woman so young and inexperienced.

The way she had her hands fisted around the sleeves of his jacket, it was as though she were unsure whether to push him away or pull him closer. His hands were too rough as they tangled in her hair to pull her in tighter against his body and he gentled his hold, still desperate to taste more of her.

She bit at his lips, the top, and then the bottom. He returned the erotic nibbles, and then thrust his tongue far into her mouth, skimming it over her teeth and around her tongue. He swore he could taste her very essence. He was so wrapped in her rose scent that nothing mattered except kissing Lady Charlotte till she was weak in the knees and begging him for more.

Her hands never moved, and his threaded through her curls, now half falling from the pins. He held her so tightly and their bodies were pressed so completely together in their sudden embrace that neither could move, even though he wanted more than anything to sweep his hands across the soft swell of her breasts to see if her skin was as soft as it looked. He would bet on his life that it was.

How had he been blinded by her youth to not realize the passion sizzling just beneath her witty demeanor?

This wasn't supposed to be happening, but Charlotte was helpless to pull away from the marquess. Unable to distance herself when she wanted nothing more than to sink deeper into the kiss. And what a kiss it was.

Their mouths were fused together, and their tongues tasting so deeply, it was as though they were of one mind in their need for more. She might fleetingly have thought she'd like to try kissing the marquess, but she had never truly planned for it to happen. She needed his help and it would be easier to accomplish her goal without any emotional entanglement between them.

His hands finally moved from her hair to slide over her shoulders and then lower to hold her about the waist. She skimmed her hands over the sides of his neck and jaw. And then he pulled his lips away from hers.

There was a raging fire of desire burning in his light blue eyes, and it was so intense she could feel the heat sizzling along her flesh exposed to the night air. Neither released the other; they just stood embracing and staring at each other.

Charlotte was a little out of breath, and her breasts rose and fell rapidly, surging against his chest with each inhalation. His eyes were focused on her lips again. Would he kiss her once more? Did she want him to? Oh, indeed, she did. But they couldn't. It wasn't right; it would change their easy friendship to something else . . . something darkly dangerous, even though she wanted to explore this because it was forbidden.

She dropped her hands away from him, and placed her fingers over her kiss-swollen lips, suddenly shocked by what had just transpired. What had she done? Worse, she wanted to do it again and again until she had her fill of this man. Could she ever truly get her fill of him?

The marquess must have seen something in her expression that disagreed with everything they'd done, for he released her, and dropped his hands to his sides despite the fact that he looked starved for more of her.

Her heart beat so fast in her chest that the sound pulsed in her ears and made her deaf to her surroundings. She could no more escape what she'd done than stop herself from wanting to indulge once again in thc sweet touch of their bodies together, and their locked lips.

Though only a couple of steps distanced them, she practically ran back into his arms, this time stealing a surprised kiss from him.

He must have read her intent, for his arms wrapped around her immediately. This time they were not idle, but pressed into her, his hands molding her hips, her waist, her back as they tasted each other for a second time.

Kissing him was so wrong, but it felt so right.

Her breasts were crushed to his chest, her arms wrapped

tightly around his shoulders and neck, her fingers tangling in his dark hair. The tresses were as soft as hers, but bone straight.

They were so lost in each other that they hadn't realized someone had entered the kitchen until they heard the clearing of a throat behind them.

Charlotte hurriedly drew herself away from the marquess and turned to the intruder, panting heavily and flushing from the embarrassment of what she'd been doing. How dare this person interrupt something so perfect, so intense.

No, that thought wasn't right.

She should thank the woman standing before them, because she'd just ensured Charlotte would not find herself ruined by the marquess.

It was the woman from Gunter's. Her dark hair was down and braided over one shoulder. She was in her nightgown and robe. She looked at odds with staying and leaving, but her gaze traveled between Charlotte and the marquess with interest.

"Bea." The marquess's voice was deeper than usual, slightly breathless from their activities. It made Charlotte feel marginally better that he seemed just as out of sorts by what had happened as she was.

"I didn't mean to interrupt . . ."

Charlotte eyed her suspiciously. Had she not meant to disrupt their kiss, she would have turned right back around and left them to their own devices—or vices, as it were—in the kitchen. Goose bumps rose along her arms at the thought. Charlotte should be praising this woman for her timely intervention. That kiss might have been an indulgence Charlotte would have liked to repeat, but it had also been wrong for so many reasons.

"I forget myself," the marquess said, stepping around Charlotte to retrieve her fallen cloak, which he wrapped around her shoulders.

Charlotte redid the frog clasp and tied the satin ribbons together beneath. She suddenly felt the need to busy herself since she could think of nothing to say to this woman she did not know. Her face was no longer hot with embarrassment. Anger filled her instead for letting her guard down and allowing the marquess to prove that he was a practiced roué and how little defense she had against him, especially when she didn't understand all that seduction entailed.

The woman stood her ground, a look of confusion puckering her pretty brows. She had the same blue eyes as the marquess. Perhaps she was a sibling?

"Can I bring you something once I've seen my guest home?"

Charlotte turned to him, unsure why he would say such a thing. She lived but two streets over and she'd found her way here, so she could find her way home, as well.

"Stay," Charlotte said to him. To the woman he called Bea she said, "I'm sorry we met this way. Please accept my apologies for . . ." For what exactly? She couldn't say for walking in on their kiss, or for being caught in the marquess's arms when she wanted to be there still.

"I'm not one to judge, but the children could happen upon you here."

She was looking at Tristan as she said that. But Charlotte wasn't sure if that reminder was supposed to upset her, or to make her realize the full depth of the stupidity of her actions.

"Understood," she said to the woman.

Charlotte nodded and turned toward the door that led to the back gardens. She didn't want to leave from the front entrance and draw any attention to the marquess's home. The servants' entrance was less conspicuous. Or at least she hoped it to be.

She couldn't look upon the marquess. Was he as angry with himself as she was with herself? Did he want to kiss her again as she secretly wanted to kiss him?

"I'll be home later, Bea," the marquess said, following on Charlotte's heels.

"Tristan," she called out. There was a measure of shock in her voice.

Tristan. How fitting a name when Charlotte wanted to use him to end her engagement to Mr. Warren.

His hand pressed to her lower back as he pulled open the heavy wooden door. It appeared she wouldn't escape him too easily. Perhaps she should act as though the kiss had never happened, otherwise everything would become awkward between them.

When the cool night air and a wall of fog wrapped around them, he said, "I'm sorry. Rest assured my sister will say nothing about discovering us. I would trust her with my own life."

Charlotte turned to him. "I've already forgotten she was there."

Her voice sounded defensive to her own ears. The marquess smiled and pulled the hood of her cloak up to obscure her identity.

"I will remind you another time of what precisely transpired between us tonight."

"I'd rather you wouldn't."

She brushed past him, not quite sure she was going in

the right direction with fog sitting heavily in the air all around them. He pushed through the clouds of white ahead of her and reached up to unlatch a gate. At least she'd been heading in the right direction.

"The fog will aid us in getting you home without discovery."

"I made it here undiscovered. I would have remained in the shadows till I was safely back in my own home."

"What kind of man would that make me, if I let you walk the streets alone at the midnight hour?" The marquess clucked his tongue and shook his head in a scolding fashion.

She snorted and couldn't help but tease him. "Despite what many might think, you really are a gentleman."

"I like to believe so." He puffed up his chest and smoothed one hand down the front of his jacket.

She nearly laughed. He was having fun at himself to put her more at ease.

"You're not anything like what I imagined."

"Is that so?"

"I thought you would be different somehow."

"I may still prove to be the rogue you so desperately desire me to be." The tone of his voice was darker when he said that—was he disappointed that she had painted him in such a way?

She needed to change the subject of their conversation. Dissecting what was between them was unsettling; especially after the kiss they'd just shared. She needed time to think about all that had happened.

"I didn't know you had a sister."

"I suppose you're too young to have read her woes in the rags."

"Scandal runs in the family, does it?" she teased.

"Her story isn't mine to tell." There was an edge of protectiveness in his voice that brooked no argument. So she wisely left it alone.

"You're a very interesting man," she observed aloud.

"You think? No different than my peers, really."

"Yet you go about society as though no one matters."

"That is where you are wrong." They turned onto Grosvenor Street. "Don't describe me as heartless, my lady, when I *do* care about the things that matter most in life."

When he didn't seem inclined to continue, she prompted him. "What kinds of things . . . ?"

"My children, my sister, Jezebel, my closest friends. Is that enough to appease your curiosity?" he said drolly.

She looked at her toes peeking out from beneath her dress and cloak as they walked. She should be ashamed that she had asked; of course he cared about his family, how could she ever assume or think otherwise? "You make me feel shallow."

"We are merely at different stages in life. And I certainly can't blame you for wanting to dissolve your engagement." He took her arm in his and patted her hand.

"My cousin reminds me often that I'm lucky to have caught Mr. Warren's attention. Though it's being arranged by my father." The betrayal of her father could not be forgiven, not while Papa was willing to ruin the rest of her life to make one small political alliance. Shouldn't she mean more to her father than to be a mere pawn that would be stolen by the first piece to cross over her square on a chessboard?

They stopped walking. Her house was close, and because he wasn't cloaked as she was, he would have to retreat into the fog before long.

"I'll be fine going up to my house alone, my lord."

"Do not walk the streets unescorted again. You don't know what dangers lurk in the shadows. And you're far too precious to subject yourself to any kind of danger."

"My maid escorted me to your house."

He smiled at her and reached beyond the hood of her cloak to cup her chin in his hand.

"Will I see you again before I go?" Her voice was wistful and she wished she didn't sound quite so eager to see him again, but it was too late to take back the question.

"Something can definitely be arranged," he replied earnestly. "You're here for a while yet."

She gave him a smile, not that he could see it beyond the hood of her cloak, but his thumb brushed over her cheek and across her lips, stopping her breathing once again.

"Write me another letter to let me know."

"I'll only pen another note if you promise to return the favor," he said.

Her eyes widened. She opened her mouth to ask if he honestly wanted her to write to him again, but his thumb pressed over her lips.

"Shh," he whispered. "I'd kiss you good night if I thought we could remain unnoticed."

Tendrils of light from the gas lamps and the moon that shone bright above them were trapped in the fog swirling around them, and for the briefest of moments, they could see each other clearly. There didn't appear to be anyone around, and she was tempted to throw him off his game by giving him another kiss, but she didn't dare. Not after what had happened in his kitchen. Really, she might not be able to stop at simply a kiss.

"I'll be attending the opera tomorrow," she informed him.

"Alas, I have a dinner engagement I cannot break."

She was crestfallen by this news. But it was for the best.

"What are we doing, Lord Castleigh?"

"Does it matter so long as we are enjoying each other's company?"

"I suppose not." She stepped out of his reach and stared at the servants' entrance where she would steal into her own home like a thief. She didn't want to go, but remaining out here with his lordship was also impossible.

"Good night, my lord," she finally said, and turned away from her very own midnight temptation.

Chapter 9

A stream of correspondence between two prominent households has been noted. All that's left to figure out is whom the letters are being passed between and how illicit the words contained within might be.

—The Mayfair Chronicles, June 1846

Dear Lord Marquess,

At your request, I'm penning you a letter— hopefully the first of many. What should I detail for you? My daily activities of late are all rather dull. I still haven't had word on the particulars of our next meeting. Surely you won't keep this lady waiting in suspense for your next move?

Ever the victor,
C

Dearest C,

One day is simply not enough time to plan what I have in mind. I shall send you the details once they are worked out.

And it was nothing more than beginner's luck that saw you nearly a victor—I feel I should remind you that our game never officially concluded; therefore, no victor can be named.

I would also like to draw your attention to my very unoriginal address. Really, you must be more discreet.

Lord Marquess

P.S. I'm very interested in your mundane daily tasks.

Dear Lord,

If you wish for me to be original and discreet, perhaps you should not sign yourself as, well, yourself in your correspondence with me.

There is no such thing as beginner's luck. It's what poor sportsmen tell themselves when they cannot outwit a worthy opponent.

Lady C

P.S. My morning was spent being fitted for new dresses.

Madam,

I think I prefer "dearest Lord Marquess" to your most recent salutation. I will show you that beginner's luck is very real. Now stop distracting me with these rose-scented letters of yours while I make arrangements for us to meet once more.

Lord Marquess

Sir,

If you wish to drop formal salutations, then I, too, shall do so. You are taking too long to make arrangements and I grow impatient for your next move. Perhaps we should bring out an hourglass to hurry you along at a pace I would be more content with? Need I remind you that I will be leaving Town in a few days' time?

Lady C

My dearest, most gracious lady,

Impatience is a failing of youth. Allow me some time, and I promise to make the wait well worth your while. Now, tell me what you've done to keep yourself busy—when you aren't driving me insane with a constant stream of parchment.

Lord Marquess

She did not respond further, which oddly enough agitated him. Perhaps something had taken her away from her pen and paper. Hopefully that something wasn't another carriage ride around Hyde Park with Warren. Tristan smacked his hand against his desk, tossing his pen in the process. The man had no chance with Lady Charlotte, so the thought of him taking her around in his carriage shouldn't have this effect on him.

He was annoyed by his own idleness and his indecision as to how precisely he should handle Lady Charlotte. Why was he courting her as though she were a match? A friend, definitely, but she had already turned down his offer of marriage. And if he were truthful with himself, her refusal did vex him a great deal.

Was he truly ready for a wife? Or did he just not want to give up Lady Charlotte to a man like Warren? He shrugged to himself, unsure. He had plans to make for this evening. And Lady Charlotte would not be informed because he intended to surprise her yet. He could picture her smile and it prompted him to leave the house before the lady in question had a chance to send him another letter and further delay him in doing what needed to be done.

Mr. Warren was waiting for Charlotte in the drawing room. Why in heavens was he calling upon her now? They rarely tarried indoors and Charlotte had assumed that was so he could declare his ownership of her and warn off any other suitors that might fancy the idea of courting her.

Genny walked down the stairs with her. "Do be kind. I'll be right outside the door," her cousin said.

"Do you know why he's here?"

Genny shook her head. "I thought we were to go around Hyde Park this afternoon."

She leaned forward and pinched Charlotte's cheeks to add some color. "Promise me," Genny said, her hands holding each of Charlotte's arms.

"Promise you what? That I won't frighten him off? If only that were a possibility. I'd be more than happy to be rid—" Her cousin gave her a look that had Charlotte snapping her mouth shut. Instead of making a snide remark, she looked to the ceiling, perturbed. "Fine. I'll be as sweet as Cook's cherry pie."

She left her cousin standing in the corridor with her eyes narrowed and her arms crossed over her midsection.

With a smile she did not feel, she entered the parlor. "Mr. Warren, it's a surprise seeing you here so early in the day. I hope I haven't kept you waiting overlong."

He was smartly put together in gray trousers and jacket, with a black waistcoat and a gold fob hanging from the pocket. He wore a cravat, impeccably starched. His gray eyes locked her in place, stopping her just inside the door. Was he angry with her? What could she have possibly done to receive such a cold glare?

"It's no trouble at all. I came unannounced though I hope you take care to hurry your pace the next time I visit. I'm a very busy man, Lady Charlotte, and it wouldn't do to keep me waiting too long." He pulled out his watch. "In less than thirty minutes I'm expected elsewhere."

She wanted to tell him that perhaps he shouldn't have come at all, but bit her lip hard instead. "Why are you here if you have another engagement?"

"I came because I have to cancel our ride through Hyde Park this afternoon. Something more important has come up."

Despite the fact that she disliked Mr. Warren, it still stung that she ranked so low on his list of priorities. She needn't think about him much longer; the marquess and she would come up with a plan to end the engagement. She would not rest until she was free of the man standing across from her.

"It's wonderful to hear that I rank so highly. You've even paid me a visit in person instead of writing a note." Which would have been much easier for them both, so why hadn't he just sent a missive instead?

"That tongue of yours will need to be tempered once we are married." His tone was very serious, with an edge of anger.

"I'm afraid that will be impossible." She glared at him, daring him to rebuke her.

"I wanted to see you in person before you left. I have business that takes me away from London."

"You've already said there are more important things; you should have saved us both the trouble."

"Your father wants to make our engagement official when you are back from your trip."

Why was her father rushing this along? He'd always doted upon her, given her everything she wanted, and now he was selling her to the highest bidder like a prized mare. She would seek him out when she was done with Mr. Warren.

"I see," was all she could say.

"I also wanted to say that you should comport yourself above reproach while at the Carletons'. I do not wish to make enemies of them but their house parties leave much to be desired."

She wondered, then, why her father let her attend any social event held by the Carletons. Perhaps Mr. Warren could answer that question for her.

"It's obvious how much you dislike them, yet you don't object to my attending their summer party." She stepped farther into the room; her fingers absently ran over the top seam of the settee. "Why is that?"

Mr. Warren brushed his hand through the thick mass of dark hair. "Not that you will understand the significance, but Lord Carleton holds sway over nearly half the seats in the House of Lords. It would be a foolish thing to cut his wife, and probably lead to social ruin for anyone that dared breathe an unfavorable word about them."

Everything always came down to politics. "Rest assured, I'm always on my best behavior when making my rounds in the evenings."

"Be sure to exercise the same prudence during the day, my lady."

"Is that all you came to tell me today?"

"Your father has asked that I formally offer for your hand."

She made a face; she couldn't help it. "It would be best if you didn't. It's dreadful enough that we find ourselves in this position to begin with."

He seemed taken aback, and stared at her agog.

"I'll only say no," she clarified. "Then where would that leave us?"

"Do you mean to make a mockery of me at the altar?"

She crossed her arms and gave him a level stare. "I'm sure I'll work up the courage to say yes by the time we get around to the marrying part."

"I see I've overstayed my welcome," he said, putting his hat back on. Did he not know he was never welcome in her presence?

"Why are you so adamant that we marry?"

He stepped close to her. Too close, and she suddenly felt uncomfortable. "For starters, I need a young wife. I do hope you'll ensure the Fallon seat doesn't end with me."

He meant to have children right away. All the saliva from her mouth dried up and she felt a panic overwhelm her.

"Children. So soon." The distaste was palatable in her voice.

"But that will be your greatest duty as my wife."

"That cannot be the only reason you want to marry me; we despise each other."

"I have three houses. We only need to see each other for the propagation of the title."

So he did intend to hide her in the country. Bile rose in her throat before she tamped down her emotions. She clucked her tongue. Why didn't he want to tell her the real reason he planned to wed her?

"There are plenty of young ladies that would willingly take my place, so there is more to marrying me than you've let on." She took a seat on the settee and stared up at him. "You don't need my dowry since you have your own fortune. You'll also be coming into the Fallon estate and all its entailments this year."

"I have an agreement with your father. I cannot discuss men's matters with you, but you have asked for details so I'll tell you this much: your father and I will prove to be a force to be reckoned with when my influence in the House of Commons meets his influence in the House of Lords."

She wondered what kind of an alliance could have formed between her father, who'd always been a kind, loving father, and Mr. Warren, who hadn't an ounce of kindness in his soul. Maybe she didn't really know her father as well as she thought? He had given her to a man she abhorred even though she'd protested the match right from the start.

"So I was no more than a bargaining chip," she said, knowing full well what the answer was.

Mr. Warren shrugged. "I need to be off. I have important business to attend to."

She didn't wish him well; she just stood in the middle of the parlor staring at nothing and feeling . . . numb. She would not sit here and feel sorry for herself, though. She needed to speak with her father. At least understand his reasons for picking *that man* for her husband.

With bravado and determination, she headed toward her father's study.

She knocked when she reached the white-paneled door.

"Come in," her father called out.

She poked her head in, and saw her father's head bowed, reading through a stack of papers on his wide mahogany desk. "Papa. Am I interrupting you?"

"No, not at all. Come, child."

He beckoned her closer with one hand, and took his reading glasses off with the other, folded them, and stared up at her. Blue eyes met blue eyes as she walked into the study and took a seat in the turquoise velvet wingback chair directly across from him. She remembered coming in here as a child and curling her feet up under her in this very chair. She was not so comfortable in her father's presence to do that now that she'd grown up.

Aside from their eye color there were no similarities between her and her father's appearance. Charlotte had seen a painting of her mother, and knew her to be a petite woman with dark hair and brown eyes. She had been very beautiful and had had the same heart-shaped face as Charlotte, a small button nose, and the most welcoming smile she'd ever seen on anyone. Her father, on the other hand, was tall and robust, with a strong nose and short gray hair where he was not balding.

"Mr. Warren just left."

"I know. He came to see me first."

"Did you ask him to come here today?"

"We had matters to discuss."

"Matters regarding me?" she prompted, not wanting to talk in circles but to just get on with what needed to be said.

"Partly." With his elbows placed on the edge of the desk, her father steepled his fingers in front of him as he contemplated her. "Why do you ask?"

She took a deep breath. "Would you reconsider me having to marry him?"

A severe frown creased her father's forehead. "Postpone the wedding until . . . ?"

"Indefinitely?" she asked in a small voice. As much as she disliked Mr. Warren, she also detested seeing disappointment in her father's deep blue eyes.

"Arrangements have already been signed off on paper. They cannot be changed now. Nor do I wish to stop this marriage." She watched her father's emotions shut off, something that only happened when he was incredibly angry.

She swallowed against the lump in her throat. "I do not like him, Papa. He's cruel to me, and he plans to hide me away in the country once we are married."

Her father let out a dark laugh that sent a chill over her arms and had goose bumps rising along her exposed skin. "Do you think I'll believe your stories? Charlotte, you were a sweet, biddable child. Your grandmamma said I spoiled you too much as a child. I never wanted to believe it, but now I question the amount of freedom I gave you. You've grown into a defiant woman."

She bowed her head. Her father knew how to properly chastise her. "I want nothing more than to please you."

"Then you'll marry Mr. Warren and stop arguing with me about it. I grow tired of your disobedience. He's a decent man and you can rest assured that you and any children you have will be well looked after. That will be a comfort to me when I'm an old man."

"Being well looked after requires more than a few thousand pounds. He'll never make me happy, Papa."

Her father smacked his hand down hard on his desk, making her jump in her seat. Some of the papers atop his desk fluttered in the wake of his violence.

"You will do this or the consequences will be dire."

In a smaller voice yet, she said, "Just tell me why you insist upon this marriage."

"I do not need to justify myself to you. I am your father and my duty was to raise you and arrange the best possible future I could for you. I've done both of those things."

Her eyes flooded with tears. Her father loathed tears so she took a deep breath and hoped they did not trickle down her face.

"I wanted romance, Papa. Someone to sweep me off my feet and ask you properly for my hand in marriage."

"Romance is for the poor who have no prospects in life but to have love to fill their bellies." Her father took a calming breath and sat back in his chair, regarding her curiously. "I've known Mr. Warren for nearly ten years. Since he first took his seat in Parliament. He's a shrewd businessman. He's dedicated and determined to succeed no matter the odds."

"Did you ask him to marry me?" The very thought horrified her beyond reason.

"No. He approached me. I suggest, child, that you use your persuasive powers to gentle the man. I suspect he was worried he'd never find a wife with his gruff manners. Also, he doesn't have the time for social functions where he could woo a woman to become his wife."

Why would Mr. Warren want to marry her? She'd always assumed it was her father's desire for the match, not the other way around. This was so much more confusing. "Why would he want to marry me? He doesn't even like me."

"It's just his nature. I wouldn't marry you off to a man I couldn't trust."

But *she* didn't trust him, she wanted to scream.

Instead, Charlotte looked down at her lap and stared at the yellow and purple embroidered flowers decorating her skirts. What did all this mean? And why had Mr. Warren chosen her? He did not fancy her. He did not look at her with mischief in his eyes like the marquess did. He did not find occasion to subtly caress her hand or arm. He was cold, distant. And not once had he shown an inclination to open up to her. She would not accept an emotionless, unkind man for a husband.

When she looked up at her father again, his gaze was pensive.

"I'll leave you to your work now, Papa." She stood, went around his desk, kissed his cheek, and headed out of the room a little dazed by her father's revelation.

She wandered up to her room. When she opened the door to her bedchamber, her maid was standing there with a letter held between her hands. Her eyes were wide with excitement. "Another letter, miss."

She took it and tore it open, anxious for any good news that could help her forget the conversation she'd just had with her father.

My dearest, most impatient lady,
   All necessary arrangements have been made for us to meet tonight. Trust Lowes when he approaches you. He'll lead you directly into my safekeeping. The time and place will be a surprise. I look forward to seeing you.

                                        Lord Marquess

She sank onto the chaise that formed part of the small seating area in her chamber. The yellow velvet embraced her as she rested her head on the soft curled arm. Tonight seemed so far away. Maybe she should accept the marquess's offer of marriage? She snorted. He hadn't been serious. He'd been trying to make her feel better.

There was always the possibility that he'd figured out a

solution to her conundrum since he had plans to meet with her this evening. And wouldn't that be fabulous? She needed a miracle now.

Tristan stood behind the curtain on the stage. Both he and Hayden were frequent visitors to the opera house; a friend managed the theater and had given Tristan access to areas not seen by the outside world—not unless an admirer was invited to visit after the performance.

Lady Charlotte sat in the Carleton box tonight; she was too far away for him to make out the color of her gown, but he thought it a deep burgundy with black lace overlay. Onyx beads adorned her bosom and a strip of black velvet was wrapped enticingly around her throat. Her hair wasn't done in the usual style; loose curls were pinned up and away from her heart-shaped face and braided back in an elaborate arrangement. Her skin was porcelain white, and her lips were stained with a red pigment. She was definitely a vision of the perfect woman. And he couldn't wait to steal her away from the rest of her company.

He could have taken a seat in his own box, but had thought it too bold considering his plans for the evening. He did not want anyone to know he was here, though surely Lady Charlotte had realized this by now. She looked to her lap as Lady Carleton spoke to her; she seemed unhappy about whatever they were discussing. Soon enough her gaze flickered over the rest of the audience in the opera house.

Was it possible she was searching for him? He had to admit there was a certain amount of satisfaction in thinking she preferred his company to that of all other men.

She stared at her lap again, a quizzical look on her face. Without a doubt, she was reading the note he'd had an usher give to her when she'd been shown into the box. The instructions were detailed but simple. All that remained was for her to follow through with his plan.

He fell back into the shadows behind the stage and made his way past the dressing rooms and through the hallway that the singers and dancers primarily used. There was a wide network of tunnels beneath the stage and the seating in the theater, leading out to street level. The interconnecting passageways were used chiefly by the staff and opera singers to get from one side of the theater to another without detection. And now they would serve to aid him in stealing away his lady.

He paused on that thought. She wasn't precisely *his* lady, but she had become important to him over the short time he'd known her. It was odd that a friendship had formed so quickly between them.

Or perhaps not.

Lady Charlotte was an intriguing and intelligent young woman . . . More importantly, though, he enjoyed being in her company, whether to steal a kiss or simply play a game of chess.

When the music stopped, he counted out the minutes for everyone to exit their boxes and seats, waiting patiently.

He stared through the decorative grill that covered a portion of the wall just under the box seating. A small latch was level with his elbow on the inside, and the hinges were well oiled so he could exit without revealing the secret passage. He would only need a few seconds to succeed in his planned game.

Pulling out his watch, he checked the time. Intermission was nearly over . . . and then he heard her distinctive laugh, delayed behind the rest of the patrons returning to their boxes—she was following his instructions to a T. He grinned and counted each step she took toward the stairs going up to her box.

"I can't believe I didn't do this sooner," Lady Charlotte said to her cousin and Lady Carleton. "I need to make use of the retiring room. Go on up without me; I won't be overlong."

She didn't give them the opportunity to tell her no, and made her way down the stairs and then along the empty corridor toward the retiring room.

"Hurry back to us," Lady Carleton said as she took Genny's arm and led her chaperone back into the private box. Her tone seemed almost conspiratorial. Did she suspect Lady Charlotte was seeking out an admirer?

On the heels of that thought his body tensed—had he been discovered? And which was he . . . an admirer or a friend? He'd worry about those details later. Right now, he had a lady to steal away, and he moved into action.

Turning up the latch, he pushed the screen out that covered the hidden passage and reached for Lady Charlotte before she could wander farther away from him. He was quick to place his bare hand over her mouth and said in a low voice meant only for her, "It's me," so she didn't cry out in fright and give his presence away. Not that anyone aside from a few ushers down the hall would take notice.

When he had Lady Charlotte safely ensconced in the servants' walkway, he released her, turned her about while holding both her upper arms, and pressed a finger to her lips to bid her to hold her tongue. With a motion of his head, he led her along the tunnel that would take them to the dressing rooms, though they wouldn't be going so far as that. Once they reached the belly of the theater he turned her around to face him once again.

Her eyes were bright with mischief, her smile secretive.

He tore his gaze away from the temptation of her lips. "We don't have much time," he said. "But I wanted to see you once more before you were off to Hertfordshire."

"You did?"

"We had an agreement, my lady, and I would not renege on it."

His reassurance had her visibly relaxing and at ease. "Have you come up with a plan, then?"

He put his hands out, indicating the dim tunnels around them. "You are in the midst of it. What will everyone say when you arrive back at the box late?"

"I simply said I would freshen up in the retiring room."

"Yes, but you managed to come unescorted. How do you suppose that will look to all those in the audience that keep tipping their opera glasses in your direction?"

"That's a good point." She brushed away a loose tendril of hair from her brow. "So I'm to create a stir in the gossip columns with my mysterious disappearance for all of fifteen minutes?"

"My dear, dear lady. This is only the start of you stepping out of line in society." He rubbed his hand down the length of her arm. "We will take it slowly."

"I don't have time to take this slowly, Castleigh. Come to think on it, I'm surprised Genny didn't escort me." She chewed worriedly on her lower lip.

He stepped closer, wanting to touch her. "She's probably regretting that choice right now."

"No doubt. And should she come looking for me, and I'm not where I'm supposed to be . . . Well, hell hath no fury like my cousin deceived." She ran her fingers along the wall as she walked deeper into the tunnel. "Where does this lead?"

"To the dressing rooms."

She turned back to him, giving him a shrewd look. "We could be caught together in a dressing room."

"I can promise you that no one of importance would take note of it. I thought we had already discussed this?" He pointedly adjusted his cravat. "I also recall telling you that I liked my head attached to my neck."

She sighed and stepped closer to him once again. "Breaking a few rules here and there simply won't work. It won't be enough to end my engagement."

She rubbed her fingers over the lapel of his jacket, stopping mid-waist before leaning her face closer to his. If he stole a kiss, would it rekindle the fire that had burned so deep in them only a few days ago? Would she pull away from him this time? He decided he would wait her out, have her initiate the kiss once again.

"I think you should ruin me," she whispered close to his mouth.

She didn't know what she was truly asking for. Perhaps he hadn't heard her right.

Her gaze dropped to his lips and then turned back up to meet his eyes. Her pupils were dilated and it wasn't simply because of the dim light. "My father won't call you out."

He gave a slight shake of his head. Charlotte underestimated the lengths to which a man like her father would go to obtain what he wanted—he was ruthless in all his dealings.

"If you were my daughter—and thank God you are not—I would call out any man that dared to lay so much as a finger on you."

She inched closer. The press of her skirts against his shins and the heat of her body were a welcome intimacy.

His body tightened with anticipation, with a need so strong to pull her against him that it took everything he had to hold back.

"Are you thinking of touching me?" she asked in a husky voice that nearly undid him.

He slid the tips of his fingers over her jawline until they reached the soft point of her chin. Her head was tilted up, her lips parted in invitation.

"The things I imagine doing to you . . ."

She pressed her lips together and swallowed. "I think it's very hard for you to resist ruining me."

"No man could resist your charms for long, my lady."

"Except you," she had the audacity to point out.

His eyes narrowed. Was she goading him into making the first move? She had less than ten minutes to find her way back to her seat. A lot could happen in ten minutes. A kiss could happen, a whole conversation could happen . . . He could press her against the wall, hike her skirts up around her thighs as she locked her ankles around his back . . .

When he did nothing more than stare at her, she let out a sigh and looked away from him. "Stealing me away tonight won't be enough to stop my wedding."

"This meeting wasn't intended to stop your nuptials. I wanted to see you again before you left to rusticate in the countryside."

She gasped and her attention snapped back to him. He could no longer wait for her to make the first move. There was no sense in delaying a pleasure they both wanted.

He bloody well wanted her but didn't know how he would ever be able to keep her without her father putting an end to it. Drunk on his own thoughts of desire and need, he stole her next breath with a kiss, and wrapped his arm around her, placing the flat of his hand to the small of her back. He walked her back a few steps until she was pressed to the brick wall. Her lips were just as soft as he remembered, her tongue shy as his explored her mouth. The tentative thrust of her tongue against his had all the blood in his body rushing south.

Oh, he wanted more. He wanted complete possession of her.

One of her hands wormed its way beneath his starched cravat, and the other hand squeezed his upper arm as she pressed deeply into the kiss—allowing herself to be consumed by the fervor that seized them.

What was he doing kissing Lady Charlotte in the dark of the theater? What did he intend for their future and that of Mr. Warren?

He released her mouth and turned his head aside. One of his hands was wrapped around her back, the other rested on the wall next to her head. The only sound to be heard was their heavy breathing.

"What are you doing here?" she asked.

"I thought that much was obvious." His voice was sardonic.

Pushing off the wall, he summoned the strength to take a step away from her. He stared at her in the dark, trying to make out the puzzlement in her expression. She didn't move; she just stared at him as though she didn't know precisely what to say.

"Say something," he said in a more placating tone.

"I don't understand you, nor do your actions shed any light on your intentions. You confound me, sir."

Tristan scratched his head and blew out a stream of air. Hell, he himself couldn't figure out his intentions. "You'll be leaving for three weeks. I wanted to see you. I can only come up with one solution where you're concerned."

"Marriage," she whispered, and looked away from him.

"Can you think of a better alternative?"

She shook her head, never breaking her gaze from his. "I need to think on it even though it is the most logical solution. I never wanted to marry in the first place. So why should I say yes to you? It's all so sudden."

Her words stung his pride. Was it so difficult to contemplate marriage with him? "Have you got another plan up your sleeve that you aren't sharing with me?"

"If I did, I'd certainly not be as worried about my predicament as I have been." She stepped away from the wall, a frown creasing her forehead. "I don't know how to respond to your offer. It's generous, but extreme."

"Say no more." Tristan took her hand and led her back through the tunnels in the direction of the private box she occupied. Was she purposely unmanning him? Or worse . . . perhaps she only saw him as a means to an end. Did she care so little for him despite their similarities?

Now he had to question his sanity in coming here in the first place. When they stopped at the small door that opened to the stairs leading to her box, he turned her to face him.

"Write to me while you are gone." His request sounded like a plea to his own ears.

"I cannot refuse the opportunity." She pressed her hand over his upper arm. "We'll have to be circumspect."

"I assume your lady's maid travels with you."

She nodded.

"Is she trustworthy?"

"Yes," she said, barely above a whisper.

After a pregnant pause, he said, "Think on my offer."

Not being able to withstand another no, he opened the latch, ushered her out of the small passageway, and closed it before anyone noticed his presence.

A handful of questions bombarded him the second she was gone. Had he made a mistake in seeing Lady Charlotte tonight? Would she refuse his offer of help if he could think of nothing other than marriage? Would she cut him off after he'd been so bold with her tonight?

He inched back into the shadows, never so unsure of himself in all his life.

Chapter 10

*A romantic opera spurs foolish lovers into rash deci-
sion making. There were two notable absences at the
opera during the second act. One Lady C—— disappeared for more than a quarter hour. And would you
believe that Lady H—— never returned to her box for
the second half of the opera? That is quite odd considering her companions were still present.*
      —The Mayfair Chronicles, July 1846

Dear Lord Marquess,
 *Should I describe my daily activities or would
you prefer an accounting of everyone here and who
I think they might be smitten with? I'm not sure what
else to say other than . . . I have been thinking
about your suggestion. I cannot thank you enough
for your assistance with my . . . predicament.*

                C

My dearest lady,
 *It would do you well to take lessons in letter writ-
ing. Still using "Lord Marquess"? I certainly hope*

*the person handling your letters is discreet. My last
two days have been spent in idyllic amusement: a
picnic in Hyde Park with my children, then dinner
and cards at a friend's. Sadly, my daughter convinced . . . No, rather she coerced my son and me to
sit at tea with her this morning. I wasn't forced to
wear an apron; my son, on the other hand, will
certainly be traumatized at the very thought of tea
with his sister again. Did I mention that the other
guests were a porcelain creation from Paris—very
sophisticated—and a brown bear wearing a dress
that hails all the way from Russia?*

                                                       T

Dear T,

*I haven't quite decided how I should address you
in my letters. "Lord Marquess" seemed most natu-
ral since you appear larger than life to all the ladies who cannot spot a rogue at twenty paces. I on
the other hand have proved much wiser than my
age might suggest. I do wish I could have attended
your tea party, only I would have made you put on
an apron. How can you truly play along without
stepping into the role completely?*

*The only idyllic pleasures to be had at present in
this dreadful heat are walks in the garden with my
dearest friend and Mr. T——. The man is always
three steps behind us—I fear we'll have no time to
ourselves because of his constant presence. He's an
odd character, but kind to my friend, so I cannot
complain about his poor attempts at poetry.*

                                          Your friend,
                                          Char

My darling C,

You really must be more imaginative than "T."
Perhaps I will start calling you Lotte? Mayhap my
given name is best. So long as you do not start quot-
ing from Tristan and Iseult, *unfortunately where*
my name derived from—my mother's favorite story
or some rot.

Is there no gossip to be had yet? Already a week
has passed, and not one scandal has been printed
in the rags. I'm almost disappointed. Perhaps I
should have attended.

T

Dear T,

What happened to being discreet about our
names? If you address me as Lotte, I'll be forced to
address you with an equally horrible rendition of
your name. I have a strong aversion to Lotte. Lady
H—— used to call me Little Lotte as a child. I felt
like one of her corgis when she called to me in her
shrill voice.

Char

"To whom are you penning another letter?" Ariel leaned
over Charlotte's shoulder.

Charlotte turned to her friend. They had escaped to
Charlotte's room to have an hour to themselves—an hour
without Mr. Torrance hovering close at hand. "You can't
guess?"

"Oh, let me have a look, then." Ariel slid the parchment from the desk so she could read the correspondence. "You are using tales about our childhood to
seduce your marquess?" Her friend tsked. "You must be

a temptress if you are to succeed in the plan we devised for you."

Charlotte took the paper back from her friend. She hadn't told Ariel that the marquess had refused to be caught in a compromising situation. And she definitely hadn't told her friend that he'd offered marriage.

"I'm working my way around to that. These things take time, Ariel."

There was an excited gleam of challenge in her friend's eyes. "Let me help you pen something fabulously scandalous."

"For a young lady with a mother that is the paragon of all that is virtuous, you should be—"

"More prudent in life?"

Charlotte grinned at her friend. "No. Just a little more innocent than you are."

"Well, it's a good thing we befriended each other at so young an age, otherwise I might have turned out exactly like my mother." Ariel visibly cringed.

"And that would have been such a waste of a brilliant mind." Charlotte pushed the paper toward her friend and stood from the vanity that faced the open window in her room. "You can replicate my handwriting. Sit." She motioned to the now empty chair. "We'll write it together."

Having Ariel write her correspondence, at least this once, helped Charlotte put distance between her and the marquess. She was developing a *tendre,* which simply wouldn't do. It was those damnable kisses that had started her feelings in that direction. In fact, that first kiss had changed everything between them.

"How is he supposed to take you seriously, when you compare yourself to Mama's corgis?"

"But it's the truth. And I really can't allow him to

address me as Lotte. So it stays. What do you think we should write next?"

"What has he said to you in previous letters?"

She didn't want to mention that he had talked openly about his children right from the start, which was silly on her part. She truly was developing an attachment to him. Worse, she hadn't even been able to tell Ariel that she'd been well and truly kissed by the marquess, and on two separate occasions.

She wasn't sure why she had kept that a secret, but she didn't want to tell anyone about what had transpired because she was still trying to make sense of it all. Maybe Ariel could make better sense of it than she? What Charlotte needed to do was detach her feelings from those kisses and not think of the marquess as a suitable match. She pressed her fingers to her mouth and sat on the edge of her bed. But what if those kisses had meant more to him, too?

Ariel looked up at her, tapping the top of the pen against her lips. "You should talk about wanting to see him again."

"He'll get the wrong impression." She flopped back on her bed and stared up at the sprigged white canopy. "What if I tell him that his correspondence is in competition with Mr. Warren's? Would the attention of another man draw his interest to me?"

"That might well work. But of course it's a complete lie since I know for a fact you've received no correspondence from Mr. Warren. Why don't you tell him about the letter your father sent?"

She squeezed her eyes shut and threw her arm over her eyes. She hated to think about that letter. It had been short, concise, and demanding. If she told the marquess that her father was moving up the announcement of her engagement, what would he do? She'd already turned down his offer of marriage—not that he'd properly thought through what he was asking. He couldn't have really wanted such an outcome.

"I'm not ready to talk about my father's demands," Charlotte said. "I wish I could convince Papa how wrong he is to rush this."

"But your impending marriage to Mr. Warren is precisely the reason you befriended the marquess—he's to help you stop your engagement."

"Neither of us have come up with a way to end the engagement. He won't publicly ruin me. I've practically asked that of him outright."

Ariel gasped. "I cannot believe you were so frank with him and that he said no. He's damaged so many other reputations."

"Are you so sure about that? His name is tied to the scandals in the rags, but I can't think of one woman he's been associated with—not by name."

Ariel tapped the pen against the edge of the table. "You know, you're right. How odd that we didn't realize that sooner."

"Not so odd, he has children out of wedlock. They live with him."

"My mother mentioned that not long ago to one of her friends." Ariel turned in the seat and looked down at the letter. "You should move on from the name drivel and write 'I long for your company, someone who understands me completely.' "

Charlotte cringed at the very thought of putting something of that nature in the letter. "Absolutely not. He would think someone had hit me over the head if I wrote in such a desperate tone. We must think our words through carefully."

Ariel tapped the end of the pen against the table. "May I see his last letter to you?"

Charlotte's first instinct was to hold it back, keep it private. It was addressed to her and not Ariel. And to share the correspondence she'd received to date felt like a betrayal to the marquess. Although why should it feel like that?

"You don't want to share his letters, do you?" her friend said.

Charlotte pushed herself up on her elbows. "It's not that."

Ariel's mouth dropped open in shock, as though something had suddenly dawned on her. "That is precisely it. You are interested in the marquess for more than just the plan we devised."

Charlotte started to protest, but not much more than "I'm not—" made it past her lips.

"We've known each other practically our whole lives. You cannot finagle your way out of this. What precisely has happened since our visit to the zoo? You're withholding some pertinent information."

"Nothing has happened. I've merely grown to respect the marquess for his . . ."

His kindness? For the kisses she thought about far too often? For his refusal to ruin her even though he insisted it was to save his own head? She knew better than that; he wanted to protect her.

"Oh, my. He's kissed you, hasn't he?" Ariel threw down the pen in her excitement at discovering Charlotte's secret. "I can't believe you didn't tell me!"

"Am I so obvious?" Charlotte was horrified that she

was so easily read. She covered her face with her hands, embarrassed.

Her friend sat next to her on the bed with a bounce. "What was it like?" Ariel's voice was dreamy.

"I was taken by surprise." She really had no desire to share details of her kiss with anyone, but this was her best friend. "It was wonderful, Ariel. It was so much more than I imagined." She fell silent. She was giving away too much of her feelings.

Charlotte took a deep breath. She needed to stay detached, as though the kiss hadn't mattered, because she didn't want her friend overanalyzing the situation. It didn't feel right to share something so private, especially when Charlotte was still sorting out her feelings about the kiss. Especially since he'd offered marriage—and his proposal was far more tempting than Mr. Warren's.

She began to wonder whether or not she could marry the marquess. It would be a grand solution to her predicament, but she wanted to marry for more than necessity. She wanted to be swept off her feet and to fall madly in love with the man who offered for her hand. Realistically, though, that dream wasn't likely to come true.

"When did this happen?" Ariel prompted her again.

Should she lie and say it happened at one of the two events where they'd met the marquess or tell her friend what she'd been up to in the evenings, sneaking out of her house in a cloak to disguise her? The truth was better, because she realized the impossibility of lying to her dearest friend.

"He was testing me. I think he wanted to see if I would back down if he treated me more intimately. I did ask him outright to ruin me." She looked away from her friend, unable to meet her gaze.

"Yet he's told you he won't put you in a compromising position," her friend mused. "We put him on the list because he's smart and known to be kind. I think he has more morals than my mother can imagine."

"You can't say a thing, not even hint at this secret, Ariel."

"Do you trust me so little? Is that why you didn't tell me?" Ariel frowned.

"No, it's not that. I was just surprised by the kiss and I wanted to sort out my feelings before telling you. I wouldn't have kept that information a secret indefinitely."

"Your *feelings*?"

Charlotte was revealing far too much. But now that she'd said that, she'd have to explain what she meant. "Before your imagination runs wild, I think I need to clarify what happened."

They both lay back on the bed and turned to face each other. "I visited him under cover of night, about two weeks ago. I surprised him; he honestly never expected me to show up at his house."

"You went to his house?" Ariel's eyes were wide. "Have you gone mad?"

"This is why I haven't told you anything yet. He was—believe it or not—the perfect gentleman."

"Yet he kissed you," her friend pointed out.

"He was testing my resolve. Nothing more."

"So you've said. But I think there's more to it than that. What was it like?"

"I can't really describe it. One minute we were talking, and before I knew what was happening, his arms were around me and our mouths were fused together."

Ariel sighed, as though picturing it. "How long did it last?"

"Long enough for his sister to interrupt us."

"He has a sister?"

Charlotte nodded. "I had no idea, either."

"Oh, I wonder if I can find out from my mother what her story is."

"You mustn't, Ariel. Promise me you'll ask no questions about the marquess. I do not want anyone to suspect my plan." She sat up and folded her arms around her bent knees. "Not that I've figured out what my plan is yet."

"You really are acting strange. Before meeting him, you would have thought differently about this. I thought you wanted to be caught in such a compromising situation that you'd either be forced to marry him, or retire to the country indefinitely."

"I seem to have developed a friendship with the marquess."

"Friendship?"

"Well, not technically, but I haven't anything better to call it."

Ariel gave a wide grin as she sat and folded her legs under her on the bed. "He's very much your secret admirer."

"Somehow I don't think he'd appreciate that description," Charlotte said wryly. "He has a reputation for being a great seducer of women, and you call him a mere admirer."

"Don't tell him, then. Why do you suppose he was testing you?"

"You really won't stop questioning me until you have all the information."

"We planned this together, Charlotte. Why should you not include me now?"

It had been Ariel who'd suggested taking the names of every rogue from Charlotte's collection of *Mayfair*

Chronicles, which she kept stashed beneath her bed where no one aside from her maid knew she had them.

"I should mention that I wrote a letter to him without ever intending to deliver it. It was a way to sort out my thoughts after I first met him. I told you I saw him at Gunter's when Mr. Warren took me for a carriage ride a few weeks back."

Her friend nodded.

"I wrote out the details of our plan in that letter."

Ariel's mouth dropped open. "Why would you do such a thing? He must think you a childish ninny."

"I can promise you that he doesn't think that." Charlotte shook her head. He wouldn't have kissed her so thoroughly had he thought her childish. "I originally wrote to him because I was afraid the marquess was not interested enough in me to continue what I had started at the duchess's ball. He said I was too young to understand what game I was playing. I never thought myself sophisticated enough or old enough to capture the attention of a man like him. But I have."

Ariel tapped her finger against her chin. "We did notice that not a single debutante was tied to his name."

"Exactly. So I thought he might side with me if I gave him reason to." Charlotte paused and took a deep breath. It wouldn't do to only offer half the story to her friend. "I might have told him that stopping my upcoming nuptials with Mr. Warren would damage his clout in Parliament when he came into his title and moved to the House of Lords."

Ariel gasped. "You didn't dare."

"I did. I had no choice. It's selfish, I know. My father wants nothing more than to make a political match with my marriage. I understand fathers do this all the time, and it would be perfectly acceptable if Mr. Warren were a decent man and I at least liked him. But that simply isn't the case."

"I'm in awe of your boldness. What did the marquess say when you appeared at his house?"

"I definitely surprised him. I think he thought I was there for an entirely different purpose."

"You mean . . ." Ariel's eyes widened.

"Yes. I think the kiss was to scare me off, but when I didn't leave afterward . . . I might have returned his kiss with one of my own." She looked away from her friend, embarrassed to admit that truth. Her skin didn't blush from embarrassment, but from the thought of the marquess embracing her, and making her feel things she'd never felt in all her life.

"I still can't believe you didn't tell me any of this."

"I think when his sister walked in, and I didn't run frightened at the idea of being caught, he realized I could handle the plan I had set in motion."

"What did his sister say?"

"She apologized for interrupting."

"What do you think the marquess would have done had she not come into the room?"

"I guess I'll never know. When his sister left, he walked me home. We agreed to correspond while I was at the Carletons'."

Her friend stared back at her quietly for a few moments. "This is very interesting."

"It is, but I've been at a loss for what to say when I write to him. He's teased me about how boring my letters are."

"I think he likes you, Charlotte."

"Don't be a ninny. He appreciates my situation and has

temporarily agreed to help me. He has everything to gain in my ruin—at least politically. Ruining Mr. Warren's good name will lose voters for him and my father."

"What would you do if your father forced the marquess to marry you?"

"He won't. Papa despises him. I've heard him over cards talking about the marquess and Lord Barrington. Even the Carletons."

"How can he hate the Carletons when he's sent you to their annual summer party?" Ariel said, disbelieving.

Charlotte shrugged. "Maybe it has something to do with Lady Carleton's position? An invitation from her is more highly coveted than anyone else's."

"You're right, of course."

"And to be in her disfavor means all doors close to you. Not even my father can risk that kind of censure."

"I suppose that explains why your father let you attend the events in Town, but not why he let you come to *this* particular house party. The worst scandals are born here."

"You know as well as I that my father could never refuse the invitation. I think he hoped I wouldn't receive one, but that wasn't the case, and I'm glad for it because it means I won't have to keep company with Mr. Warren."

Their conversation called to mind the words she'd had with her father shortly before leaving Town. He'd made it clear that he would be furious if he found out that she was corresponding with the marquess. That knowledge wouldn't stop her from carrying on, though. She just needed to decide what exactly she planned to do with the marquess. Could she accept a *permanent* solution? Marriage? Why must she lose her freedom? Life was cruel to women; they never had a say in their own future.

Charlotte stood from the bed. "Come, we should write this letter and go back down to the rest of the company."

She convinced Ariel to keep the beginning of the letter.

Dear T,

What happened to being discreet about our names? If you address me as Lotte, I'll be forced to address you with an equally horrible rendition of your name. I have a strong aversion to Lotte. Lady H—— used to call me Little Lotte as a child. I felt like one of her corgis when she called to me in her shrill voice.

Because you are waiting so patiently for the latest on-dit, let me tell you that there is one scandal brewing. For the sake of the persons involved, I hope that they are vigilant and not caught out. They seem to have developed strong feelings for each other over the past week. I think I'll keep you in suspense a while longer about who is involved. I would hate to be responsible for the leak that ruined their sojourn in the country.

Your friend
Char

Dearest C,

I will keep in mind that we must be ever vigilant. We don't know who could be watching the post coming to and from the Carleton estate.

Town is equally hot, and the stench off the Thames grows unbearable, making me crave an escape of my own. Perhaps I should retreat to my estate up north if the weather doesn't cooperate and turn into something more civilized soon. But first, I await your return. We've much to plan in person since we haven't planned anything on paper.

I can think of a few people who might be engaged in a scandal as well. Perchance do you refer to mutual friends engaging in wickedness? My oldest friend was acting odd before he left for the country. "Smitten" and "distracted" are how I would describe him.

Your dearest friend
T

My dearest friend,

I'm not sure it is safe to discuss our plans in our letters. I fear that the only solution to my conundrum is what you've previously suggested—and neither of us wants that outcome. We are too free-spirited to be confined—especially by what you once mentioned.

Yes, a scandal is brewing between mutual friends. Though I must say my friend seems blind to the man seeking her favor, who has been sincere and kind beyond measure. I've only seen such behavior in a man desiring a permanent place in a lady's heart.

I do hope the weather treats you more kindly in Town. I would hate for you to leave before I am home. I've news to share with you—about a mutual foe, the very one to precipitate our friendship.

Your
C

My darling,

   You cannot end your letters as you did the last. I'm waiting for further explanation. Has our foe paid a visit to you? Have plans changed?

                                              Your
                                                 T

My friend,

   Everything has changed. I'm sorry I can't provide you with more details just yet.

   You should know that something has happened at the party. I've been confined to my room—all the young unmarried ladies have. I don't know what is happening, but I fear this could be my last letter before I come home. It's becoming increasingly difficult to get posts out safely. Please don't write me any more notes. I can't be caught out when there is scandal afoot.

                          Longing to return to London,
                                                Char

Chapter 11

Someone was seen lurking about in the shadows of Lord R——'s last night and every night before that for a week. Perhaps one of his many daughters has a secret to keep? This writer will certainly uncover all the answers in due course.

—The Mayfair Chronicles, August 1846

Her father had arrived twenty minutes ago. He'd called for her to come to the small parlor. She was too nervous to remain idle and so paced the room, fingering the decorative ornaments on the mantel and on the side tables. There were only a few reasons her father might come to the Carleton estate—none of them good.

When the door opened, the sound of other guests could be heard from the corridor beyond. Charlotte turned to face her father, still surprised to see him here of all places.

Her father's arms were outstretched so she could walk into them and hug him. "My dearest," he said, patting her hair as he used to do when she was a child.

"What's happened to have brought you here? Is Grandmamma well?" Her cousin had advised against leaving the old woman in Town during the hottest months. And her failing health was one of the three reasons her father might be here.

"Your grandmother fares very well. Her sister's presence has lightened her spirits these past few weeks without you to brighten our home."

"Has something terrible happened to bring you here?"

"I cannot lie to you, not about this, but you should hear the unpleasant details from me and not anyone else at this shameless house party." Her father visibly took a reassuring breath—this was not like him at all. "Your chaperone is to be removed from the party for a transgression that cannot be ignored."

"You can't do that to Genny," she argued.

Her father raised his hand to stop her protests. She snapped her mouth shut, knowing he was out of sorts, and she hugged him, hoping to lift his mood.

"I already have done exactly that. And I've done it to protect you, poppet."

Tears prickled her eyes. She was angry and sad and felt so many conflicting emotions she couldn't list them. How could her cousin not have been more careful? She was smitten with Lord Barrington and had been for the duration of their stay at the Carletons', but the earl had left today . . .

She pulled away from her father's comforting embrace and searched his eyes, hoping she could read the truth there. She didn't need to hear it from him; she could guess that her cousin had been caught by another house guest. Who would dare call her father here?

"We will be leaving together tomorrow."

"But the house party will have concluded by the weekend. Can we not stay as long as that?"

"Don't argue with me. I've had to push up your engagement to cover the scandal that's already stirring talk in London. It was too much to ask for Lady Hargrove to keep her mouth shut. She's told anyone of worth what's transpired."

Her mouth dropped open with his cool announcement. With a ferocity quite unlike her, she suddenly despised the older woman who had taken her under her wing when she was only a child.

With her anger came a realization to what her father said. "What exactly does pushing up the engagement entail?"

Her father puffed out his chest, his pride so crystal clear she knew what he was going to say before the words passed his lips, and she silently screamed on the inside. "The banns will be read this coming Sunday. You'll be married before summer ends."

"Papa, it's too soon. You promised me one season." Tears threatened to fall, but she swallowed against them. Her father disliked tears more than anything, and crying would have him sending her back to her room without argument.

"I know, dear, but the circumstances surrounding our family . . . The scandal arising from this might blacken our name."

He shook his head as though he were at a loss for words—well, that made two of them. How could she possibly find a way out of her current circumstance?

"Papa." She felt her heart drop in her chest. Marry in four weeks' time? She couldn't. She wouldn't. She pressed her fist to her chest, unable to take in a decent breath.

This was the very thing she feared he'd come to the country-side to tell her. It was the *worst* of her imaginings.

"I've already discussed the sordid situation with Mr. Warren. We'll make preparations for an intimate wedding party—family only," he clarified with a stern look. "Your grandmamma is eager to make all the preparations and her sister has agreed to stay on to help with the wedding arrangements."

She could swear she saw black dots floating across her vision and blurring her sight. Her laces were too tight, and she wanted them off, but she was trapped. Trapped. She felt faint. This was so wrong. This was all wrong. She needed to get word to the marquess. But it wouldn't be safe to do so now; her father would certainly be watching all the post coming in.

She'd have to send her maid to the nearest posting inn as soon as she returned to her room.

"Calm yourself, my darling."

He squeezed her shoulder as though it would comfort her. The only thing that could possibly comfort her at the moment was a repeat of yesterday—when everything was still carefree and any unpleasantness in the distant future.

"The gossips will leave you alone when you are married to such an honored member of society. And when Mr. Warren takes his seat in the House of Lords next to me, you'll be the talk of Town, my darling girl. Just imagine, you'll be as respected as the Countess of Carleton."

Her father was beaming. How could he be so blind to her panic-stricken state?

She really did think she might faint, yet what she needed to do was escape this place. Escape her father. Run as fast as she could from Mr. Warren. She could not marry him. Would not. How dare he agree to any such arrangement with her father when he disliked her as much as he did. He was a cruel, stupid, selfish man.

"You look pale, child." He stood above her, worry carved in the lines of his aged face. "Do you need water? Should I call in another of the ladies to assist you?"

She attempted to stand, but her head spun and her vision was so compromised that she was forced to seat herself back on the settee and take a calming breath. She must control her emotions. She must act the perfect daughter— no matter where her thoughts wandered.

She took in a slow, deep breath and felt marginally better as she reined in her emotions. She would find a way out of the marriage her father had his mind set upon.

With one final deep breath, she felt her nerves slowly calm. She would make it through today just as she had every other normal day. Her anger and resolve to find a solution slowly replaced the fear that had momentarily crippled her.

"I'll be fine, Papa. This has all been such a shock that I can't think of what to say or do." Her voice was firm. "I'm sorry if I alarmed you."

Her father sat next to her on the settee. "I understand." He pulled on one of her corkscrew curls at her temple, and let it bounce back up and hit her cheek. "I'm so sorry I ever allowed that woman into our midst. Had I known or even guessed at the scandal that would fall at our feet . . ."

She reached for his arm and squeezed it reassuringly. "Don't apologize."

She stood slowly this time and didn't feel any dizziness. She couldn't listen to such talk against her cousin a moment longer. Taking her father's hand once she was finally steady on her feet, she gave him a sad smile.

"I need to rest, Papa."

"We'll get through this," he said reassuringly.

She wasn't inclined to believe him. "I'll see you for dinner, Papa. Just think about delaying our departure till the end of the week. There will be gossip surrounding us no matter when we leave; more speculation could arise from leaving the Carletons early. What if the gossips should think I was involved in some wrong-doing if I'm removed from the house before the party ends?"

Her father shook his head. "I should never have let you come here."

"You could not refuse the invitation," she reminded him, which was the complete truth.

"Go on up and rest," he finally said. "I'll see you down to dinner."

She leaned closer to her father so she could kiss his cheek—she was rewarded with a smile. How she hated herself for the betrayal she would deliver to her father. But it must be done. He could withstand a moment of irritation compared to a lifetime of sorrow for her. Couldn't he?

When she had made her way to her room and locked the door behind her, she went to her writing desk without delay. Could she safely send one final note to the marquess? Her engagement had gone from being announced on her return to London to banns being read this very Sunday.

What kind of person did it make her that her first thoughts when her father explained the situation had not been of Genny but of the marquess. Genny would weather this incident, whatever it was she'd been caught doing. Charlotte liked to think she'd come to know Lord Barrington during the past few weeks, and there was no question in her mind that the earl would do everything in his power to protect Genny.

The marquess needed to know everything that had transpired. Would he find a solution to her problem now that her situation was so dire? Or would he walk away knowing there was little he could do to stop her upcoming marriage? There was only one way to find out.

Tristan had grown fond of the letters he and Charlotte exchanged. Though there hadn't been that many, they were quickly filling up the top drawer of his desk. His little temptress was a witty and amusing woman. But the last few letters had him worried and anxious for more news than she provided. Her most recent letter was more worrisome than ever. He looked down at the parchment that had been sitting on his desk the entire afternoon.

> *My friend,*
>
> *It's with great urgency that I write you this letter. Scandal has finally touched the Carleton summer party and my father has come to escort me home earlier than anticipated. I do not know what I can ask of you, but I need your help to stop my marriage in four weeks' time to Mr. W——.*
>
> *I'm at a loss as to how to accomplish my goal in so short a time, so I must turn to you for guidance. In all likelihood, I'll be home before Saturday. Can we see each other as we have in the past?*
>
> *Do not write another letter, for any mail will certainly be intercepted before it finds its way to my morning tea tray. I will come to you soon. Please don't abandon our plan now that the timeline has shifted and come so soon.*
>
> *Yours,*
> *Char*

So she was in a bit of a pickle. And he apparently was to be her knight in shining armor. What in bloody hell was he supposed to do? Steal her away from the Carletons? Whisk her out from under her father's nose when they arrived back in Town? He liked Charlotte; he didn't want her to have an unpleasant marriage. His original plan was looking more and more appealing, but he wondered how Charlotte felt about *that*.

Opening the drawer in front of him, he tossed the newest letter on top of the rest. What if he petitioned for her hand? He nearly snorted. Her father wouldn't allow him entry into his house. There was no hope in hell he'd be given a fair opportunity to court her.

Did he want a courtship?

"What has you thinking so hard?" His sister stood in the doorway. Her gray, high-necked dress with its lace fichu was unflattering, but perfect for a governess, he supposed—although she was not a governess.

Odd that he hadn't heard her open the door to the study. Was he so worried about Lady Charlotte's predicament that the outside world couldn't penetrate his thoughts?

"A friend is in difficulty," he said. "I'm trying to find a solution but I'm not having any luck. Which, you must admit, is highly unusual for me."

Bea stepped into the room and walked toward the chairs that flanked his wide mahogany desk. "Is this a female friend or a male?"

He smiled. His sister knew him too well. "I suppose that would make all the difference to you."

She stood before him, fingering the edge of the ornate molding of the desk. "I do sort the mail, you know. I've always done so at your request."

"So you haven't failed to notice the letters coming from Hertfordshire." Why was she fishing for information? It wasn't like Bea to act coy; she usually asked him outright about anything she wanted to know.

"She doesn't write her name on the envelope, which is always a clear sign that she does not want her letters discovered. Is it the same woman I found you with in the kitchen?"

Tristan crossed his arms over his chest and leaned back in his chair. He realized he should have taken better care to protect his and Charlotte's correspondence.

"I've also noticed that you haven't been catting around for some time," his sister said with a cheeky grin.

He raised one eyebrow at her comment. Did his sister take note of everything he did? Since she ran the household, in all likelihood there was little she wouldn't notice. Damn. He should be more careful regarding Lady Charlotte.

"Yes, it is the same woman you saw in the kitchen. And I don't *cat around*."

"Do you want to discuss her?" Bea sat in a chair opposite him, clearly not intending to let him say no.

"You're exasperating," he said. "I really wish you wouldn't meddle in my private affairs." A frown formed on his face.

"Is she more than a friend to you? Or just a passing amusement?"

"You'll not let this go, will you?"

"You could marry, you know. Start a family."

"I have a family."

"I know. But you'll eventually need an heir."

He sat forward, elbows resting on his desk as he stared back at his sister, shocked by her suggestion. "Are you afraid I won't want you in my life anymore?"

His sister's expression became somber. "There will come a time when you marry, brother. And at that point, we three may not be wanted."

"That won't happen, Bea. Don't think for a moment that I would allow anyone to dictate what I should and shouldn't do, especially where my family is concerned."

"Only time will tell." Bea stood. "I came here to invite you to the sitting room. Ronnie painted the most beautiful garden scene and you must see it."

Tristan walked around the desk, and side by side he and Bea went up to the sitting room the children occupied for their lessons. He had a couple of days to decide what to do about Lady Charlotte. And maybe his sister did have a valid point about marriage.

The last thing Charlotte wanted to do on her return home was face Mr. Warren. Her father had given her no warning that her *affianced* expected to see her the moment she returned, and that betrayal was like a heavy weight around her heart.

Once her valises were brought up to her room, her maid helped her change out of her travel-worn clothes. She took her time readying herself, even after another maid had come to inform her that Mr. Warren had arrived, was speaking with her father, and had requested an audience with her in ten minutes. He wished to discuss appearances that they were to make together about Town in the coming weeks. She took thirty minutes to have her hair redone and had a cup of chamomile tea to settle her nerves.

Finally ready to face her foe, she all but glided into the parlor where Mr. Warren and her father sat. They both stood on her entry.

"I'm so sorry to keep you waiting. Traveling does not

agree with me, and my dress did not fare well in the carriage back from Hertfordshire."

She approached her father and kissed his cheek. "Dearest," he said. "You cannot keep your guests waiting so long."

"I apologize, I know it was dreadful of me, but the last few days have been arduous." She nodded to Mr. Warren.

"My lady," he said coolly.

She'd angered him with her tardiness once again. Good.

"I'll leave you two for a moment to discuss your nuptials." Her father took Mr. Warren's hand, and offered a nod of farewell. "I'll see you tomorrow at the club."

"At the scheduled time." Mr. Warren bowed cordially to her father before he left the parlor. Charlotte didn't like being alone with Mr. Warren. Her father served as a barrier; it was as though his presence offered a bit of protection.

"I've already said that unnecessary delay is one of the great faults that I disapprove of in anyone."

Of course he wouldn't offer her a civil word or ask how her trip had been. He disapproved of the Carletons as much as her father did.

"You'll have to get used to it, Mr. Warren. I find it difficult to work up any sort of courage to sit with you."

"So you insist on making our marriage miserable?"

"I think that is your preference, sir."

"I could care less." He waved away the harsh words as though her opinion mattered not. "I'll soon have the Fallon estates at my disposal and will require a wife to run those households. It won't be difficult to see very little of each other."

"You should wait till the seat is rightfully yours to take."

"You know what has precipitated our marriage. And waiting makes me wonder if I will have a wife tainted by scandal—that would be unacceptable to me."

"You don't think I'm tainted by my cousin's recent actions? She was my chaperone and she was thoroughly compromised. And as distracted as she was, who was to say I didn't find trouble of my own?"

He came forward and grabbed her upper arms in a strong grip, a look of rage filling his storm-ridden gray eyes. His grasp was firm, but it did not hurt—he was proving his superiority, that he had the control in their current situation. Without a doubt he had only to release a little more pressure to cause her a great deal of pain. His actions were meant to intimidate her. She was not easily cowed and glared back at him, daring him to do his worst.

"Are you suggesting you are not pure, Lady Charlotte?"

She shrugged. "I'm merely pointing out that there are so many things that can taint a lady's view on life."

He released her and paced angrily away.

"There are so many young women you could marry. You haven't given me an adequate reason for why I have to be that unfortunate woman."

He stormed back toward her, his face only a few inches away from hers. He was clearly seething. "Because I prefer to marry a woman I despise."

She gasped, taken off guard by the honesty. Who in their right mind would ever want such a thing? "I think you mad, sir."

"No more than you. It won't matter once we're married. After we make the obligatory appearances around Town, you'll be sent to my cottage in Yorkshire."

"I will not be shipped off." She was shouting now and stopped to take a calming breath. She could not allow him to get under her skin. He wouldn't matter, and her marriage would be a moot point once she paid a visit to the marquess. She had to remember that.

Mr. Warren gave her a dispassionate smile. "You'll do exactly as I bid."

"Would you even try to like me as a friend?" She wanted to know for the sake of curiosity. Surely there was some redeemable quality in this man.

"You are not a friend, madam, you are to be my wife; they are two very different things. I do not care to have a loving relationship with the woman who only needs to bear children for the sake of the title."

"You're a callous, cold man."

"I've been called worse," he said matter-of-factly. "There is nothing you can say to change this outcome."

"You're right, of course." She'd not let him believe she had a plan to change that. An ill-formed plan, but at this point it was better than nothing.

Mr. Warren seemed taken aback by her assent. He gave her a sharp look. Was he looking through the lie and seeing her deceit? Her stomach balled up into a knot as she waited for him to say something.

"Finally, we agree on something."

She released the breath she'd been holding.

"Then there's nothing else to be said. Shall I bid you a good day, Mr. Warren?"

"I will pick you up at precisely ten on Sunday. I'll be in an open carriage, so we can ride to church together."

"I always attend with my grandmother."

He raised a hand to stop her complaint. "She'll arrive

with your father. This will be an important day and also the first day the banns will be read for our upcoming wedding."

No, the banns would not be read.

She ducked her head, afraid her expression would give away her intended deception. "Until Sunday, then."

"Good day, Lady Charlotte. And please ensure you are not late."

"I will do my best to make sure you'll never have to wait for me again."

With one last distrustful glare, he left. Charlotte slouched back on the sofa. Her time was running out. She had to find another viable option so that she didn't have to spend the rest of her life with Mr. Warren.

Drastic times called for drastic measures.

Marriage to the marquess was looking like the better choice. Why hadn't she said yes and eloped when he suggested it? Her biggest question was, had he been seriously suggesting that as a solution? There really was only one way to find out. She'd have to steal out of her house tonight to see him again.

Chapter 12

Lord B   has finally shown his true colors. I never thought he'd be the type to publicly ruin someone, but I am proven wrong by his most recent escapades at Lord and Lady C——'s annual summer party. I'm disappointed that more scandal hasn't yet been revealed from the most talked-about house party every season—surely there is something to be ferreted out. All in good time, dear readers. All in good time.

          —*The Mayfair Chronicles,* August 1846

"My lady, let me go with you. It's not safe for you to be out alone so late at night. You can't go by yourself," her maid, Sophie, said once again.

Charlotte squeezed Sophie's hand as she took the unassuming cloak that would aid in her midnight jaunt. She couldn't allow Sophie to come this time in case any of the other servants saw her accompanying Charlotte. She would not endanger her maid's position.

"Miss, I'm worried about your safety at such a late

hour. I came with you the last time, let me accompany you again."

"Oh, Sophie, you've been my confidante all these years." Charlotte hugged the woman who wasn't more than two years her senior. "But you can't go with me. I'm leaving this life behind, and I might find it too difficult to do so if you are with me."

She was positive the marquess wouldn't turn her away.

"No one in their right mind would let you leave like this. What will your father think of me when you're not to be found come morning?"

She had told Sophie what she planned. And had given her specific instructions should her father find himself in a rage and sack any of the staff that worked closely with her. If the marquess turned Charlotte away, she intended to travel abroad. But before she left London, she would ask the marquess's help for any servants that required it. She could not predict how her father would react when he heard what she had done to escape a marriage she never wanted.

"You know what to do should you find yourself in difficulty."

"Don't you worry about me, I'll be fine. It's you I worry about."

Charlotte pulled Sophie into a hug. "I'll miss you dreadfully. But should everything turn out in my favor, as I hope, I'm going to send for you."

"You're too kind, miss." Sophie's arms wrapped around Charlotte in a brief embrace.

"I've known you most of my life, Sophie. I won't ever forget all you've done for me."

They stared at each other for a minute.

"I hope you can trust this gent. I don't want to see you

hurt. And I really don't like what you've read to me about him in the rags."

"I have a good feeling about this, and my instincts have never let me down." Charlotte smiled and squeezed Sophie's hand. "Besides, it's better to leave now than to wed that awful Mr. Warren."

"I don't like him any more than you, miss."

Charlotte threw the cloak around her shoulders and cracked open her bedroom door. There wasn't a soul about. With one last look at her maid, she pulled up the hood, slid through the door, and crept down the hallway.

She hoped the marquess wouldn't send her back home once she explained what she had done.

A knock came on his study door. "Come," Tristan called out.

"My lord, you've a visitor in the kitchen." A wry look of amusement was on his valet's face.

Tristan raised one brow. "Has she been settled in?"

Dixon nodded.

"Does my sister know that anyone is here?"

"No, my lord. I came straight here upon her arrival. I was locking up the house for the evening when she knocked upon the back door."

Tristan stood and buttoned his vest. As he unrolled his shirtsleeves, Dixon came forward, plucked the cuff strings from the desk to help with the cuffs of his shirt, and then assisted him in straightening his rumpled clothes.

"Be sure none of the servants are about, Dixon. I want complete privacy this evening."

"I'll ensure nary a soul is about, my lord." Dixon bowed and left to do as he was bid.

Tristan had been expecting Lady Charlotte to visit

him, as her letter had implied. He had in fact noted the arrival of her family carriage earlier in the day when he'd been out running errands. He hadn't seen her, but he'd known she was back in Town.

He strolled down the hall and headed toward the kitchen. The door was ajar so he pushed it open.

Lady Charlotte had her back to him, her hands outstretched over the coals that were cooling in the grate.

"We really should stop meeting this way."

Charlotte turned suddenly, her cloak clinging to her form and dripping from the rain she'd been through on her way to his house. She took a few tentative steps in his direction. Was she unsure about her welcome? He'd secretly worried about her since her last letter. He shut the door behind him and came far enough into the room that they stood at arm's length from each other.

"As you know, I had no choice." Her voice was barely above a whisper.

"One might wonder why you're here in the middle of the night."

Her gaze snapped to his. "You know precisely why I'm here."

Charlotte pushed the hood of the cloak away from her face.

"I'm not sure if the problems you create for me are good or bad."

Why couldn't women seek him out for a simple friendship, just as Jez had? It irritated him to no end. Was he worth so little as a man? He should take it as a compliment that women threw themselves at his feet on a regular basis, but when it seemed he was only good for bedding women that wanted a walk on the wilder side of life, it started to grate on his nerves.

"I don't understand your meaning."

"Charlotte." He shook his head as he stepped forward—only a foot separated them now. "We have laid the foundation for a long friendship and you want me to destroy that so you don't have to marry someone you dislike?"

"In this instance, it would be a friend helping a friend."

"So naïve." He caressed the side of her face before dropping both hands to her throat so he could release the frog clasp on the damp cloak and remove it from her shoulders. He took the heavy, wet material and draped it over the back of a chair.

"Why don't we go to a more comfortable room? You'll need something to drink that'll warm you from the inside out, you're soaked right through."

She nodded her agreement.

He took her hand and led her through the house to a comfortable sitting room. He bade her to sit on the long sofa with a motion of his hand and went to the sideboard to pour out a small amount of brandy.

"Tell me what you couldn't tell me in your letters." He handed her the tumbler. "Here, drink this. It's just enough to warm you but not hamper your judgment."

"Thank you," she said, and drank back the contents in one swallow. He took the glass from her and set it on the sideboard before finding his way back to the sofa and settling in next to her.

"Genny was having an affair with Lord Barrington," she said in a rush. "I was forced to stay in my room when it was first discovered. And my father insisted I stay there until Genny finally left."

"So that's what prompted your father to attend the summer party?"

She nodded. "It must have been a great shock when he

found out that my chaperone was engaged in an illicit affair. Now he thinks that if I marry Mr. Warren sooner it will save our family from more gossip."

Of course the old man would think that. Goddamn it. Why did everything have to move so fast when he was enjoying the slow seduction between him and Lady Charlotte? He supposed he couldn't keep at it forever.

It was either ruin her and face a duel with her father—there was no question in his mind the old man would call him out—or marry her. Though her father might still take aim with his pistol. And it was said that Ponsley had excellent aim.

"It might salvage your reputation to marry sooner rather than later."

"I cannot—"

He placed his finger over her lips. "Shh," he whispered, not wanting her to continue because he knew perfectly well there was little choice left for her.

Her lips were soft to the touch, so soft he rubbed his thumb over the bottom one, parting her lips.

"Tristan," she whispered. "Ruin me, it's the best option I have. The only option I have. I will not marry that man, and my father won't listen to reason."

God, he loved hearing his name come from her lips, her soft breath brushing over his thumb. He pulled away and stood up from the sofa.

"Do you know where your cousin is?" He paced in front of her, one arm behind his back and using his other hand to gesticulate. "How will she fare now that she is whispered about in society as though she's a pariah? Do you understand the repercussions of ruin?"

"I will come into my inheritance in a few years. The

funds will see me well settled; my cousin is not so lucky. Yes, I have always understood the repercussions of my ruin."

He stopped suddenly, took her shoulders in his hands, and brought his face level to hers. His hold was gentle, he didn't want to truly frighten her, just make her understand what her plan would mean for her future. "What do you intend to do before you have your inheritance?"

When she didn't answer, he continued, "You hadn't thought that far in advance, had you?"

"My father will not turn me out. He might send me away, but he will not turn me out."

"You're a fool to believe that, to have so much faith in him merely because he is your father. He cannot protect you. He will have to choose between his political career and his daughter. Which choice do you think will win?"

She glanced away from him and pinched her lips. She hadn't thought of that. When she looked at him again, there was a resolve in her dark blue eyes that tolerated no refusal.

"Why are you stopping me now? You've known all along what I have to do to secure the future I want."

"Court me in public and gain yourself a reputation as a girl with no morals? Sleep with me and not worry about ever having to marry a man you despise?"

She opened her mouth to argue. He was right; she'd never truly thought this out.

She stood and faced him. Her chest puffed out like an angry, ruffled bird. "I admit it, I didn't have a solid plan in place and I was going to rely upon you to help me out of my predicament."

"What happens, Charlotte, if I bed you? Do you waltz

out of my house come morning for all to see? Do we go about Town together in my carriage to start speculation that you have become my mistress? What exactly do you think happens to a woman who has fallen from the good graces of society?"

He wasn't sure why he was growing angry. Maybe because she preferred social ruin over marriage to him. Because, really, what society woman in her right mind would choose to marry him? He mentally scoffed at that.

She covered her face with her hands, then rubbed her eyes. He was being too hard on her. But she needed to understand how dire the consequences would be if she stayed the night.

"I can't go home, Tristan. Please, if you won't let me stay the night, help me in another way. I have enough pin money to see me to the Continent where no one will find me. I'll rent a room in Paris."

Tristan shook his head and took her chin in his hand. "You're a foolish, foolish girl."

She pulled away from him and walked over to the banked fire, keeping her back to him and her arms crossed in front of her defensively.

"Do you have another suggestion?" she asked quietly. There was defeat in her voice, something he'd never heard from her before.

"I've offered once before, and I'll offer it again: you could marry me." She could choose to accept that fate or go home to her father and her fiancé, because he would not allow her to leave London alone.

She turned, her eyes focused on him. "You can't be serious. My wish was to not marry at all."

"Am I so terrible an alternative? While you and Mr.

Warren have your differences, we have grown to be allies. We think a great deal alike, Charlotte."

"You're asking too much in this instance. What about—"

"My children? My sister? They make the idea so repugnant to you?"

"No, I didn't mean that."

"I think you do." And that shouldn't disappoint him, but the truth was, it did.

"Don't put words in my mouth; don't tell me how I feel." She came toward him, a determined fire blazing in her eyes.

"I will not help you find your way to Paris. You'll flounder on your own."

Her nostrils flared and her jaw tightened. She had to know he was right. She wouldn't make it a day trying to navigate in society there. Their pace was faster, their gossips more vindictive and cruel. She couldn't possibly understand if she'd never been there before.

Her face fell as she realized the seriousness of the situation she'd put herself in. "It was not supposed to happen this way. I was to be given a year to plan an escape."

He pulled her into his arms, needing to comfort her. "Running away will only have your father chasing you across the Continent."

With a defeated sigh, she pressed her cheek against his chest and relaxed in his arms. One of his hands caressed her back, the other cupped the back of her head, his fingers tangled so deep in the tresses of her hair, he could feel the pins that held the arrangement in place.

She had one arm wrapped around him, her other hand resting flat over his chest, under her cheek.

"Help me find a way," she all but begged.

"I no more want you to marry that scoundrel than you do."

"For my sake, or do you have a personal vendetta against him?"

"He's not a man deserving of you. He is known for leaving bastards in his wake."

She raised her head and looked up at him. "The information men are privy to."

"We know more than we let on."

Her lips glistened; she'd obviously just licked them.

"I don't want to go home. Can I stay the night with you?"

"And have you thought about what that might mean for tomorrow?"

She nodded, even though she couldn't truly understand what she was asking. Staying the night meant he'd have to marry her come morning. Whether she agreed to that right now or not.

Despite wanting to thwart Warren at every opportunity, there was something the man had that Tristan coveted, and she was currently in his arms. Tristan wanted Charlotte for his own, and though she did not feel the same now that he'd given her friendship, and she'd accepted that all too eagerly, he still wanted to win over her affections.

"For tonight, the only thing I care about is us. Not my father or my imminent marriage if I were to go back home," she said.

That cemented his decision. Tristan allowed his desire to rule him from there on out. He scooped her up in his arms and hastily carried her up to his private chambers. It was late enough that his children were abed, and his sister would be tucked away in her own room sound asleep.

Charlotte was all his, at least for tonight. He wasn't sure what to make of his desire to keep her to himself, but he would analyze it tomorrow when he obtained a special license for marriage.

He pushed his chamber door closed with his shoulder and leaned there for a moment. Charlotte's feet slid down to the floor and he helped to steady her. She looked around his room, which wasn't overly large, but comfortable. The bed was a dark cherrywood, and the walls were papered in a moss-green diagonal pattern. There was an ivory-striped damask bench at the end of the bed, and a chaise longue under the window.

Charlotte took it all in, fingering the tassels on the bolster pillow in the corner of the bench. She didn't face him. Was she unwilling to look him in the eye because she did not know the rules in the bedroom? He vowed he would teach her every one of them.

After clicking the lock over, he walked slowly toward the first woman to ever see the inside of his bedchamber. Though she would have no way of knowing it, Charlotte was the first woman to be invited into his private sanctuary. No woman had ever set foot in his house, and certainly not in his private rooms. This was his home, where his family lived, not a place for idle amusements.

When he stood directly behind her, he slid one hand over her abdomen and pulled her back a step so she was flush against the front of his body.

"I can still arrange to have you delivered safely home," he whispered in her ear. "It's not too late yet."

She shook her head. He still wasn't sure she understood what it meant for her to be here so he slid his hand higher, cupping her breast softly through her dress and corset. Her breath hitched, but she did not step away.

"I like you, Charlotte. I have since the first time we danced. You're bold. Daring. A troublemaker to be sure. All admirable traits."

Her head turned to the side, her temple brushing against his chin. "I wouldn't be here if I didn't count you among my friends."

His hand traveled still farther up, holding her neck, keeping her head turned to the side as he kissed her cheek. She thought them merely friends . . . He'd show her the meaning of friendship and more.

"You understand the consequences of what we are about to do?"

"I do."

She didn't. She couldn't possibly understand. He would marry her on the morrow because she was that important to him. He would have his revenge on Warren and Charlotte's name would be protected. It was the best he could offer. And while she had refused him earlier, he would convince her otherwise over time.

His free hand released the buttons down the back of her bodice. When the last button fell loose and the bodice dropped forward on her slender frame, Charlotte pulled it from her arms and tossed it on the bench, and he worked methodically to remove her overskirt, releasing the ties individually. Charlotte's breath hitched at each slight jerk back. With all the ties now loosened the material slid from her waist to pool on the floor at her feet. He made quick work of his vest, tossing it to the floor, and went about removing his cuff strings.

Needing to see her face and expression, he turned her around. Her gaze met his boldly. There wasn't an ounce of trepidation or fear. She didn't smile, nor did she frown. She just looked at him with a measure of trust that awed him. Had anyone ever given him such a look? He couldn't recall a single person outside of his family that trusted him as thoroughly as Lady Charlotte did in this moment. He would not disappoint her; and he certainly wouldn't give her a reason to not always look at him that way.

She held herself still for his perusal, standing proud with her chin up, unafraid of revealing herself to a man for the first time.

"It's not too late."

"Yes it is. I'm not going anywhere, Tristan."

Her hands went around her hips and untied the under-skirt. It dropped in increments as she released each tie in slow succession. They continued to gaze at each other as she let the soft linen swoosh to the floor to join her outer skirts.

Unabashed, she stood before him. Her corset was cinched tight, the flare of her hips and the curve of her breasts making her shape a perfect hourglass. The strings on her corset wrapped around her waist and tied at the front. He reached for them, pulling one of the tied hoops until it unraveled from its knot. She didn't flinch or try to hold the corset from opening ever so slightly.

"Turn around," he said.

She did so without hesitation. Because he wanted to enjoy undressing her to the fullest, he slowly threaded his finger around the middle strings and pulled. The corset loosened enough at the back so that he could squeeze the two ends of the busk together to remove the waist-cinching contraption. It was on the floor with the rest of her clothes in the next moment. Nothing but a chemise, pantalettes, and stockings stood between him and her naked skin. His mouth watered to taste her bare flesh.

As she turned, his hands slid from their hold about her

hips, went around her back and stomach and then to her hips once more.

"You can still save your reputation and let me take you home. No one will ever know you were here. Only Dixon knows you arrived through the kitchen, everyone else is abed." He needed her to be one hundred percent sure that this was what she wanted. Because come morning, she would become the lady of Castleigh. There was no way around that ending.

Shaking her head, she said huskily, "What comes next?"

He pulled his shirt from his trousers and lifted it over his head so he could toss that on the floor, too. "Whatever you like," he responded.

She sucked in her bottom lip, and her gaze dropped to his naked chest.

Taking one of her hands, he pressed her flattened palm over his chest. "Touch me if you like," he offered.

She looked into his eyes once again. "Will you do the same?"

"Yes."

Her breath hitched as he cupped her breast through the cambric. Her nipple was distended, and her pulse raced so that he could feel the strong beat of her heart where his thumb rested on her chest.

Her eyes closed as he brought her nearer with his free hand at the base of her spine. "I want you naked, your heated skin pressed against me."

Her mouth parted, her palm slid higher until it reached his bare neck. "Then strip us bare," she said just as her mouth met his.

She kissed him slowly, her lips pulling gently at his as their breaths mingled and their bodies came together chest to chest.

The soft give of her breasts against him had him fully hardened in but a second. He needed to have her so badly, yet he also wanted to spend the whole night learning every inch of her body.

Grabbing her buttocks in each of his hands, he tilted her enough that her core rubbed against the steel-hard length of his erection as he thrust his tongue inside her mouth. He almost wished he were already inside her, making her delirious with pleasure. But this would be her first time, and he didn't intend it to end too soon.

She caressed the length of his back, stopping just at the edge of his trousers. He swooped her up into his arms again and strode purposefully toward his bed. He pulled away from their kiss long enough to sit her on the edge of his bed and rid her of her pantalettes and stockings. Her chemise he left on, wanting to watch her take it off as she'd watched him remove his shirt. He released the buttons on his trousers and loosened them from his hips, but stopped from removing them altogether. He never wore underclothes, and he wasn't sure what Charlotte would make of his jutting erection.

He dropped his hands to his sides, and in a rusty voice thick with ardor said, "Take your chemise off."

Charlotte had never wanted anything as badly as she wanted to please the marquess. When she'd asked to stay the night, she'd known it would be her ruin. She'd known that she would never be able to go home and be the innocent daughter again. She should care more about her reputation. A woman's status in society was based on her actions. But when she looked at the marquess, his eyes blazing with desire for her, she could only think about the here and now.

When he asked her to remove the last stitch of clothing she wore, and reveal herself for the first time in her life to a man, she didn't hesitate. For some reason that surprised her, even though she'd been orchestrating her ruin ever since her father told her he wanted her to marry Mr. Warren.

She pulled the soft cambric over her head and dropped it on the bed next to her. Tristan visibly swallowed, his gaze narrowed on the tight peaks of her rosy nipples where the cool evening air kissed them. The way he looked at her made her feel as though he were already touching her. His hands were fisted over his thighs, still covered with his trousers. Would he remove all his clothes as she had?

"So beautiful," he said as his gaze dropped to the dark thatch of hair at the vee of her thighs. His raw assessment of her had her face flaming and her heart pounding erratically in her chest. She hadn't been shy a moment ago, but she certainly felt as though she should cover herself now.

Maybe if he were as bare as she currently was, it would put them on an even footing. "You wanted us to lie together naked, yet you have not shed your trousers," she pointed out.

Blue eyes met blue eyes and she leaned forward on the edge of the bed to help him remove his clothes since he didn't seem inclined to do so just yet.

Instead of helping her, though, his knuckles ran down the side of her face, her jaw, and her neck until finally he was caressing the tip of one of her breasts. He stood from the bed so she could help shed his trousers.

She'd never seen a man naked before and wasn't sure what to expect. She took her time, feeling the strong line of his hips as she slid her fingers beneath the soft material and slowly pushed it down. All the breath left her lungs when his manhood thrust out in front of her in bald proof of his desire. Because surely a man did not normally sport such a thing beneath his clothes; it would be noticeable.

When she hesitated to push his trousers lower than his thighs, he chuckled, stepped back, and shucked them himself. By the light of a few candles around his room, she could see that his body was lean but strong, much like a racehorse with its whipcord muscular lines, the power and strength evident in the way he moved.

She wanted to feel all that strength beneath her fingertips. He let her study his form with her eyes. He was perfection, like the Greek statues on display in the museum—only their private parts had been strategically covered when she'd gone to see them with Lady Hargrove. Now she understood why; that part of the man was almost mesmerizing. She'd never desired to touch the statues and busts, but this man standing naked before her was a thing of perfection and surprising beauty. She could barely tear her gaze away from his manhood, but she did manage to stand from his high bed and take a few steps toward him. She didn't stop till the tips of her breasts brushed against him ever so lightly.

"Do you trust me?" he asked. She looked up at him, her heart racing, her nerves unsteady, and her stomach full of butterflies. His question had been earnest, as though this were the most important answer she would ever give him.

"Completely."

His fingers lightly skimmed over her lower back, making her shiver with the tickling sensation.

"You understand that we cannot go back from this? That once we have truly joined, you will never have another."

She nodded. She knew without doubt that she'd never lie with another man after tonight. She would not turn into a lusty wanton like so many young widows seemed to do—well, according to the *Mayfair Chronicles* at any rate. "I understand."

He walked her backward until her thighs hit the edge of the bed.

"Sit," he said. And she did so.

She reached out and ran the flat of her hand over the muscles in his stomach, marveling at how very different their bodies were.

"This will be a night to remember." The conviction in his voice was a promise she believed with all her heart.

"I want tonight to be special for us both, Tristan."

"And it will," he said.

His body was warm, almost hot to the touch, as she learned the dips and lines of his torso.

"Open your legs to me."

This time she did hesitate for a moment. It would reveal a part of herself he hadn't seen yet. His finger went under her chin and lifted her face to look up at him.

"Let me see all of you, Charlotte."

She slowly parted her thighs, feeling exposed, vulnerable.

The marquess leaned over her so that she was forced to go back on her elbows. His body was centered over hers, his manhood lightly brushing the top of her belly. A bead of fluid came from its tip, and had she been more sure of what she was doing she might have reached out and touched it.

Light kisses rained over her face, lips, and neck. His tongue tasted a trail from behind her ear to the middle dip of her throat at the top of her chest. He trailed his mouth lower, around the soft plumpness of one breast and then the other.

Charlotte fell back fully onto the bed, and tried to absorb all the sensations of the marquess naked above her, doing very wicked things with his tongue against her body. She felt hot, needy, her body anxious to be touched all over and crushed against his.

The marquess cupped her other breast in his hand just as he kissed the nipple, capturing it between gentle teeth to blow a hot stream of air on the distended tip before sucking it deep into his mouth. She made a sound then, not quite a moan, not quite a surprised squeak, but something foreign to her own ears.

When he released her, he grabbed her by the waist and hitched her farther up the bed so he could join her. He spread her thighs wider apart with his hands, and stared down at the most private part of her. She lowered her hand to shield herself.

"Don't," he said in a gravelly voice. She stopped and stared at him curiously.

He captured her eyes with his, and in the next moment he was touching her so intimately that a startled squeak left her throat and she nearly slammed her thighs closed.

"Hush, I promise to do only what you like."

He spread her inner folds and touched her softly, as though he'd done this a thousand times and knew how to wring more pleasure out of her than she'd ever experienced in her whole life. Her head fell back on the bed, and her eyes closed, as she trusted him to do exactly as he promised.

His fingers moved faster the more comfortable she seemed and the farther her legs spread for him. The sensations he was drawing from her were inexplicable and eye-opening. Before she wanted him to, he removed his hands and pressed her thighs wider still as he leaned in close to her. His shoulders were between her legs, and his mouth . . . Oh, good Lord, his mouth was doing such naughty, naughty things to her body that she felt her skin flush three shades of red. But she was helpless to push him away when the pleasure was so intense that the only thing she wanted was *more*.

"Tristan," she moaned, throwing her head back and reaching down to tangle her hands through his hair. She wasn't sure if she should push him away or pull him in tighter to her body. His shoulders were a firm weight keeping her legs pressed wide.

She felt light-headed from the pleasure he was wringing from her and a fine sheen of sweat broke out on her brow as the sensations escalated and her body tightened, her thighs squeezed around his head to hold him nearer yet. He didn't seem to mind, for he sucked at her with a fervor that astonished her. Later she might be embarrassed by her unabashed display.

"Tristan." She was nearly shouting his name now, and the sounds that came from her throat would surely add to her embarrassment later. But right now, the only thing she could think of was how his tongue licked between the folds of her private area, giving her the greatest pleasure she'd ever felt.

As her moans grew louder, he reached one hand up and put the side of his hand in her mouth. She bit down lightly on him, knowing he wanted to muffle her screams of pleasure, as the feeling in her belly grew stronger and stronger. She swore her body was floating from all the sensations bombarding her. She was on fire and Tristan coaxed the flames higher and higher, until she was sure she touched the clouds. She hit an apex so pleasurable she never thought she'd come down again.

She was panting when it was over, and the marquess slowly came over her body, his manhood a firm reminder that their evening was far from finished. He was kissing her face, her neck, squeezing her breasts, and drawing more moans from her. And though her legs spread wide around his hips and she knew instinctively that he would soon put himself inside her as he had done with his tongue, he did no more than kiss and caress her, letting her slowly glide back into her surroundings.

Feeling more like herself now that the intense pleasure had ebbed to a deep unfulfilled throb in her body, she massaged his shoulders and back in their intimate embrace.

"Are you ready to feel that again?" he asked.

When she tried to speak her throat was so dry that she coughed instead and nodded her agreement. He chuckled again and was suddenly up from the bed and going to the next room. He lit another candle, illuminating the room. It looked to be his dressing room. A ewer and washstand rested inside the door. He procured a tin mug and poured some water into it and brought it back to the bed. Charlotte sat up as he approached.

She pointedly stared at his manhood. "Why did you stop?"

"On your account. Drink up. We are about to engage in more."

She drank nearly half the contents of the mug and handed it back to him. He took a sip from the same mug before placing it on a stand next to the bed. When he turned back to her, she could see the hunger in his eyes had not ebbed.

He clasped his hands around her ankles, and pulled till she was laid full out on the bed. He was on his hands and knees, and pressed light kisses on her body and teasingly tasted her mouth with his tongue.

"I will love you so thoroughly tonight that you'll never be able to get me out of your head."

"I think you have already done so."

"I've hardly begun."

His arm hooked under her thigh and pressed her knee up; the position had her legs spread wide open. She felt the wetness at her core press against his abdomen and swallowed back her nervousness.

"You make me feel so out of my element . . ." she whispered.

"I'll take that as a compliment."

She cupped his head in her hands and looked him in the eye. "I can't thank you enough."

"No thanks required, my lady, I've wanted you from the moment you stole into my house that first time."

"We barely knew each other then."

"You aren't nearly distracted enough if you can think rationally right now."

"Then what does that say about your abilities as a great seducer?"

"I am questioning my capabilities, actually." He pressed his mouth to hers and any thoughts she had vanished as she felt a new spark of arousal.

The ridge of his manhood slicked through her feminine juices, rubbing that part of her that was already sensitive from his earlier ministrations. She felt lost in his touch again, wanting more, but not really knowing what that entailed. He continued to kiss her, sucking her tongue into his mouth when she retreated, and then lowering himself so he could flick his tongue gently over the tip of her breast.

His fingers touched her core again. Her thighs were slick, her center throbbing for more of what he'd already given her. She would never get enough of that sensation. She would be a happily ruined woman.

When his hand moved away from her center, she felt a completely new sensation, that of his manhood pressing against her. He didn't enter, but hovered above her as he grabbed each of her wrists in his hands and held them at the sides of her head. His head lowered to take the tip of her breast in the hot cavern of his mouth and to lick a trail of kisses across her sternum, then gave her other breast the same attention. Her body ached in a way she didn't know how to relieve, but Tristan seemed to understand her mounting desire, for he pressed himself forward, lodging the head of his manhood within her then going no farther.

Her breath caught in her lungs and she looked at him with her mouth parted and her body ready for more.

He pulled out and thrust a little farther the second time. Her hands were immobile and she wanted to hold him, feel the crush of his body atop hers as he claimed her, but she did not ask it of him. His hair fell forward. She wanted to push it back and feel the rub of his facial hair against her sensitive, overheated skin.

"Trust me," he said with a gentle kiss at her mouth.

"Always," she found herself saying without any thought to the depth of meaning that single word held. But it was in her actions, too, for her legs fell completely open to him and her pelvis tilted in such a way that she felt him slide deeper still inside her.

He pulled out of her again, never breaking his gaze,

and pushed in farther with a groan. She didn't think he was fully seated, but liked that he took his time, letting her body grow used to his.

She clamped her thighs around his hips and pulled him fully atop her, till their pelvises were pressed tight together and they were completely joined.

She wanted nothing more than to rub against him, and couldn't help the small rotation of her hips, as he stayed motionless inside her. "I need more."

He kissed the tip of her nose. "My impatient little wanton." He released her wrists and held her hips to still her motions. "You'll rush us to the finale too soon."

"More," she demanded this time, shocked by her determination to get what she wanted.

Tristan didn't stop her, though he probably could have. Instead, he went up fully on his knees, his hands holding her hips elevated, and rocked in and out of her body slowly. She still twisted in his hold, needing to reach that fever pitch she'd felt before.

The thrust of his body against hers grew faster, stronger. She uttered little mewls of pleasure as he brought her to the precipice again. Her body felt as though it were spiraling out of control. Her heart drummed loudly in her ears as her body tightened and screamed silently for more. Always wanting more.

Tristan had her hips lifted so high off the bed that he bent over and nibbled an erotic path of kisses down the center of her ribs, never letting up on the pace as he thrust into her body again and again. His thrusts grew more frantic, and she knew that it would be over soon. She'd been on fire before, but now her body exploded like a shooting star blazing through the night sky.

He collapsed on top of her, their bodies sated and slick

with sweat. They both breathed heavily, their chests rising and falling. Tristan rolled to the side, half on her, half on the bed. He tucked her head against his chest and languidly caressed her buttocks and thighs till their breathing regulated somewhat.

Her thoughts were jumbled and confused. She'd just given herself to a man. She was a ruined woman, just as she had wanted, but it felt wrong to have gone about it this way, to use a man who had become a good friend in the short time they'd known each other.

"You'll sleep in here with me tonight."

"I hadn't thought to sleep anywhere else." She wasn't sure what the morning had in store for her. Exhaustion swept over her despite the thoughts that weighed heavily on her mind.

"Good," he said, and the last she remembered was him kissing her temple and saying good night.

Chapter 13

As far as I know, the Marquess of C—— has never allowed a woman into his home. I know for certain he still owns a discreet townhouse where his mistresses and lovers meet him under cover of night. So why did he allow his cloaked visitor to stay in his private home last night?

—*The Mayfair Chronicles,* August 1846

Tristan hadn't slept since Charlotte closed her eyes and exhaustion finally overtook her. His thoughts were too occupied with the woman who slept in his arms and what would come of her future.

Their future.

He had done the one thing that would ensure she could never marry Warren, yet he felt like the biggest ass for going about it the way he had. She'd asked him to lie with her, yes, but that didn't make the weight of his actions any lighter.

He disentangled himself from her just as the sun started to rise. After dressing, he went straight to his sister's room, and knocked softly. She was a light sleeper so he gave her a few moments to answer.

His sister opened the door bleary-eyed.

"I'm sorry to wake you so early. But I require your assistance . . . urgently."

"What can you possibly need from me before six in the morning?" Bea rubbed at her eyes and gave a big yawn as she retreated into her room to grab her dressing robe and cinched it fiercely around her waist.

Tristan leaned against the frame of her door and crossed his arms over his chest. "I need you to pay a visit to our uncle. I'll have a horse and groom readied while you dress."

Her gaze snapped up to his. "Why would I need to see him so early in the day?"

"He has the ear of the archbishop. And I require something that only the archbishop has the authority to issue."

Bea's eyes widened as she stared at Tristan in astonishment. "What have you done?"

It was his turn to rub his hands over his eyes. He hadn't realized how exhausted he was until he stood under his sister's scrutiny. "I can't leave the house for obvious reasons."

"And those obvious reasons would be . . . ?"

"There is a lady in my chambers who cannot wander freely about the house once the children are awake."

His sister went to her wardrobe and pulled out a frock, tossing it on the bed. When she faced him again, she sighed with exasperation. "This isn't like you."

"The situation could hardly be avoided. I take it you'll visit our uncle?"

"I will, but why can't you go?"

"Because the lady in question will not stay if she finds me absent once she wakes."

"Maybe you should let her leave."

"You're the one who's been insisting on my marrying these past weeks. Now that the opportunity has presented itself, you've changed your mind. Not very sporting of you, Bea."

"I didn't expect you to go to these lengths. Can nothing in this house happen under normal circumstances?"

She referred to their living arrangements and the children. "There wouldn't be much fun in doing the expected thing."

Bea sat heavily on the edge of her bed. "Does she know you intend to marry her?"

"No. We discussed it too briefly. I think she thought my offer wasn't sincere."

"Was this before or after you spent the night with her?"

He smiled. "Before, if you can believe it. Now, enough questions, I'm going back up to my room. When the children are up, have Cook deal with them until you arrive back. And have her send up breakfast for two. I'll explain everything when you get home."

His sister reached out and clasped his shirtsleeve. "Are you sure this is wise?"

"I've never been more sure." And that was the honest truth.

"How did she come to be here?"

"She came of her own accord, I can assure you." Did his sister think he had lured her here? That he'd planned all along to ruin the young lady?

Her head tilted to the side as she looked at him. "Is this the lady you've been writing to?"

His grin widened. His sister was as observant as ever. "The one and only."

"I do hope she knows what she's gotten herself into."

"That's my worry, sister. Now I must get back." He patted Bea's cheek before heading back to his bedchamber.

He paced his room for some hours, not wanting to wake Charlotte, even when she slept past ten. A sweet breakfast for two with pastries, fruit, and scones lay ready for when she woke up. There was a bath off his room that he'd readied with hot water. Lady Charlotte would surely be stiff and sore from their evening together, and she'd probably want privacy while she thought over the events of last night.

He sat on the edge of the bed, and brushed his hand over Charlotte's shoulder. "It's time to greet the day, my lady."

She let out a big yawn and stretched like a cat that had lain curled up for too long. Her eyes slowly opened, her expression neutral as she stared back at him, pulling the sheets tighter around her as though to protect her modesty, something that had thankfully been absent last night as they had made love.

He couldn't blame her since the light from outside shone brightly into the room and he'd dressed in trousers and a shirt.

"I've drawn a bath for you."

"You needn't be so kind."

"Charlotte . . . about last night."

"It was beautiful." She sat up, making sure to pull the sheets tightly around her, shoulders and all.

"Yes, but there are consequences to face the next day," he said.

She stood up from the bed and went to the tray with sweets and fresh berries. She took a raspberry and popped it into her mouth.

"I could just dress myself and leave through the front door, I suppose."

"I'm afraid it's not so simple as that."

"Why not? I'm a fallen woman now, aren't I? Mr. Warren certainly won't have me now that I've lain with another."

"Nor do I think your father would so easily accept you back into his home."

"My father adores me." The conviction of her statement had him shaking his head. He'd explained last night how this would affect her relationship with her father, but she seemed to think Ponsley would ignore the reproach society would aim at his daughter. "My father could not stay angry with me for very long. He's a very forgiving sort."

"You're too sure of yourself, my lady, and you forget that your decision to stay with me last night means that you are now judged by society and not simply by your father."

"You're wrong. My father has influence and cannot be so easily dictated by society's opinion."

"Had I realized you were so misguided last night, I would have sent you home so you could cause no harm to your reputation."

She picked out a few more berries, and gave him a long assessing look before she shrugged her shoulders. "I will find out soon enough."

"I'm afraid that is impossible. You made your choice last night, Charlotte, and I'll see to it that the consequences are resolved satisfactorily."

"What do you mean?"

"I'll not be used for your little child's game. We'll discuss what happens next after you've had a chance to wash up." He pushed open the door to the bathing room. "I ran the bath for you a short while ago. It should still be warm."

She pushed past him in a huff, but turned to him on the

threshold of the door, her eyes narrowed. "There is nothing further to discuss."

He put his hands in his pockets. He'd save his argument for later.

"I've borrowed some fresh clothes from my sister; yours were damp from the rain last night and didn't fare well on the floor. There is plenty of soap and other bathing accoutrements for your use in the bathing room."

She shoved the door shut in his face and he could hear her grumbling some nonsense about him being annoyingly impossible.

He didn't think today would go well. But there was nothing to be done about it right now. He'd given her plenty of opportunity to return to the safety of her home and the life she was used to last night. And though she'd scoffed at his offer of marriage, he'd never been surer about giving her the means to avoid marrying that cad Warren. Theirs might not be a marriage founded on love, but Tristan had a great deal of respect for the lady currently residing in his room, and he would not take no for an answer. He hoped she felt the same type of respect for him. And that would have to be a good-enough foundation for beginning their marriage.

Who did he think he was that he could order her about as though he had a say in what she did? The hot bath had been a welcome sight, as was the tray of sweets and fruit when she had awoken. She dropped the sheet she'd grabbed from the bed and stepped slowly into the water. Her body ached in places that had never before ached. Her body was tired, and some parts were more sensitive than usual. She sank chin deep into the bathing tub and leaned her head back against the edge, closing her eyes.

How should she proceed today? Did she leave Tristan's house in full light hoping her reputation sufficiently ruined that her father would cancel the reading of the banns?

Did she let the marquess escort her around Town with no maid or chaperone in sight? Surely gossip about her cousin was already circulating.

When the water cooled, she pulled the stopper for a short while and turned on the hot tap to warm the water again. She wasn't quite ready to face the day. Though she wouldn't mind filling her stomach with the sweets on the breakfast tray—she hadn't eaten well before arriving at the marquess's house because her nerves had been on edge since she'd been back in Town.

She took the soap from the tray on the table close by and dunked it in the water, the sweet scent of bayberry filling the steamy room. After rubbing a washcloth with the soap, she washed her body. She didn't bother taking down her hair even though she was sure it was a tangled mess. She'd put it up in a simple chignon once she was dressed. There were a multitude of bath linens to choose from as she stepped from the tub. The marquess had thought of everything, wanting her to be comfortable.

All the clothes she'd need for the day were before her. Stockings and pantalettes, freshly laundered and smelling of lavender, a corset that looked a tad large for her but would do until her clothes could be brought from her father's house, a chemise that was made of a fine linen with lace trimming the sleeves. His sister's clothes were of the finest material. Why it surprised her she couldn't say, but she supposed his sister was well looked after since they seemed to get on well living under the same roof.

And then there was the dress . . .

She stood and walked over to the door where it hung,

and fanned out the satiny material. It was no simple day dress; it looked almost—dare she think it?—like a wedding dress. It was ivory with no other color adorning the full, rounded skirt. She would need a crinoline to wear it properly. The sleeves were capped and trimmed in lace. The bodice was cut with a deep vee at the front, and a fine overskirt of lace fanned out around the back, falling in a delicate train.

She eyed the dress she was to don as she pulled on her underclothes. The long corset covered her from chest to hip and she felt the burn of the laces as she cinched it closed too fast.

She didn't bother with the dress. She left it hanging as she yanked the door open and stormed into the next room.

The marquess sat in the chair next to the window. His elbows were on his knees, and his gaze focused on her as she stopped in front of him.

"What is the meaning of that dress?" She pointed back toward the bathing room.

He stood languidly, as though he'd been expecting her outburst. His expression was calm, certain. Too certain for her liking. "It is exactly what you think."

"I already told you that I would not marry you."

"I don't remember giving you a choice in the matter."

"You cannot force me."

"Do you know what will happen if you go home now?"

She took a step back. Admittedly, she hadn't the faintest clue. She hadn't thought much beyond dissolving her engagement to Mr. Warren.

"Let me inform you about what your actions have ensured." He turned her, directing her toward his dressing room with his hand placed possessively at her lower back.

There was a small mahogany table with a mirror. Shaving accessories were neatly lined up along the back.

"You have ensured your removal from society by coming to me last night." He placed his hands on each of her shoulders and pushed her gently down into the seat. "You have effectively changed your status from debutante and a diamond of the season to a pariah."

"My father will not turn his back on me." Though she was feeling less sure about that the more she thought on it.

"As I have already said, you've given him no choice but to act according to the rules of society."

He started removing the pins in her hair. The messy curls fell around her bared shoulders one at a time until the pins were stacked in a neat pile in front of her. The marquess leaned over her, his face next to hers in the reflection that stared back at them. He reached around her, his forearm brushing against the side of her breast as he pulled out a small drawer that contained combs and brushes. He reached for the silver-handled brush and shut the drawer with an audible snap.

His head turned, his mouth but a half an inch from her ear as he whispered, "You, my dearest, dearest Charlotte, are left with but one choice." The heat of his breath on her skin made her shiver and had her remembering the way his unshaven face had rubbed over her body to create the most delicious sensations the previous night.

She closed her eyes, turned her head away from him, and picked up the brush.

"Why marry me when you've never married the women you were associated with before?"

"I told you not to believe much of what the gossips have said. Besides, we've developed a friendship these past weeks and I will not let a friend languish on the fringes of society—despite your determination to do just that."

There was more to the picture than she was seeing, she was sure of it. "What do you gain in marrying me?"

"I get to ensure that Warren is made a laughingstock. And haven't you told me that he would lose favor before he was appointed a position in the House of Lords?"

She pinched her lips together and parted a section of her hair to brush the knots from it.

"It's not advisable to play games with politics when you don't know the outcome of one wrong move."

"This isn't about last night, is it? You're not marrying me because you took my innocence. You're marrying me because you have a personal grudge against my father and Mr. Warren."

"We didn't meet by chance, or because of your unwavering desire for self-ruin."

"I hate you."

"For now, maybe. We wouldn't be the first married couple to be at odds with each other, and certainly not the last when you have to conform to society's rules or feel the sting of their wrath."

"You cannot force me."

He stood behind her, his arms crossed over his chest, clearly not amused by her antics. She would not be his pawn.

What had she done?

"I wouldn't dare force you. But you have to understand that you can't go home now. You'll be denied entry and forced to turn around with only the clothes on your back. Did you think for one moment how you would make off with your precious pin money?"

"This is under your misguided assumption that I will be barred from the house I grew up in."

"I promise you that that is exactly the case."

"I'm afraid you don't know my father as well as I do."

"I see we will get nowhere this morning. I have some business to attend to in my study. In the meantime, I advise you to get yourself dressed. I'll send my sister up the moment she's back from her errands, and you can talk to her about what being the Town pariah truly means."

With that, he left. She had been about to tell him how wrong he was again, but the door to his chambers clicked shut behind him. She looked in the mirror. Her eyes were wild, her color high. For the first time in months, she began to question her decisions.

Had Tristan spoken the truth? Could she not recover her reputation from all that had happened last night? She'd never thought to go this far, but she'd been spurred on by the repugnant thought that she'd be married to Mr. Warren in four weeks' time. She'd acted without considering what would happen after her night with the marquess.

She sat there for some time staring at her reflection, thinking about the consequences she would have to face head-on today. She'd brought this upon herself. She wrapped her arms around herself when a sudden chill swept through the room and cut right through her heart.

Furious didn't begin to describe how Tristan felt. His reluctant bride was probably plotting his death upstairs while his friend looked ready to throttle him if he didn't have an update on Miss Camden's whereabouts.

Tristan didn't have time for Leo, but spared him a few

moments to tell him what Charlotte had relayed to him the previous evening.

Leo, however, proved difficult to get rid of. Though Tristan couldn't explain what had happened in the twenty-four hours since they'd seen each other last, he did promise to send a fast rider out to the Carleton estate to find out the fate of Miss Camden. This was no longer about the wager they had. They'd both deviated far from the path of revenge for Jez, to outcomes neither expected. Leo seemed taken with and was searching for Charlotte's chaperone, and, well, Tristan was about to become a married man. He was sure Charlotte would come to her senses once he sent his sister up to talk to her.

He could return her to her house tonight, and pretend that nothing had happened. But he wouldn't. She'd made her choice by coming to him last night. And truth be told, he wanted her even though she might despise him at the moment.

Seeing Leo off, he went into the breakfast room to say good morning to his children. They'd have a mother by the end of the day. Well, Ronnie would at any rate; Rowan, despite not knowing it, had one in Bea. There would come a day when they'd have to tell him the truth.

"Papa," Ronnie shouted and launched herself into his arms.

For a moment, he worried that they wouldn't like Charlotte. He hadn't thought much about their feelings in the mess he'd made. Even more important, what would Charlotte think of his children? Did she even like children? She'd been favorable when they'd discussed them while corresponding. Certainly, she would be welcome to the idea of sharing a house with his motley crew.

He held Ronnie two feet above the ground and smoothed his hand down her blonde hair. "Darling, I'm sorry I couldn't come down for breakfast. I have a surprise for you, though."

Ronnie jumped down, eyes wide. "A present?"

"In a sense. Do take your seats, children, I have wonderful news to share with you."

Rowan shoved his mouth full of croissant, his eyes wide in anticipation. His daughter didn't touch her food, but put her elbows on the table and rested her chin in the palm of one hand. Her foot tapped in excitement.

"How would you feel about a mother?"

He should have discussed this with Charlotte, and prepared his children sooner . . . but time had run out.

Ronnie screwed up her face. "You're going to get married?"

He gave her a warm smile and patted the side of her face. "Today, in fact."

Rowan's chin dropped, his mouth full of food. "Rowan, chew your food properly," he scolded lightly. Instead, Rowan picked up his glass of water and chugged the whole thing down.

"Really, Papa? We're going to have a mother? What's she like?" he asked.

Temperamental, furious at the moment, and a woman of her own mind. He would never say any of those things aloud to his children, of course.

"She is a perfect fit for this family," he settled on, knowing there would be a few bumps as they adjusted to family life together.

"When can we meet her?"

"Today. We'll be going to church later on and have a nice small wedding ceremony. Bea will help you get dressed just as soon as she's had the opportunity to meet Lady Charlotte herself."

Ronnie stood from the table, walked over to him with a stubborn pinch of her lips, and then stormed out of the room. He stared after her, sorry to have upset her. So his children might not be ready for a mother. They'd not had the opportunity to prepare themselves for the change, but they were young and he was in charge of the household, whether they believed it at times or not. It took a lot of willpower not to go after his daughter and try to make her feel better about the situation.

In a perfect world they would have had the opportunity to meet the lady he would marry, get to know her, and grow to like her before any changes were made. But he knew all too well how far from perfect the world really was.

He let out a heavy breath and rubbed his hands through his hair roughly.

Bea walked in at the next moment, an envelope clutched in her hand. "Did I just see Ronnie storming out of here?"

"I'm afraid so. She didn't take my news very well."

"Was it wise to tell her?"

"We will be there as a family as my vows are taken."

"Has your reluctant bride agreed, then?"

He turned to Rowan, not wanting him to hear any more. "Rowan, go find your sister."

"Yes, Papa." He stopped in front of Tristan before leaving and threw his arms around his shoulders. "Thank you," was all he said before he ran out of the room in search of his sister.

"Lady Charlotte is not agreeable to the idea, but she really hasn't any choice after the events of last night."

"There is always a choice, Tristan."

"Should I send her on her way as though nothing has happened and have her marry Mr. Warren in a month's time?"

Bea pinched her mouth shut and glared at him.

"I thought not," he said.

"If she's said no, you can't really force the issue."

"That's why I need you to go and talk to her."

"She is a stranger to me, Tristan."

"Yet she doesn't have a brother to lean upon. She cannot be saved from her mistakes as you once were. And I'll take no chances in case she carries the next heir of Castleigh."

"How dare you do that to her! Why would you take away her choice like that?"

"Our night together was mutually agreed upon."

Bea was shaking her head. "You knew better. She has no experience with men like you and couldn't possibly have understood the consequences."

"I gave her plenty of opportunity to change her mind."

His sister's forehead puckered as she came forward. There were tears pooling in her eyes and a fury so great he'd never seen the likes of it before. "You have robbed her of her innocence to fulfill your own desires. You had no right."

"I had every right, Bea. Warren—"

"Warren will find another bride. And now that you've chased one woman away and are making her marry you . . . How do you suppose you'll stop him in the future?"

"There will be no need. The Fallon name will not save him now."

Bea's fists clenched and unclenched at her sides. "You don't deserve her," she said, and spun around to stalk away from him.

He sat there stunned, wondering about his determination to claim Lady Charlotte as his own. The truth was he didn't want to give her up to anyone else. Last night had cemented that feeling.

Chapter 14

Dear readers, I have the most salacious news for you. Wedding bells rang for a certain marquess and his mysterious lady friend. Her identity has been revealed finally, and what an uproar it has created.
—*The Mayfair Chronicles,* August 1846

Charlotte had put her hair up in a simple bun with a braid wrapped around it. She pulled the dress down from the bathing room door to spread it out in front of her, and sat on the edge of the bed to look at it. There was a soft knock at the door. She ignored it; she was too furious to deal with Tristan just yet.

The knock came louder. She marched over to the door, uncaring that she was still dressed only in her underthings, and whipped the door open.

It was his sister, Bea, standing on the other side. Her expression was stoic, unsurprised. Charlotte stepped away from the door, inviting the woman in since it didn't seem she had a choice right now.

"My brother wanted me to help you dress."

"Did he now?" She didn't turn to face the woman as she went over to the window to stare down at the garden below.

"Fighting me won't get you anywhere. Believe it or not, I don't agree with my brother's tactics."

"I'm sure you don't want someone usurping your position in this household. And more than anything I wish I could forget the last two days of my life and go back to a time before I met your brother."

The rustle of material sounded behind Charlotte, but she did not turn to face the woman who would be her sister-in-law. Charlotte had come to realize that there was no escaping marriage, but that didn't mean she had to like the idea of it.

"Why aren't you married instead of taking care of your brother's children?"

"There is no other life available to me, Lady Charlotte. Unlike you, I was never given a choice about what would become of me after I trusted the wrong man and was shunned by society."

"With your brother's fortune, surely you could have done anything you pleased."

Charlotte turned to face the other woman. She looked close in age to Tristan, somewhere just shy of thirty years of age. She was pretty and looked much like her brother. Her hair was dark, her eyes the same light shade of blue that was eerily beautiful. She was about the same height as Charlotte but her form was more curvaceous.

"Tristan does not make important decisions lightly," she said.

"Ah, so you don't like this arrangement any more than I do."

"I don't. But I don't see how you have much choice."

"I can go back to my father, ask his forgiveness."

"And tell him what you've done? Tell him that you spent the night in the arms of a man he despises? That man you are so anxious to turn your back on is my brother, and he's willing to marry you because of the stupidity you both displayed in your hasty actions."

"Why does everyone assume my father will turn me out? I'm his only child."

"And what a disappointment you will be. Your Mr. Warren loathes scandal. He will not have you now."

"I dislike him so I could care less if our arrangement is dissolved. Assuming my actions are found out." Charlotte stepped away from the window and walked over to the bed, fingering the fine lace on the wedding dress.

"I was once as foolish as you," Bea said. "Your father will have already made up his mind where you're concerned. I have heard of your chaperone, Miss Camden. Do you know that she's been forced into hiding? Who knows if she'll survive the scandal long enough to carve a new path in life."

"And what about you?" Charlotte asked.

Bea turned to her suddenly. "I was never offered marriage, Lady Charlotte. You should keep that in mind. I am nobody to those who used to be my friends. Forever forgotten in their eyes because I fell in love with the wrong man."

"Who was he?"

"You mean you don't know?"

She shook her head, curious to find out the answer, but not sure this woman would reveal her secrets to a complete stranger.

"I do hope you have a strong constitution, because my

brother can be difficult. You should also know that he will never allow his children to be banished from this household."

"I would never . . ."

She knew without a doubt that Tristan loved his children. It had always been evident in his letters. His children were innocent of any wrongdoing; she would not punish them because she was forced into marriage by her own stupidity.

"I suppose I won't find an ally in you."

"You haven't earned my trust, so I'm afraid not. If I don't have you dressed, my brother will think I'm aiding in your escape. Turn around so we can get this dress on you. We need to be at the church in two hours' time."

"So he truly intends to marry me. And so soon?"

"Before your father can find you, yes."

"I'm not of age to marry whomever I please. My father can object to the marriage regardless of us speaking our vows."

"You will see that he won't. Your father cannot save you from what you've done."

Charlotte wanted to argue with her, but the more she thought about it the more she realized she had ruined any opportunity she had to have her freedom. She'd brought this on herself in a thoughtless, selfish moment. There was no going back, only forward, and in a direction she had not planned.

She could do this, she told herself. This was a better alternative than marrying Mr. Warren. It was an opportunity to put her life on a path of her own making. Tristan had become a friend since they had met; surely he wouldn't cloister her and hide her away from society.

"I don't know what I've done to make an enemy of you, but I do not wish to start off on the wrong foot if I'm to marry your brother and to share a house with you."

Bea looked at her long and hard as she released the ties at the back of the bodice so they could start dressing Charlotte for her wedding day. That thought left her a little dizzy and she had to sit on the bench in front of the bed.

"I'm sorry we couldn't meet under different circumstances," Bea said.

"So am I." Charlotte looked over her shoulder at the other woman. "But this is the hand we've been dealt, and we should make good use of it, don't you think?"

"I couldn't agree more. And I'm not angry with you, only disappointed by my brother's actions."

"He was not alone in this decision."

"But he knew better." She sighed heavily. "Stand up so I can tie the petticoats in place."

She did as she was told, threading her fingers together and holding them out of the way. She was slightly unsteady, and her legs wobbled. She'd never been the nervous sort, but this was an unusual circumstance. She stood there listening to Bea's instructions every now and again and tried not to focus on the consequences that were sure to come with their wedding today.

"What will happen after the wedding?" she asked, hoping Bea at least had some idea about what was to come.

"I suppose we'll come back here for brunch. I haven't really discussed the plans with my brother. But I assume he'll want to contact your father to inform him of the nuptials."

"Shouldn't I be the one to see my father?"

"It's probably best you don't see him straightaway. I can't imagine he'll be very forgiving about what's happened, at least not for a while."

"So Tristan will visit my father?"

"That's assuming gossip hasn't made its way to your father by the time we are back here. The moment you step out our front door and into a carriage with my brother, me, and the children—as he insists they witness the ceremony—tongues will be wagging. It's really only a matter of time before your father learns what has happened."

She swallowed the lump in her throat. This was proving to be too much for her. She needed a little more time.

"I see you are already having second thoughts."

"It's not that."

Bea came around to face her and gave her a questioning look. "You're a terrible liar."

"I suppose I am. It's just that I have never planned anything so poorly."

"Rational thought tends to be absent when intimacies are involved. If there is one thing I can promise you, it's that my brother has a kind heart. While the gossip columns have been cruel to him, and although he seems not to mind the negative attention, he really does want nothing more than happiness for those in this house."

"I don't for a second doubt you. But I'm sure he wishes me to the devil right about now." She meant it jokingly, but the truth hurt.

She was now the woman he was forced to marry.

Bea tugged on the front of the bodice and fanned out the train so it lay evenly around her. Charlotte felt silly to be dressed for her wedding with no guests but the woman before her. Why would Tristan go to the trouble of having her wear such a beautiful gown? She looked down at herself, and ran her hand over the front where cording shaped the bodice into a deep vee.

"It was our mother's."

Shocked, Charlotte's head shot up and she searched the other woman's eyes. "Why—"

"I told you, my brother has a kind heart. He has already accepted you into this family. Had he not, he wouldn't have woken me before dawn to obtain the license you require to marry this afternoon." She smiled at Charlotte, suddenly a different woman from the angry one who had stormed through Tristan's bedchamber door not twenty minutes ago. "I must go ready the children. They'll need to be in their Sunday best since their great-uncle is going to be marrying you and Tristan."

She really didn't know what to say other than, "Thank you for helping me."

"You're welcome. I'll see you in an hour. My brother will probably be up shortly to ready himself."

Charlotte nodded. Wasn't there some superstition about the groom not seeing the bride before she walked down the aisle? She wouldn't be walking down the aisle on her father's arm, though. Too afraid to wrinkle the dress, knowing that it was Tristan's mother's, she stood in the middle of the room and counted the minutes that passed.

So many thoughts flitted across her mind that her nerves were on edge as she stood there and waited. She could not leave the room to go and look for Tristan; this was not her house, though it would be in a few short hours.

What would his children think of her? Or his servants who hadn't had the opportunity to prepare for the change today was about to bring? What a muddle she'd put herself in. What a muddle she'd put Tristan in, for surely this was not the outcome he'd planned, either.

She walked over to the tray of food that had been brought up for breakfast. She hadn't touched it since eating those berries this morning, and though everything looked delicious, her stomach protested the idea of eating anything. She hated waiting.

If Tristan didn't come to see her, would he send Bea in to bring her down to the carriage? Would she have to go outside alone? She was breathing heavily, as though she'd just run for a sustained period of time. She didn't like uncertainty, or this inability to predict what would happen next. She turned away from the food tray since it didn't tempt her and instead focused on the closed bedchamber door.

She needed to make the next move. It would give her a modicum of control.

She stepped forward and tried to regulate her breathing. She was feeling a bit light-headed and that simply wouldn't do. She lifted the handle on the door and paused when it clicked open. She closed her eyes and steeled herself for whatever was to come next. She could do this. She would do this. She pulled the door open slowly, waiting for the sounds of the house to fill her ears. Servants were rushing to and fro, a maid ran past her with an armful of linens.

When Charlotte stepped out into the corridor, a footman was giving instructions to another maid. He looked at her after a short while, finished his instructions to the maid, then came toward her and bowed. "My lady. I'm Clarkson. How can I assist you?"

"Where is your master?"

"He's with his valet."

"And where would I find him?"

"He does not like to be disturbed while at his toilette."

His reluctance to answer her had her sticking out her chin. "Show me to him immediately."

He ducked his head. "Yes, my lady." His arm pointed to the right. Charlotte preceded him in the direction he indicated. There were a number of doors at the top of the stairs, all facing the upper landing that looked down into the foyer. The floor was carpeted in a deep maroon, the walls papered with a heavy floral pattern. She counted six doors, including the one she'd come out of. That meant he'd taken a guest room while she'd been waiting for him.

She turned to face the footman, who led her to the door closest to the landing.

"In there?" she asked, feeling her resolve waver.

He nodded and bowed again, taking a few steps back. She knocked and didn't wait for an answer within before barging through the door. Tristan was in the middle of the room, shaving cream coating his face and neck with his valet standing behind him.

"So eager to see me, my bride-to-be?"

"No, but you left me alone and I don't like to be kept waiting."

He motioned to a chair. "Take a seat and wait out the hour with me while I get ready."

He looked her up and down before tilting his head back for his valet to rub the blade along his neck and jaw. "The dress fits you well," he said when the valet wiped the blade on a towel folded neatly over his arm.

She placed her hands over her midsection and sat on

the edge of the chair. "We need to set some parameters for this marriage."

The scrape of the blade was the only sound in the room for a few more moments. When Tristan sat up, the valet passed him a damp towel that he used to wipe his face. "I don't see why there have to be boundaries. You seem to forget that you came to me for help. And that is exactly what I'm doing."

"I realize that. But marriage wasn't something either of us wanted."

"Yet I've gone to the trouble of getting a special license for the day."

"Tristan . . ." She needed to turn the topic to her father. "What will you say to my father?"

"I will tell him it was necessary for us to marry. He'll probably have already heard the news by the time we arrive back here."

"So quickly?"

"How little you know of the seedier side of society. I guarantee you that the betting books will be filled with Ponsley residence gossip the moment we leave this house. First your cousin, and now you traveling with a man who is deemed untouchable for marriage."

"Untouchable?" A smile touched her lips.

"In a sense."

"I never took you for a narcissist."

"I'd be disappointed if that's how you viewed me."

He stood from his chair and started to release the buttons on his shirt. His valet came up behind him to assist in the removal of his clothes. Charlotte turned around, even though she'd familiarized herself with his body last night. She was sure her face was flame red beneath the spattering of freckles she had no way to cover this morning after her bath.

"Dixon, leave us a moment, please," Tristan said.

The valet walked past her and out the door.

"Charlotte."

"Yes." She still couldn't turn, unsure whether or not he was dressed.

"Turn around and look at me. You weren't shy last night."

"You're indecent."

"I hope our marriage is full of indecency," he said, a wickedness in his tone that sent her pulse racing.

She spun on her heel, not in the least amused by his shamelessness. "You are being intentionally vulgar."

"Quite the contrary."

His shirt had been replaced, but it remained open and she could make out the dark trail of hair that led beneath the seam of his trousers where they sat on his hips. She swallowed and tore her gaze away from him.

"Marriage will give us a lifetime to learn to understand each other."

"What are you hinting at?"

He shrugged as he pushed the buttons through the holes on his shirt. "Just making an observation. We're to be married in a few hours, my lady. You might want to get used to the idea of seeing me in a state of undress. My parents didn't even take separate rooms."

"Lying together for one night does not mean you truly know me intimately."

He reached out and cupped her arms, giving her a steady look. "I would never expect to know you so thoroughly after one night, but I like to think I know you somewhat through our correspondence."

"This is all happening so fast, Tristan."

"I warned you last night."

"I couldn't go home and face Mr. Warren another day."

He pulled her into a hug and caressed her back. "I'm glad you came to me last night."

"You're taking this very well." Her comment was muffled against his chest.

"I've been thinking about it since you left. So I've had longer to come to terms with marriage than you."

"Why are you doing this?" she asked in a small voice.

"There are a lot of reasons, some I can't even explain."

She pulled away from him, feeling silly to have allowed his comforting embrace. "Try."

"You know my feelings toward Warren."

"Which you haven't fully explained to me." She walked farther into the room, and took a seat in one of the damask chairs next to the fireplace.

He rubbed one hand through his hair and let out a frustrated breath. "I'm sorry I can't be more forthcoming. In time, perhaps."

"Why else, then?"

"You remind me of a very dear friend."

"The Dowager Countess Fallon?"

"The very one."

"But she's your friend, and I can't imagine you'd want to marry your friend."

He laughed. "I suppose not. And I didn't mean because she was my friend, but because she has a larger-than-life personality."

She couldn't hide her grin. "Larger than life?"

"You're simply the most beautiful, most frustrating, bold, and daring woman I've ever known." He paced purposefully toward her, and lifted her chin with his hand.

Charlotte swallowed back what she'd been about to say. Did he really think those things about her?

"Now," he said, releasing her. She missed the heat of his touch almost immediately and frowned down at her lap. Today felt unreal, like a dream she was about to wake up from at any moment. "You can either help me dress, or I'll call Dixon back in here to assist."

"I'm afraid I don't know the first thing about men's attire."

He smiled and went to open the chamber door and call his valet back in.

Chapter 15

The Archbishop of Canterbury received two visitors today before two o'clock. Would you believe that one of those gentlemen was Lord C——?
—The Mayfair Chronicles, August 1846

Bea had thought ahead and arranged to have an early dinner readied for their return. There was an array of food to select from, but no one seemed inclined to eat much, aside from Rowan. Tristan watched Charlotte, disturbed that she was visibly uncomfortable. She looked out of sorts, an expression he was not used to seeing on her. There was a small sliver of quail on her plate together with mixed vegetables. She pushed it around with her fork. Did she even like fowl? He couldn't have a decent conversation with her in the carriage with Bea and the children sitting so close. It had been a long silent ride to the church.

"Is there something more to your liking?" he asked, indicating the trays on the buffet along the back wall. Footmen and the butler stood ready to serve her whatever she wished.

"It's been a long, busy day and I find I have little interest in food at present."

He couldn't agree more, since he ate without really tasting his food.

"Ronnie," he said, noticing his daughter still hadn't taken a bite of the food on her plate. "Are you truly not hungry?"

She crossed her arms over her chest and narrowed her eyes at her plate. She had refused to look at him since they'd arrived at his uncle's church. Not a good first family meal together, but there would be other nights to practice a new routine that included Charlotte.

"Will you honeymoon?" Bea asked.

Charlotte's gaze shot up to his. They stared at each other for a silent moment. He could see a yearning for exploration spark in her eyes, eyes that had been somber for most of the afternoon. It was a good change, but a honeymoon wasn't possible right now. There was too much going on in his life. Also, two significant bills were up for passage in Parliament, and the House of Lords would be in session this coming week.

Besides, his children wanted to spend time with him while their lessons were suspended for the summer. Then he also needed to become accustomed to being married. Had they had time to plan their wedding, circumstances might be different. But that was not the case, nor could it ever have been possible.

Charlotte didn't say a word; she seemed just as curious as his sister. Rightfully so, he supposed. Good Lord, he'd have to get used to having another person in his house. This all felt so strange and not quite real.

His sister's fork was halfway to her mouth, one eyebrow cocked as she waited for his answer.

"Parliament resumes again in a week." He wiped his mouth and tossed his napkin to the table. What was the sense in eating when it all tasted like dirt? He couldn't take the four sets of eyes looking at him as though he could magically fix everything that was wrong at the dinner table right now.

Bea pushed her chair out. "I'll take the children up and give you some time alone."

Rowan stood and ran over to Tristan. "Today was wonderful, Papa." He seemed to be the only person to think so. "She's so pretty, you know. Not like the stepmothers in the fairy tales."

Tristan chuckled and smiled up at Charlotte, who was still expressionless.

A door slammed open in the hallway, drawing his attention to the dining room entrance.

"Castleigh, you bloody bastard. Show yourself!" came an enraged shout.

Tristan looked heavenward. He wasn't to be given a reprieve. If something could go wrong, it was going to go wrong. Pushing his chair out, he leaned over to kiss Rowan on the head.

"Go with your aunt." He walked over to his daughter, but she'd jumped out of her chair and was stamping away from him.

He was sure she'd come around in a few days. Wasn't that what everyone needed—a few days? "Good night, Ronnie. I'll see you at breakfast tomorrow."

Charlotte was already standing, her hands fussing with her dress. Bea was ushering the children toward the door when it burst open and Ponsley barged through, face red, teeth bared. His beady eyes were pinned on Tristan in an instant.

"What have you done to my daughter?"

"Father." Charlotte spoke quietly and stepped forward.

Her father turned to face her instead of Tristan. Tristan didn't like the look on Ponsley's face, and feared the man would actually hurt his daughter. He stepped between them, drawing Ponsley's focus back on him.

He really should have seen the fist coming, but he was preoccupied with Charlotte standing behind him, and his sister ushering the wide-eyed children away.

The old man had a strong right hook that put Tristan on his ass in an instant.

He'd have to chalk this experience up to his own stupidity. He put his hand to his nose. It bled like a son of a bitch down his face and all over his hands.

"How dare you ruin something so pure!" her father shouted.

Charlotte rushed forward and pulled her father off Tristan before he could go for his neck.

"Father, please," she cried.

"How could you do this to me? You knew your duty."

Charlotte had tears in her eyes as she reached for her father. He sidestepped her, as though she were something dirty to touch. "I couldn't, Papa. I just couldn't marry him. You wouldn't see reason, and I had no choice."

Tristan slowly stood, grabbing up the extra napkins on the table to staunch the flow of blood from his broken nose. His whole face throbbed from the hit and his vision was blurry.

The old man pointed at him. "She is coming home with me until we can sort this out."

"It's too late, Father. Whatever the gossips have said, it's true. I'm married to the marquess now."

"It can be undone. You're not of age."

"This can't be undone. What would you do with me? Hide me away in the country for the rest of my days because I'll no longer be marriageable?"

"You chose this man over Warren?" The look of disgust her father wore stung Tristan's pride. "Where's your head gone, child? You're a disappointment to our family."

Charlotte rubbed the back of her hand over her tear-damp eyes. Her lips trembled as she reached for her father, as though she wanted to wrap her arms around him. He stepped away from her, his gaze darker than when he'd first stormed into the dining room.

"I acted hastily because I knew you could not be convinced to change your mind."

"So you chose to lie with the biggest scoundrel society has produced in two decades."

"It's not his fault. I asked him to help me." Tristan was surprised she defended him at all.

"No daughter of mine would defy me this way. You are nothing to me." He turned around then and walked out of the dining room, and out of the house, slamming the door behind him.

"Charlotte." Tristan spoke softly, because she was silently weeping where she stood, staring after her father. He wished he could wrap her in his arms, but he didn't want to bloody his mother's wedding gown. "He cares for you a great deal."

Her sharp gaze was full of anger and he was sure it was directed at him. "So much so that he nearly called me your whore."

"He'll forgive you in time."

"Don't pretend you can understand my father. You don't know him like I do. I can see now that there will be no forgiveness from him."

He reached for her, wanting to at least squeeze her arm in consolation. She jerked out of his reach and turned to face him.

Her hands came up to cover her gasp too late. "That bad, eh?"

"Oh, Tristan. I'm so sorry this happened."

"The only thing I'm sorry about is that I didn't move away in time."

"We need to get you upstairs and cleaned up. You'll frighten your children looking like that."

She cared enough about his children to shield them from this. That brought a smile to his face, but it hurt too much and his frown slipped back in place. She took his elbow to help him along. He didn't need to be guided like this, but she seemed less angry with him at the moment so he let her do as she pleased.

"Where would we find your valet? He's going to need to set your nose to rights."

"Of all the opportunities to break it when I was younger, I had to break it now." He shook his head, then stopped when his nose began to throb fiercely.

"Now you will look dangerous to all the ladies. They'll fawn over the bump you'll have on your nose."

"Don't be silly." He didn't like the idea of her thinking he wanted to please any woman besides the one who had become his wife a few short hours ago. "I'm beginning to think we should escape the bustle of the city."

"I've only just returned from a sojourn in the country-side."

"Hertfordshire isn't nearly far enough away to be considered the countryside. I have a comfortable house in Birmingham."

Charlotte opened their chamber door. It was odd how

everything had suddenly become theirs and no longer his. He liked the idea that he was sharing his life with her. "I'm going to ring for your valet. What was his name again?"

"Dixon."

She guided him over to a chair, forced him to sit by nearly pushing him down, then went in search of an extra hand. He wasn't helpless, and probably could have fixed the break himself, but he would let her have her moment to fuss. She seemed truly concerned that he'd been injured, though it probably looked worse than it really was.

Dixon charged through the door a moment later with Charlotte on his heels. "My lord, I heard the maids tittering, but I didn't expect you to look quite this bad."

He'd need a mirror to see what everyone was fretting about. He pulled the cloth away from his face as Dixon came forward. His valet cringed but didn't hesitate to reach toward Tristan's face.

He clasped his head with both hands and looked him in the eye. "It'll only hurt a moment," he said a second before cracking his nose back in place. A fountain of tears streamed down Tristan's face.

"Shit." He winced. His face throbbed, his head pounded, and his vision was still a bit blurry. His lady wife had disappeared. And he was sorry she had left so soon. The idea of a wife appealed to him a great deal—and that surprised him since he'd never really seen himself as the marrying sort before meeting Charlotte.

"I'll have the maids bring up some fresh linens. We'll need to get you out of your clothes, the blood is liable to stain them."

He was a trifle wobbly on his feet since his head throbbed in time with his heartbeat. "I can't believe I'm about to ask for your assistance in undressing me on my wedding night."

Dixon laughed low, and released the buttons on Tristan's jacket.

"I don't think my head has ever hurt as much as it does now."

"You can sleep it off, my lord."

"Right, then. I'm sure my new bride will appreciate me retiring early on our first night wedded."

"You aren't going to be standing much longer, my lord."

Black spots swam across his vision and his head bobbed back. "I think you're right. Can you have the house packed up, Dixon, I think we'll leave first thing in the morning for Birmingham."

"I will have all the preparations made."

"Just make sure I make it to the bed before I pass out." Because there was no question in his mind that he was about to fall over.

Dixon chuckled again.

"You must have charmed your way out of every fight in your school days," a soft voice said. He cracked his eye open—it felt quite swollen. Bea had come with a basin and linens, and not Charlotte as he'd hoped.

"I suppose it was too much to ask to have my wife tend to me."

"The maids are helping her change out of her wedding dress. She fretted over getting your blood all over it."

That news made him smile just before he fell back to the bed and knew no more.

"Do you think we should wake him?" Charlotte asked. Her sister-in-law was already attending her brother while she'd been changing into a borrowed dress.

"He's never been fond of the sight of blood. Not once in his childhood did Tristan resort to using his fists to fight his way out of trouble. Charm and wit have gotten him by just fine for the whole of his life." Bea shook her head. "He'll be so disappointed that he fainted at the sight of his own blood."

Charlotte placed her fingers over her mouth. She couldn't help the giggle that came from her lips. It was too funny.

"Don't tell him I told you. He'll have my head."

"I don't think he will, Lady Beatrice. He might faint at the sight that makes."

Bea laughed and wrung out the rag she'd used to clean the blood from her brother's face. He lay atop the bed they'd slept in last night, half-clothed.

Charlotte should be cleaning him, shouldn't she? Wasn't that a wife's duty? "I can help," she said, feeling the need to step in and assist.

Bea turned to her. "I don't mind. Besides, he'll need someone to help put on his dressing robe at the very least. I'll let you do that with Dixon."

As far as she knew Dixon was in the dressing room picking out his master's clothes for his wedding night. The thought of the rest of her wedding night had a blush heating her face.

Bea dabbed at Tristan's face, mindful of his swollen nose and eyes.

"We'll need to pack. Tristan won't want to be around Town looking as he does. You'll have enough speculation circulating and when he has two black eyes in the morning it will certainly make it worse. You'll have to borrow my clothes until we can arrange to purchase you a new wardrobe. There's a quaint village near the estate grounds where we can arrange a new wardrobe for you."

"You are too kind." She took the bowl from the bed and held it closer to her husband's face so Bea wouldn't have to trail blood across the bed. "I cannot believe my father struck him."

"I'm sure any father would have done the same."

Bea finished wiping the blood from Tristan's face and dropped the cloth in the bowl. Charlotte took the bowl over to the bathing room and dumped the bloodied water down the drain. There was a ewer full of water, so she rinsed out the bowl, refilled it, and went back into Tristan's—nay, it was their bedchamber now, not only his.

"I think I should take over. This is part of being his wife, especially if he has any more run-ins with my father."

"You don't have to." Bea gave her a sympathetic glance.

"I want to. I haven't really had the opportunity to talk to Tristan since we said our vows. So now is as good a time as any."

Though it wasn't a typical wedding night, it was still Charlotte's wedding night. Bea seemed to contemplate the request before standing from the bed and tilting her head in farewell.

"I'll leave you alone then. And I'll pack clothes for our trip north for us both."

"Thank you, Bea. I can't tell you how much I appreciate your kindness right now. Even though we started the day off on the wrong foot."

"My brother would not have married you if you were not a good match. He's an excellent judge of character."

Bea left the room, shutting the door softly behind her. Charlotte stood holding the cloth for a moment, staring at her unconscious *husband* on *their* bed. Would they be expected to share a bed tonight? Despite having participated actively in her ruin the previous evening, she felt suddenly shy at the thought of baring herself to this man a second time. Her emotions had been high last night, her situation dire . . .

She let out a laugh. "Yes, Charlotte, because you haven't created an even more dire situation for yourself by practically forcing Tristan into marriage."

She walked toward the bed and stared down at Tristan. She shook her head. She still couldn't believe that she was the Marchioness of Castleigh.

Her father had done quite a bit of damage to Tristan's handsome face. Since the valet had set it the swelling had receded, but his eyes were starting to turn a deep shade of purple. She grimaced as she reached out to wipe the last of the blood away from his cheek. His eyes cracked open and he stared back at her.

"Should I take that expression on your face as a sure sign that I look like I've been in a tavern brawl?"

She winced because yes, that's what she imagined he looked like. "It will heal in time," she reassured him.

"Maybe I should avoid a mirror for the rest of the night."

At least his good humor was still present and he wasn't angry with her about his face—at least not yet, but he still hadn't seen how awful it truly looked.

Charlotte leaned over to put the bloodied linen in the water and rinsed it out. When she was done, she folded the cloth and laid it over the edge of the bowl that she'd placed on the nightstand. She was at a loss for what to say so she picked up the bowl again and brought it into the bathing room.

"Thank you," he said.

"It wasn't I who cleaned you up. After Dixon put your

nose back in order, your sister washed away most of the blood. I had the maids help me into another dress."

"I don't think I told you that you looked lovely today in my mother's dress."

"I wanted to change so I didn't get any blood on it." She dumped the water.

"And it's appreciated." His voice was much closer than it was before.

She spun around and nearly dropped the bowl into the tub. She jumped at the sight of him so suddenly close to her.

"I didn't mean to startle you."

She looked at him a long moment, contemplating what needed to be said.

"We were friends only yesterday, why should everything have to change between us?"

He scratched at the rough underside of his jaw. "I imagine the next few weeks won't be easy. And I'm sorry we couldn't think of another way for you to avoid marriage to Warren. We might have been able to if things hadn't gotten out of hand last night."

"I brought this on myself."

"It takes two to make love, Char. We were both *very* active participants." He took the bowl from her and placed it on a bench. "We were both consenting and we both knew the consequences."

"I'm usually better at planning things in my life. I'm not one to act without a thought to the consequences. At least not under normal circumstances."

"I can imagine." He reached for her then, not to embrace her but to squeeze her arm at the elbow. "This change in both our lives will take time to get used to."

She didn't say anything, only nodded her agreement.

"I'm going to give you some time alone and take the guest room tonight. We'll decide on our sleeping arrangements when we arrive in Birmingham tomorrow."

She nodded again, happy that she would have privacy tonight. It would give her a chance to digest the events of the last twenty-four hours. So much had happened and changed that she really hadn't stopped for a moment to think what impact these events would have on her life and Tristan's. Goodness, she was a stepmother now. Never had she thought to utter such a word.

He turned away from her, proving his intent to give her the privacy he had promised. She reached out and took hold of his arm before he could leave her completely.

"Thank you. Not just for tonight, but for the sacrifice you made in marrying me."

He took her chin in the palm of his hand. "It wasn't a sacrifice; never think that again."

She gave him a smile and clasped his hand in return. "Good night, Tristan."

He gave her an elegant tip of his chin. "Good night, lady wife." And then he was gone.

Charlotte sat on the edge of the bathing tub. She felt out of place, which was probably normal since this wasn't technically her home, at least not yet and probably not for some time. She curled her hands around the lip of the tub and closed her eyes. She wanted to block everything unfamiliar for a moment and embrace what she knew, but there was nothing here that she knew. It was a shame that everything couldn't be normal when she opened her eyes.

The night was early, but she was surprisingly tired, so she went into the next room to ready herself for bed.

* * *

Tristan wandered down to his study, intent on wrapping up any unfinished business. He'd have to send a letter to Leo, telling him he hoped he fared well in his search for Miss Camden, for he could no longer be of service to him since he was headed to his Birmingham estate. Goddamn the mess he had put himself in. Yet he couldn't imagine any other outcome. Charlotte was his wife, and that felt more right than anything.

Chapter 16

If the archbishop received two visitors in one day, it shouldn't be a surprise that two households have packed up to retreat for the country when the start of the little season is around the corner. There were two notable absences when the House of Lords took their seats. Perhaps it was the stench and heat of the day that kept them away—but I hardly think that to be the case.
—*The Mayfair Chronicles,* August 1846

It was imprudent of him to assume he could escape Town without a friend paying him a visit. He'd received Hayden first thing this morning. Hayden preferred to deal with business in person, and wanted to go over the outcome after the reading of a new bill in Parliament that Tristan had missed—the tax levy on sugar imports that had partially started this whole charade regarding Charlotte.

"So the levy passed through both houses in Parliament?" Tristan asked.

"We always knew it would." Hayden crossed his ankle over his knee as he settled deeper into the wooden chair.

Tristan shook his head. "Bloody stupid bill."

"All it does is enable those with plantations run on the backs of slaves to profit further."

While Tristan didn't rely solely on the income of his sugar imports, the new tax would hurt other plantations in the West Indies.

A footman came into the room, and served Cook's famous coffee as they stared at each other across his desk. Tristan hadn't found sleep easily last night with his head throbbing and his face still hurting. The cold cloths resting over his eyes to bring down the bruising from yesterday's run-in had helped a great deal, but he still looked like he'd been beat to a bloody pulp.

"I can't believe you let him get a hit in," Hayden said.

"I assure you, had I ever thought he could pack the punch he delivered, I'd have moved quicker. But he had the right to do far worse."

"I'm surprised he didn't call you out. Pistols at dawn seems more like Ponsley's style."

And guns would be far messier than the blood from his broken nose. Thank God the old man hadn't called him out. Despite it being illegal, it was still done on occasion by the older generation and the pompous asses who treated it like the newest fad for the slightest insult.

"And leave his daughter a widow in the thick of a scandal?" Tristan took a sip of his coffee. He drank it black this morning, and it was truly heaven in a cup. "I was surprised he asked his daughter to leave with him."

"I'm not." Hayden placed his cup on the desk and undid the button on his jacket so he could sit more comfortably in the overlarge chair. "Had she gone home with him, he would have annulled your marriage and then had her married hastily off to that prig Warren."

"Might have." He was glad she'd chosen him instead. There had been a moment yesterday when he thought she might choose her father.

"Now that you've accomplished what Jez set out to do, what happens with the next lady to catch Warren's eye?" Hayden asked.

Tristan leaned back in his chair and put his feet up on his desk. He wished Warren's true nature could be exposed. Not that he'd explain that to Hayden. There were only two people in the world that knew of Warren's past.

"I am officially out of the game, my friend."

Even if Warren didn't deserve a decent marriage . . .

Ever.

"His misdeeds will eventually come out and hang to dry in the public eye," Hayden said.

Tristan raised his eyebrow and stared back at his friend. How far had Hayden dug into Warren's past? Did he know about Bea? It wasn't possible. God, not even Warren knew the truth about Rowan.

"Will they? I have my doubts. The man at times seems invincible and the Fallon fortune will ensure he's never turned away from a table."

Why could no one make out the horns hidden just beneath his scalp? It was true that Tristan had more of a reason to despise the man than most—but Warren had had torrid affairs and flings with actresses and dancers since his time with Bea, yet hardly a whisper was peeped about Town.

Hayden raised a skeptical brow. "So you are just going to leave Town and you'll pretend your marriage never happened overnight?"

"It will definitely have happened."

"You took even me by surprise," Hayden admitted.

Tristan grinned. He had wanted Charlotte all to himself

and now there was no refuting that she belonged wholly to him. Warren could never get his hands on her, nor would any other man.

"It's best to leave London. At least for a few weeks to let the worst of the scandal die down and be replaced by someone else's misfortune."

"Did you want to marry her? You don't sound or look like a man trapped by indiscretion."

Tristan drummed his fingers along the edge of the desk. It wouldn't hurt to tell Hayden how he and Charlotte had come to be on such friendly terms.

"Charlotte and I grew to be friends after meeting at the duchess's ball. We have been exchanging letters since then. And I have no regrets in the decision that had to be made."

"Ponsley is your father-in-law, though. Surely you took into consideration what that would mean in the long term."

Her father was well loved by the Tories in the House of Lords, the party being antiquated and in need of serious reform—they *did* after all support the plantations where slavery ran rampant. Charlotte's father was also a hypocrite and didn't believe the same standard applied to him as to everyone else.

"He matters not." Though that wasn't the complete truth. Eventually, his lovely wife would want to make amends with her father—hopefully when the old man grew used to the idea that Tristan was a permanent fixture in the apple of his eye's life.

Hayden voiced his thoughts exactly. "He'll matter to your wife eventually."

"When that time comes it will be dealt with."

And not a moment sooner. The longer he could put off coming to terms with Ponsley the better. The old man would not forgive him easily for stealing away his only daughter.

"I won't keep you long." Hayden put his empty coffee cup down and stood. "I only came to see which of the rumors was true."

Tristan grinned. "All of them, I'm afraid. You know I can't stay out of the rags for long."

Hayden only shook his head. "Will you make any rounds before leaving Town?"

"That depends on whether anyone else shows up in the same fashion you did."

"Unannounced and curious, you mean?"

"Yes, that's exactly what I mean. Though you must admit, the rumor mill has been very busy since yesterday."

"One needs only to sit in his club for a quarter of an hour to be privy to the latest gossip in Town." Hayden put his hat on. "Let me know when you plan on coming back to London. Proper introductions for the new marchioness must be made."

"It'll be a long time before exception is made for my wife," Tristan said.

"Not if I have a say."

Hayden was a good friend, and had an enormous amount of power with his position. It went without saying that Hayden would find someone to hold a ball in his wife's honor once Tristan gave the go-ahead. And it was a gesture that was greatly appreciated.

Hayden's expression turned somber. "Will you see Jez before you're off?"

"I hadn't thought to pay my respects to anyone. Happenstance brought you to my doorstep this morning, old friend."

Hayden nodded, not meeting Tristan's gaze. "She's

been out of sorts, for lack of a better term. I'm worried about her."

Tristan leaned his head back against the high back of his chair. "To be honest, I've been worried about her since the funeral. She's not been her usual self, even considering the changes in her life. Her husband's death should have been something to rejoice."

"I couldn't agree with you more. But that is obviously not the case."

"I'll stop by her house on my way out of Town. It's the least I can do."

"Are you sure you want to introduce your new wife in that fashion?"

Tristan rubbed at his forehead. "No. I'll go on my own."

"How do you plan to tell her of your success in keeping the young woman out of Warren's clutches?"

"I daresay there was very little affection between the two of them." He pinched the bridge of his nose, feeling the beginnings of a megrim. His head throbbed fiercely, but there was nothing to be done about it. Not with his bruised face—but how would he explain that to Jez? "I'll tell her the truth, of course."

Hayden rose from his chair. "I look forward to your return to London. I'd like to be properly introduced to the woman who finally caught up with you."

Tristan tried to return his friend's grin, but his face stiffened and he was forced to grimace instead. "You'll like her. She has the same fire Jez once had."

Hayden retrieved his walking cane. "I miss that fire and wonder if she'll ever be her old self again. Don't forget to call on her before you leave."

"I wouldn't dream of forgetting her. Though I'm liable

to scare her off with the condition I'm in. I'm hardly fit company with blackened eyes and a broken nose. Hardly fit to make any rounds around London."

"Somehow, I think Jez will find amusement in it."

Tristan stood, shaking his head. Hayden made a good point. Perhaps Jez would not let him live this down.

He walked his friend to the door before heading upstairs to see his wife—who had not come down for breakfast this morning. The maid he'd sent up said she'd woken only a short while ago and had asked for tea to be brought to the bedchamber. She'd be free to roam the house today, but he had a rule about family meals being taken together when everyone was in residence. And she'd adhere to that rule. She had promised to obey him in her wedding vows. He'd hold her to those words for important things— family being of utmost importance to him.

He knocked on the chamber door and waited a spell before opening it since he wasn't sure how she'd feel about him walking in unannounced. He couldn't leave her alone all day. Yesterday's business with her father was sure to have her glum, and he would not have a sorrowful bride.

He strode into the room intent on laying out the itinerary for the day.

Charlotte was in a state of undress. His sister had obviously loaned her a dressing robe, the one made from fine silk and trimmed with lace that he'd brought back from Paris a number of years ago. It was simple, elegant, and flattering on her figure. Her hair was down around her shoulders in a loose spill of curls, and a blue satin bandeau held it back from her forehead.

She was standing with her hands folded in front of her. Though it was obvious she'd been writing a letter because there was a tray with those accoutrements sitting on the end of the chaise and a smudge of ink between her fingers.

"You look well rested," he noted.

She ducked her head. "As do you."

"Hardly." He laughed.

"You look much better than you did yesterday, my lord."

"No need for formalities. I didn't mean to interrupt you. I just wanted to let you know our plans for the remainder of the day."

"Your sister has been to see me. She said we would leave after luncheon, and stop at a posting inn around the dinner hour."

Now what was he supposed to talk about with his new wife? "Very good, then. I didn't mean to interrupt your letter writing."

Charlotte blushed, as she turned to look at the evidence of her letter behind her. "I wanted to let Ariel know the truth. I feel terrible that I won't see her before we leave."

"What of when we are back in Town?"

"Will we come back for the little season?"

"I defer that decision to you." He paused, thinking he should clarify his reasoning for leaving. She must think carefully about when would be the right time for her to be presented as the Marchioness of Castleigh. "Though I do believe that the longer we are absent the better it will be for your position in society on our return."

She mulled on it a moment, clearly understanding what wasn't said. "We'll have to see how we manage in Birmingham."

"We travel in two carriages. We should have some time to ourselves."

She visibly swallowed. Did she think he'd seduce her in the carriage? Or did she just not want to be alone with him?

This was damnably awkward.

"I have an errand to run before we leave." She opened her mouth as though she were going to ask what, then closed it. "You can ask what my plans are, Charlotte. Don't make this uncomfortable between us. We were on such good terms before yesterday."

"My life has changed very drastically over the last day."

He folded his arms over his chest. "It can't be changed now."

"I don't want it to be changed. I just want everything to be like it was before . . ."

Before they'd lain together or before they'd wed? Taking a few more steps in her direction, he brushed his lips over her cheek. "Today is to be your only day of reprieve from this family. You must dine with us at all meals; you cannot hide in our bedchamber for the rest of your days. You need to be a part of this family."

Charlotte pulled away with a sharp glare in her eyes. "You don't mean to dictate my routine? High-handedness was one of the reasons I reviled Mr. Warren. He assumed I'd keep my head ducked low and follow his rules unchallenged. I will kowtow to no one."

Tristan narrowed his eyes. Was she really comparing him to that wretched man?

"I will not tell you how you should go about your day, but there are rules that must be adhered to in this house for the sake of the children." He held up his forefinger. "One of those rules is that I dine with them, even though they are too young to be at the main table. The second is that activities are carried out in as normal a manner as possible for the children, and they will never be treated as though they are different from any other wellborn child."

"You will set them up for failure if they think they have the same privileges other children of the peerage have."

"Ask me if I care, Char. My children have been my world for a long time, and I will not let anyone tell them they are not good enough."

Charlotte blushed a deep scarlet. He hadn't meant to chastise her, but life was complex where his children were concerned. They'd have a difficult-enough time when they were grown; it was only fair to let them enjoy life freely while they understood little of what hindrance their parentage would cause them when they were old enough to understand society's strictures.

"I'm sorry. I thought . . ."

"You thought wrong. Don't paint me with the same brush you use for Warren." His jaw tightened as he took a calming breath. What would he do if she despised his children? "Not all men are created equal."

"Please, I don't want to quarrel." Charlotte placed her hand on his arm. "This is difficult for me. Can't you understand that?"

"And is it any easier for me? I admit I have been thinking about marriage longer than you have, but that doesn't make this any less odd for me than it is for you. We'll both have to make adjustments."

"I just need time," she pleaded.

"Time for what?" Would she look for reasons not to make their marriage work because she wasn't sure how to deal with his children? "Do you want to mope about? To think through the consequences now that we are already married? I will say this one more time; you cannot hide in our bedchamber. You are now a part of this family and will participate in its activities."

She drew back from him. "What of the adjustment for your children? Are you going to force my company on them?"

"You'll find they are more forgiving and accepting than most grown men and women."

Charlotte's shoulders slumped as she released a long frustrated breath. "All I'm asking is that you give me the rest of the day to sort out my thoughts, Tristan."

He nodded. "No more than today." He put his fingers under her chin and gazed into her dark blue eyes. "We'll have to share our chambers again soon. I don't want anyone questioning the distance between us."

She opened her mouth to protest.

"If it makes you more comfortable, I can sleep on the sofa. Now, I'm off to get ready to see Jez. She's been hiding away at the Fallon residence these past few weeks, and I want to draw her out before she becomes a hermit."

"Is she a close *friend*?" She squeezed her fists in the material of her dress.

"Yes. And before you let jealousy spark any thicker in your tone, you should know she's like a sister to me. There's nothing I wouldn't do for her."

He left her standing in the middle of the room as he went into his dressing room. He pulled a bell to call his valet up. If he dressed quickly enough, he'd have at least half an hour with Jez and he'd be home in time for luncheon with Charlotte and his children.

Charlotte followed him, standing at the threshold of his private dressing room. He should move his things out of here and into the other master bedroom. She would need a place to hang her dresses, and it wouldn't be practical to share. He'd think on it when he returned home.

"I might not know you well yet, Tristan, but I do know you have one of the kindest hearts of any man I've ever known—and that includes my father."

Dixon interrupted his response. Not that he knew precisely what he intended to say to her compliment. Charlotte retreated back to the bedchamber. He heard her scribbling out the rest of the note he'd stopped her from writing. Their first conversation since yesterday hadn't turned out too badly.

Jez was in the garden. Why in bloody hell was she here? Tristan was positive she'd never pruned a rose in her life. The footman closed the door behind him and Jez stood up from the ground where she knelt and wiped the back of her gloved hand across her forehead, smearing dirt over her temples.

Her red hair was upswept, a wide purple bandeau tied around it, but strands of hair had escaped here and there. He wasn't sure he'd ever seen her so ill presented, not even when she was under the weather. Why hadn't he stopped by sooner? They attended a ball together a week ago, but apparently a lot could change in that time.

"What's gotten into you, love? I've never seen you holding a pair of gardening shears for as long as I've known you."

There was a pile of roses and other flowers in the center of her back garden. Some were in perfectly good condition, others gnarled, twisted, and dead.

"I am pulling out all the rot left in this house."

So she was still purging herself of whatever reminders

her husband had left behind. Tristan couldn't blame her in the least; she'd had a hard life with that man—a life he wouldn't wish on his worst enemy.

"Can I help you? Or, better yet, can I fetch your gardener?"

Jez stabbed the shears deep into the ground, and smacked off the dirt encrusted on her gloves on the coveralls she'd donned to protect her . . . trousers? Since when did Jez wear men's clothes? Too many firsts today were throwing him off balance.

"I think we should get you inside, have some lemonade brought to the drawing room." He motioned with his hands toward the door. Jez only looked at him with her face screwed up tight.

"If you're parched, lemonade can be served out here. Time is of the essence now, there's too much to be done. I can't stop yet."

Jez picked up a towel, poured out some water, and washed off her face. She invited him to sit on the lawn furniture.

"What's brought you by?"

"I wanted to tell you that I am leaving for the country— for an extended stay. I couldn't leave without a proper good-bye."

"Leaving?" she asked.

"In light of the events in my household that have unfolded these last few days, yes. It's quite necessary, you see."

She gave him a thorough look. "What events would drive *you* to the country in the middle of a Parliament session?"

Her question gave him pause. "You really don't know?"

"I've not left the house for . . . a few days."

Why had she hestitated in answering? How long had it been since she'd left the house? "Are you quite all right?" Since when did his friend not know the latest gossip?

"Believe it or not, I'm starting to feel more like my old self. I'm still not sure what I'll do when I lose this house." She looked around her with a frustrated sigh. "I asked Warren to put me up in the dowager house, but he refused. I suppose I shouldn't be surprised."

"When did you speak with him?"

"He stopped by a few days ago, asked how I fared. He's probably looking for signs of whether I'm increasing or not. He is anxious to take on the title."

"He'll be doing so without a wife," Tristan informed Jez.

That got Jez's attention, for she stared at him curiously, a slow grin forming on her lips. "The new Earl of Fallon won't have an heir in the belly of a new bride? I take it you've succeeded where the Ponsley chit is concerned."

"You might say that, but I wouldn't be so callous about the situation. I married her instead."

Jez wasn't often shocked, but the way her eyes widened and her mouth dropped open ever so slightly, he knew he'd done just that—shocked her.

"When precisely did you have time to wed?" she asked in a rush.

"Only yesterday." Tristan grinned, knowing full well that he'd have to explain himself in more detail. He hadn't told Jez of his developing relationship with Lady Charlotte since that first ball—truth was, he hadn't discussed it with anyone.

"Only yesterday? You make me feel as though I've been living under a rock."

"Hastily done, it was." There was a measure of pride with the revelation of his swift union.

"You didn't waste time with the banns, I see." Jez leaned back in the cushioned wicker chair. "It's probably for the best. Ronnie is going to need a mother if she's to be given the opportunity to debut."

"You know that is impossible."

"All I know is that nothing is truly impossible. You could find her an impoverished lord. They're always looking for an heiress. By the time she's grown up, there will be more than a few titles her fortune could save."

"She's ten. Let's not make haste with my daughter's future." Tristan tugged at his cravat, uncomfortable with the direction of their conversation. "Why don't you join us in Birmingham, Jez?"

"Thank you, but rusticating is simply not my style," she said drolly. "I have a house to clean my husband's stench from. I daresay his evil has seeped into the very foundation."

He hated to leave his friend—she was somehow . . . broken. After all the years of abuse she'd suffered, the endless excuses she'd had to make for the bruises on her arms, her neck, even her face on occasion, she'd always held her head high. Was she truly defeated now that she was free of the bonds of the horrid marriage she'd endured?

"It was worth asking. And if at any time you want to join me, I'd be more than happy to entertain you, introduce you to my wife. Ronnie would love to have you, too." He reached over and took Jez's hand; it was cool to the touch. "No worries if you can't spare the time. While you're here, though, you'll have to keep Leo in line. He's after that chaperone."

Jez gave him a wide smile. "Leo has gone back to the countryside only this morning. He, too, has news to share."

Had Leo taken Tristan's advice and obtained a special license for when he found his missing chaperone?

"So Miss Camden did stay here with you. I thought the rumor balderdash when I heard it."

Jez used her straw hat as a fan to cool her reddened cheeks and neck. "What a darling creature she is. She was here less than a week, and she kept me in high spirits with her tenacity and her verve for life."

Had Miss Camden kept Jez on her feet as she had Tristan and Leo all those weeks ago at the Carleton dinner party? He smiled, knowing full well she probably had.

"You find that amusing," she said.

"I do. I'm acquainted with her and find her charming beyond reason." Tristan stood, needing to be on his way. "You don't require an invitation if you feel the need for some solitude up north."

"Your offer is kind, but I have Hayden to keep in line while the rest of you are off *rusticating*." She stood from her chair and gave him a kiss on the cheek. "You seem happy with your decision. Congratulations on your marriage, Tristan."

"I am happy." He brushed a few loose strands of hair from Jez's brow. "You really look a mess. Let your gardener handle this and spend the afternoon outdoors under an elm with an ice in hand. Otherwise, I'll worry while I'm away."

"Hayden's dragging me about Town tonight for this and that."

Hopefully Hayden could keep Jez in higher spirits, enough to return her to her old self. She was a changed woman and hopefully for the better.

"I'll write while I'm away," he promised.

Jez ushered him out of the garden and toward the

house. "You'll be here all day if you don't leave now. I'm doing much better than I was at my husband's funeral. I promise you."

He shook his head. "I hope that to be true. But honestly, Jez, what kind of man would I be if I didn't worry after my friends, especially in their time of need?"

"My time of need has passed. And luckily, I have a long future without that blackguard husband of mine. We both know that he would have eventually been the death of me."

Tristan wasn't sure if she meant Fallon would have gone too far and killed her with his hands, or damaged her in some way psychologically. Thank God they'd never have to find out the answer to that question.

"My bride is probably wondering where I am."

"I'm not the one keeping you," she pointed out.

"Adieu, darling."

He left with a heavy heart. He would have to trust Hayden to look out for her. In fact, he'd send a note to his friend on his return home.

Chapter 17

Lady H—— has been banished to the countryside. I do not imagine her daughter's prospects to be very good with all the sordid business surrounding their family right now.

—The Mayfair Chronicles, August 1846

"Welcome to Hailey Court," Tristan said as he took Charlotte's hand to assist her from the carriage.

Charlotte stared up at the house before them. It was larger than anything she'd ever had the pleasure of being in and very nearly a castle. The road leading up to the grand house must have been three miles long. Unlike the Carletons' estate, there didn't look to be any houses nearby.

The Tudor-style house stretched up three stories in yellow stone, and there was a turret and walkway atop. On either side of the center building there were two-story structures that turned into a U shape where she could just make out the deep brown wood and masonry siding covered with climbing ivy.

At least thirty staff members were lined up outside on

the yellow-cobbled road. Tall wildflowers danced along the edge of the building and trimmed hedges were lined up neatly beneath each window like tin soldiers on watch.

Tristan stopped to speak to each of the maids, kitchen staff, footmen, and finally the butler and housekeeper. He introduced Charlotte to everyone along the way. He knew their work lives and something of their personal affairs. Her father had never cared about the staff in this way and Charlotte found the marquess's personable manner refreshing.

Finished with introductions, he held out his arm for her to take. "Shall I show you around the house, or would you prefer to rest until the supper hour?"

"I'd like a small tour." She slipped her arm through his as a footman opened the Gothic double doors into her new home.

The entrance hall was large, airy, and welcoming. The walls were paneled with dark walnut that stretched the length of the room and toward a vaulted ceiling painted the lightest of blues. A rich Persian rug was centered beneath a round wooden table over the gray shale floor. A massive set of closed double doors lay directly across from the front door of the entrance hall. There were Gothic-style doors to her right and left. One was open, revealing a long corridor that stretched the length of the house; she could make out inlaid doors at various intervals.

Tristan led her straight through to the closed door ahead of them. Pushing the door inward, he revealed a large sitting room that stretched two stories high with a wall of paned windows.

"This is the garden room."

"Aptly named," she said, staring outside at the extensive grounds. There was a round, tiered fountain on display in the middle of the back courtyard.

"There are a number of gardens here, mostly consisting of wildflowers. We have staff on hand to keep them fresh and full. There is a lake on the property. It's small, but surrounded with an old wood that makes for a serene boat ride, if you like the water."

"It's quite grand and beautiful."

"My family has lived here since the house was built in the fifteenth century."

She tore her gaze away from the paned windows and toward her husband. The history such a place must have. He showed her room after room, each as richly appointed as the last. All the ceilings were high, the colors used in the paints and wallpaper light and airy.

When they finished the main floor, she said, "We can tour the rest of the house tomorrow. I'm weary from the two-day trip here. And your children haven't spent a lot of time with you these past few days, so they are probably missing your company."

He stared at her with an odd expression. "Do you say this out of concern for my children, or so that we can avoid getting to know each other better for a while longer?"

"You think me conniving."

"I do not, but we do have the remainder of our lives together. We might as well learn to get along as husband and wife. I won't live a separate life from you, so we must come to a truce."

"Right now, I'm trying to come to terms not only with the change in my life, and with our marriage, but also with the fact that I am now a stepmother." Why was he so adamant on this issue? "I don't even know what role I play in this family, let alone in your children's lives."

"I hope you can accept my children in time." His response was short and clipped.

"I've angered you."

He bowed gallantly, but his gesture was not made in a gentlemanly manner. He was dismissing her. "No, I'm not angry, merely disappointed that you are not as accepting of our situation as I thought you would be." He turned from her to address the butler. "Hobbs, have one of the maids finish the tour with Lady Castleigh. All her things should be brought up to the master bedroom. Place mine in the chambers next to hers."

"I'll have Jamie and Marshall take care of your luggage right away, my lord." Charlotte thought those were two of the footmen she'd been introduced to on their arrival.

"Tristan." She didn't want him angry with her, and now they were taking separate rooms. Not that she would dare argue over the sound judgment concerning the bedroom arrangements. She needed to know him better before she shared a bed with him again. If that made her a hypocrite considering her actions before they were married, then so be it.

His light blue eyes pierced right through her and stopped her from saying more. "The trip has been trying for us both. I will spend the hours before dinner with my children."

"Of course. I'll see you later this evening."

"We keep country hours here, Charlotte."

"That's perfect since I've only just come back from Hertfordshire." There was a little bit of defiance in her voice. She would not slink away into the shadows after being chastised by her husband in front of the servants. She would have to speak with him later on that matter—she was too travel-worn to argue at present.

Tristan could barely fight back the grin at Charlotte's cheeky comment. He liked that she was high-spirited. It must be awkward to have married into a family with children who were not your own, but she had done just that, and she would have to come to terms with it.

Ronnie hadn't spoken a civil word to him since before the wedding. Rowan was beside himself with joy to have a mother figure in the house, which brought with it a whole new set of problems. It was high time Bea and he told Rowan the truth of his parentage; to delay much longer would only hurt the boy when he was grown. Resentments could be forgiven at a young age. Children were not malicious or vengeful. He must bring up the topic with his sister while they were here. Besides, Charlotte should know the truth, too. Surely they could keep it a family secret once the truth was revealed.

Tristan rubbed his eyes before turning on his heels and leaving his wife to brood on her own. It would take time to learn to live with each other. Now all he needed to do was find some vestige of patience—which he sorely lacked at the moment.

He came upon Bea and the children in the blue salon. All the curtains were pulled back from the paned windows that stretched two stories high and gave a splendid view of the gardens outside. Light-sage damask chairs and sofas were strewn about the room, some near the windows, and some next to the fireplace where portraits of family long gone hung in a place of prominence.

The room was aptly named for the cornflower-blue paneling that wrapped around the room and the sky-blue painted walls. He remembered sitting in here with his mother while she'd read stories to him and his sister on the sofa on rainy days.

Bea and the children didn't notice that he was standing in the doorway of the room, so he listened to them chatter.

"Ronnie, you can't be difficult about this."

"Why'd he marry her? I don't like her."

"Don't be mean, Ronnie. It'll be a change for us all." His sister had the patience of a saint when she talked to the children.

"That doesn't mean I have to like her," his daughter argued.

Frowning, he took a step back, not wanting them to see him. He wanted to better understand the origins of his daughter's displeasure, but she'd clam up the moment she saw him.

"I don't see why you don't like her. She's pretty." This came from Rowan.

"Being pretty doesn't make a person nice," Ronnie said.

"Life is full of change, dearest." Bea's voice was soothing and calm. "You will grow to like her in time."

"I don't want a mother."

"She doesn't have to be your mother. You can be friends if that makes it better," Bea suggested.

"I don't need any more friends." Something smashed against the floor.

"Ronnie." His sister's voice was much firmer now. "You're acting like a baby going on in this fashion. I'm tempted to bring you up to the nursery if you'll not behave and act like a proper young lady."

"Why can't I go to school, Aunt Bea?" Ronnie suddenly asked.

"You're not of age—"

Ronnie stamped her foot hard on the ground. "I am, too."

Tristan chose that moment to enter the salon. "What's all this I hear about wanting to attend school?"

"Becky—"

"And who is this Becky?" He tried to keep his spirits high while questioning her, but her dislike of Charlotte had disappointed him.

"One of girls in the village," Rowan answered.

"Ah, now I understand. Has she been by the house?"

"Yes, her father is the local magistrate. They came before summer."

"Papa," Ronnie said. "She's going to a girls' school in the fall. I want to go, too."

"Oh, angel, you're still a bit young yet."

At least he was thankful that his daughter was talking to him. Though he had a feeling if he didn't give her whatever she wanted, she'd return to disliking him again. It was not easy to strike a balance with his children. He wanted to give them everything he could, but he couldn't spoil them or he'd ruin them. They didn't know it yet, but their lives would be filled with the unfair cruelties of the world once they understood they were not what was considered *good association* since they were bastards.

"I'm not too young. Becky is only a year older than me. I can't see why you won't allow it. You don't want me around anymore now that you are married."

Tristan sat on the sofa next to his daughter. "That's simply not true."

"Then why did you marry?"

"You'll understand when you're older." He rubbed her back, trying to be comforting. He understood this was a difficult situation for his daughter.

"I don't like it when you tell me that. Is she my mother?" she asked earnestly.

Tristan looked to Bea and gave her a nod, indicating she should leave the room with Rowan. He couldn't brush that question under the carpet this time. It was time he explained her background.

Bea stood and held out her hand. "Come, Rowan, your father needs to sit with Ronnie for a bit."

Rowan picked up his wooden soldiers and followed Bea without arguing.

"Ronnie—" Tristan started.

"Why did you send them away?"

"Because I needed to have a conversation with you and you alone. If you want to be treated like a young lady, then I am offering to treat you exactly like one."

She only stared back at him with blue eyes identical to his.

"Lady Charlotte is not your mother, she is your step-mother. Do you understand the difference?"

His daughter nodded.

"Good. Your real mother is no longer living. She died of fever five years ago." He recalled the day he'd received a letter from Ronnie's aunt detailing what had happened. She'd had another child, but both mother and babe had died after a long labor. "I know that's not what you want to hear, but it's the truth and I'll not lie to you."

"Did she live with us before that?" Tears filled his daughter's eyes.

"She did not. We lived very separate lives. She was not able to marry me when she had you because she was already married to another."

"But you're not allowed to do that."

He nearly smiled at his daughter's innocence. He wouldn't dare, though—not when the conversation was so serious. "Your mother was a dear, dear friend of mine. I like to think we were in love with each other."

He rubbed his hand over her cheek and brushed away the stray tear with his thumb.

She stared at him for what felt like an eternity. Would she understand the significance of this truth? Would she judge him for it?

He didn't expect her to entirely understand what he'd revealed, but she would grasp that what he'd done so long ago had not been the right decision. He needed to say what the harsh reality of her world would bring.

"Do you understand what a bastard is?"

"Becky called me that. She said her mother told her I was one. I understand." A new stream of tears fell from his daughter's eyes. He'd give anything to stop them, but he couldn't lie about her past.

"You know, then, that it means you were born out of wedlock?"

She nodded. "Papa?" There was no other word than defeated for her beseeching tone. "What about Rowan?"

"Same, I'm afraid."

Though he'd not explain that Rowan was not her brother but her cousin. Ronnie rubbed her tears away with the back of her hand and sniffled loudly. Tristan dug in his pocket for a handkerchief and handed it over to his daughter. She took it, and gave him a long look before standing up and running off to her room—presumably. Tristan fell back on the sofa.

He had a wife that after one night of perfect passion had changed her mind about playing the part of marchioness, a daughter that in all likelihood hated him, and a sister that was not happy about the decision he'd made. Rowan was the only one on his side at the moment and that nearly made him burst out laughing.

The tall grandfather clock that stood in the corner of

the room chimed five times. Dinner would be served in an hour. He needed to find his way to his chambers and ready himself for the evening. Who knew what the conversation over dinner would bring? The last two nights in posting inns had been filled with awkward silence accompanied by the clink of silverware at odd intervals.

He stood and headed up to his chambers. Though he and Charlotte wouldn't share a room just yet, the one he was situated in had an adjoining door. Not that she'd give him admittance just yet. What could he do to persuade his wife to like him as she had before they'd married? Was this such a great shock that she really couldn't discuss her feelings with him? They'd written letters for over a month and now they could barely have a civil conversation without arguing.

Dixon was already in his room. "Shall I suggest the navy frock coat for this evening's dinner, my lord?"

"Too warm. I need something I can move in easily."

"What evening activities do you have planned?"

"After supper? Maybe a walk in the garden with the family. I'd like to see how the gardeners have fared since last I was here. They undertook the orangery in the springtime, didn't they?"

"Yes, my lord. According to what the maids have said, the building was reinstated to its former glory and citrus trees are being brought in. Would you prefer the tan short coat and black trousers, then?"

"Sounds delightful." Tristan turned his back to his valet, so he could be assisted in undressing. Cupboards were being slammed just beyond his adjoining chamber door and he could hear mumbling. "Is my wife readying for the evening, as well?"

"Yes, my lord. Marcia is assisting her." He remembered

the dark-haired girl. She'd been hired some five years ago; she would be of an age with Charlotte.

"They'll be a perfect match." Tristan dropped his arms when his jacket was off, and stepped toward the wall separating him from his temperamental wife. He couldn't stop himself from knocking on the adjoining door. Would she answer? Or would she choose to ignore him?

He didn't have long to wait, for she flung the door open not a minute later. Had she not known it would be him? Her look was curious, her hair down and wispy around her heart-shaped face. She was wearing a blush-pink dressing gown edged in fine lace. Her maid was also in the room, an ivory silk gown folded over her arm.

"Will you be so kind as to invite me in?"

She moved aside and motioned with her hand that he was free to enter. "Marcia, please give us a few moments to ourselves," Charlotte said.

The maid curtsied and left the room.

Tristan stepped in and closed the adjoining door behind him.

"Did you walk the grounds this afternoon?"

"No, I'll walk them in the morning."

"Are you settled in, then?"

"Tristan, why are you tiptoeing around me? I feel like a delicate flower you're afraid will wilt away with the slightest touch."

"I'm not worried about you. I just want to make sure you're happy."

She smiled. "You're a very thoughtful man."

With his palm over his chest, he raised his chin and looked haughty. "Don't let that get around to the masses; I wouldn't want to jeopardize my reputation."

That had Charlotte's smile cracking into a full grin. She rolled her eyes and whirled away from him to sit at the vanity. Picking up the silver brush, she parted a section of her hair and brushed it. He watched her, enjoying the practiced motion of her hands, and wished she were touching him instead. He walked over to the bed and sat on the edge of the mattress to better watch her.

"What happens after dinner, Tristan?"

Her hand stilled and her gaze caught his in the mirror.

"We can walk in the garden or retire to the sitting room, have a glass of wine or tea, and enjoy each other's company."

"I meant tonight, when it's time to retire for the evening."

He'd known that was what she'd meant, but he had no answer to that. Any number of things could happen. It would be her choice whether to accept him or deny him access to her bed—because that was the only place he wanted to be right now.

"It's the lady's choice."

"Where do you sleep?"

"Here," he said with a shrug. "The room adjacent. I'll not force you to spend time with me, Char. Not if you aren't ready to. I understand that we rushed into marriage without getting used to each other's company first. Ours is an atypical marriage."

"No more atypical than half the ton marriages." She continued brushing her hair.

Tristan got up from his perch and went to stand behind her. He moved the hair away from her back, pushed it over one shoulder, and leaned in close with his hands resting on the chair back. "We are atypical because we were forced to marry as any other indiscreet couple would. The one difference is that we came into this marriage as friends."

"Are we friends or something else?"

"Lovers?" he provided.

She nodded.

"You don't have to be one or the other, Char. We can be friends and lovers. I'd say the best marriages are a combination of the two." He caressed the side of her cheek with the back of his hand. His eyes did not waver from hers as they stared at each other in the mirror.

She did not reject his touch, but instead relaxed back into the chair. From his vantage point, he could see the swell of her breasts. He wanted to slide his hand down along her soft skin, feel her nipples pucker up between his fingers, but he settled for going as far as her neck. She'd have to invite him into her bed for him to take this further, no matter how desperate he was to have her again. He understood perfectly well that she was still sorting out her feelings about everything that had transpired these past few days.

"I should leave you to dress."

"Stay a while longer." She captured his hand, pressing it between her fingers and neck.

"Is this an invitation?"

She turned away from the mirror to look at him directly, her mouth slightly parted. A blush settled over her freckled cheeks. "I've been fearful that our night was only a dream, and that I was making a fantasy out of what we shared."

Tristan slid his hand through the tresses of her hair, cupping the back of her head. He gave her plenty of opportunity to stop him, but instead she allowed their mouths to meet gently. It started with nibbles of each other's lips, then a shy meeting of their tongues. He pulled her out of her chair, wanting to feel the soft curves of her body pressed against his harder body. His other hand tangled in her hair, while her hands squeezed high on his arms and her breasts heaved tightly against his chest.

As much as he wanted to toss her back on the bed and make sweet love to her again, he restrained himself and settled for locking their lips together and tangling his tongue with hers. He nibbled at her bottom lip, traced the seam with the tip of his tongue, and then sucked it back into his mouth. He could do this all day and night, but forced himself to pull away. They were expected for dinner, and Tristan didn't think Charlotte was asking for more than a kiss.

"We need to dress for dinner."

She nodded. Her eyes were still closed as she sucked her bottom lip into her mouth. It took everything in him not to gather her back in his arms and take possession of her mouth once again.

"What if I said no to tonight?" she asked quietly.

He enjoyed the fact that his wife was playing hard to get and making him prove his worth. "I defer to your judgment in this. Besides, we have many years of nights to come."

He walked back toward the door, needing to put some distance between them before he changed his mind about giving his wife the ultimate say—why hadn't he tried to convince her otherwise? He could be very persuasive.

Before going through the door, he turned to her. She looked delectable the way she stood with one fist clenching the material of her dressing robe below her neck. Her color was high and her hair wispy and in disarray around her face; he'd been the cause of that.

"Perhaps you should write me a letter." She looked at him oddly. "To break the awkwardness," he clarified. "We should write to each other again."

"I think I'll take you up on that offer." She released the tight hold on the material in her fist.

"Good. I look forward to the exchange of notes. I'll see you in half an hour," he said as he shut the door behind him.

Chapter 18

*All is too quiet in Town now. It's as though a great
storm is brewing before the little season is upon us.*
—*The Mayfair Chronicles*, August 1846

Dear Lord Marquess,
*I wanted to send you a note before dinner to
say simply . . . thank you for everything you've
done.*

Char

Dearest wife,
*I'm disappointed by how you still address me.
Have we not moved past the need for secrecy? We
are married after all. Dinner was a wonderful treat.
You should know that Bea caught you not once but
twice staring at me. She teased me about it not ten
minutes ago.*

Yours,
Tristan

Charlotte smiled and pressed the letter to her chest, closed her eyes, and leaned back against the pillows in her bed. She had read his note at least thirty times. Folding it, she put it on the side table and turned down the lamp.

Something had changed between them with his simple reassurance that they would take their time to get to know each other if that was what she wanted. He was courting her. She wondered if he realized he was doing what he hadn't done before they had married—or had they courted? How else to explain the letters exchanged between them?

He was a practiced charmer of ladies—no matter their age or standing. Her last thought before falling asleep was that he was all hers and hers alone.

Whispers woke her in the morning. She knew it was early because the sun was only starting to peek through the yellow sheer curtains on the tall windows, and creeping into her line of vision. She blinked a few times and focused on the room around her. The walls were papered an emerald green with a gold-leaf pattern. The room had a large seating area: two chairs and a chaise. There were also two black-lacquered desks with gold decoration painted on them.

She wondered briefly if Tristan's parents used to take a plate for breakfast and share their mornings together in here, writing their daily correspondences. The thought sent a thrill of excitement through her body. *She* would take breakfast in here with her husband. But first, she'd respond to the letter he had written last night.

Charlotte stretched out and yawned. Something cold and smooth slithered over and around her feet. She threw the sheets back and jumped from the bed with a scream that could have shattered glass. Her breath froze in her lungs as her scream died away. She stared at the bed, her heart in her throat, then jumped up on a chair and out of harm's way. Someone charged into the room, and she swore she heard children giggling but was too stunned to look for them. Her gaze was locked on the sheets.

Tristan lifted her down from the chair and put his arms around her shoulders in an embrace. "Are you all right?"

She couldn't tear her gaze away from the bed where there were four small muddy-brown snakes slithering and twisting together. She knew there were four because they all had yellow bands around their necks. She put her hand up to her mouth, feeling slightly woozy and ready to throw up. She'd been in bed with those . . . those slithery, disgusting things. They had crawled on her as she slept. Touched her bare skin as she thought about her husband. Her vision wavered.

"I feel ill," she croaked out in a dry, frightened voice. Her head was spinning and she had to close her eyes for a moment.

Tristan caught her around the waist just as her knees gave out. He scooped her into his arms and carried her over to the chaise. He kissed her lightly on the forehead then stood away from her.

She grabbed his arm. "Don't leave me here with those vile creatures over there."

"I'll remove them for you, Char. If it's too much to watch, turn away, but they'll be gone in a trice."

Her gaze was riveted to the bed. If she let them out of her sight would she ever be truly convinced that they were gone? She couldn't help but stare. She'd been in bed with snakes and hadn't known it.

Those little imps had done this. It was probably Ronnie

since she had made her dislike known these past few days. But she'd definitely heard both children laughing when she'd woken this morning.

Tristan opened the window on one side of the bed, and grabbed the snakes up by holding them at the base of the neck. She had to turn her gaze away when their bodies whipped around in protest at being handled. When the window was closed, she turned back to her husband. He had a sympathetic expression on his face.

"Should I expect snakes in my bed in the future?" she asked, her question coming out weak and frightened.

"Ronnie. Rowan." A shuffling of feet running down the hall could be heard when Tristan shouted for them. They were making their escape because they knew they'd erred.

"I'll have a conversation with the children," he said as he sat next to her on the chaise.

"No. They'll hate me more if you do."

"They don't dislike you, Char."

"Just the idea of you having a wife." Charlotte rested her head against Tristan's shoulder, needing to be comforted. He rubbed soothingly at her back. "Rowan might not dislike me, but your daughter certainly does. Ronnie probably thinks I'm here to steal you away."

"She's just growing used to the idea of having another person of importance in our house."

Why it surprised her that she was important to him she couldn't say. But she was glad to hear him say so and it made her feel marginally bolder.

"Now, if you're feeling better, you should get dressed and come down to breakfast."

She looked around the room, nervous about what else she might find. "I don't want to get dressed in here."

"Your maid can dress you in my room."

She lifted her head from his shoulder, suddenly feeling foolish. It was the first time she noticed that he was already dressed. Though he was wearing only shirtsleeves and his vest.

"What time do you wake up in the morning?"

He gave her a crooked smile. "I had no one to keep me up through the night. I was up a few hours ago."

"What time is it?"

"Eight."

"You wake up at five?"

He shrugged. "Sometimes. I like the quiet before the house is fully awake. It's peaceful."

She gave him a smile. "You're a surprising man. I cannot wait to know all your secrets, my lord marquess."

He returned her smile and stood up from the chaise. "Come, let's get you off to my chambers, and dressed before we find ourselves indisposed on the chaise for the rest of the morning."

She blushed. "You're a rascal for saying any such thing."

"Always, my lady." He deposited her in his room. "Dixon," he called.

His valet came out of a dressing room, holding out a jacket for Tristan to slip his arms into. "Please have Marcia come to my room to assist Lady Charlotte. And have the maids check the master bedroom for any more childish surprises."

Dixon bowed and said, "Straightaway, my lord."

Before Tristan could leave, Charlotte stopped him with a hand on his arm. "Thank you for coming to my rescue." And she didn't mean just today, she meant in offering marriage, too.

He stepped close to her and wrapped one arm around her, placing his hand over the small of her back. "I have no regrets, Char. I wasn't rushed into any of this, I've been sold on the idea of marriage for some time and had only to meet you to cement that decision."

Her breath caught in her lungs. What could she say to that? Instead of a witty, intelligent response, she said, "I'll see you at breakfast, my lord."

Planting a loud kiss on her mouth, Tristan turned and left the room just as her maid arrived.

"Good morning, my lady. What would you like to wear today?"

She picked a dress and Marcia helped coil her hair. And to her delight, they found a pot of powder to cover her dreadful freckles. The day was already looking brighter.

When she went down to the breakfast parlor it was already bustling with chatter. She fixed herself a plate at the sideboard and took an empty seat next to Bea. On their trip north, Charlotte had had very little time to interact and bond with the woman, aside from readying themselves together in the morning.

"Good morning, everybody. I do hope you all slept well in your own beds." She looked pointedly at the children as she said that.

Rowan giggled and Ronnie grinned as she stared down at her plate.

"What have I missed?" Bea asked.

"A morning prank," Tristan said.

Bea put her fork down and leaned back in her chair with a stern look on her face. "I knew you two were up to no good in your morning biology lesson. What precisely did you do? Put frogs in her bed? Mud in her shoes? You were gathering something and hushed about it when I inquired what you had found."

"It was Ronnie's idea," the youngest piped up.

"Rowan!" the girl admonished. "I'll never tell you another secret again."

"Now, now," Tristan said. "You know that's no way to treat a guest in this house."

"But that's just it, isn't it? She's not a guest." Ronnie was astute, and Charlotte could respect that. Though she probably thought Charlotte was there to usurp the children's place in their father's life. She wouldn't dare, of course. Tristan adored them, as did Bea. All Charlotte needed was some time to get used to the fact that she was their stepmother.

"If you'd let me finish," Tristan added, "I would have said that if you wouldn't treat a guest in such a manner, you would definitely not treat a member of the house the way you did this morning."

The butler knocked and entered the room. He carried a salver with a letter and an opener placed neatly over it.

"This arrived urgently, my lord."

Tristan sliced the opener through the flap, reading quickly over the contents of the page. Once finished, he tucked the parchment back into the envelope and gazed at her with a concerned expression on his face. She wanted desperately to ask what news he had, but not in front of everyone else in the room.

He placed his napkin on the table and stood. "If you'll all excuse me, I have important business to attend to." He offered no further explanation, only a nod and then he was gone.

She stared after him, then looked at Bea, hoping maybe she could provide answers to the questions filling Charlotte's mind. Who had sent the letter? Did Tristan normally leave the table without telling all present what the issue pertained to? Should she go after him? Offer assistance? Ask him if there was a problem? She didn't know the answer to any of these questions because she didn't know a lot about her husband, and she felt slightly ashamed and rather useless.

Bea didn't wait long to give her the answer she needed. "He'll call on you if he needs you. Really, the letter could be about any number of things."

Her last comment was not reassuring to Charlotte in the least.

"You're sure I shouldn't follow him?"

Bea nodded. "Trust me in this. Tristan will come up with a solution to any problem he has before he presents it to someone else. He hates to burden anyone with a problem he hasn't had a chance to think through first."

Charlotte filled her fork with eggs. "If he doesn't call on me soon, I'll have to search him out whether or not he's come up with a solution."

A bloody call for seconds.

Had Ponsley grown insane without his daughter's presence these past few days? No one dueled or called another person out in this modern day and age. It was dirty, and unsophisticated.

Tristan entered his study and slammed down the letter he'd received that demanded satisfaction for the abduction of his daughter and the ruin of Charlotte's good name.

Seconds!

Who in hell would second him? This was ludicrous. An antiquated notion that was completely and utterly absurd. Under most circumstances he'd first contact Leo, but his friend was indisposed and in a similar situation as Tristan at present. Instead, he'd have to call upon

Hayden—who would strongly disagree with the whole notion of one's honor being challenged in such a fashion. How could you have any honor left if you were dead?

He penned a note to Hayden and asked the butler to have his fastest rider put it directly into Hayden's hands once in London. His rider could make it there tonight, deliver the letter, wait for a response, and be back by tomorrow evening. With hopefully an answer Tristan wanted to read.

He leaned back in his chair to contemplate his next action, his fingers massaging his temples. He would not respond to Ponsley just yet. The bloody old prig had a pair of balls to rival a bull in full rut. The bloody bastard. Well, one thing was certain, he would not make a widow out of Charlotte.

A soft knock sounded at his study door.

"Enter," he called.

Charlotte stepped into the room, a look of worry making her brow heavy. "Is everything all right? You looked as though you have received . . . disagreeable news."

How much should he tell his wife? Would she beg him to call it off? He decided not to say anything, at least for the time being. He knew he couldn't keep it from her for long, though.

"Bad news has a way of working itself out," he said.

"Is there something I can help with?"

He smiled and shook his head. She was a sweet, kindhearted woman.

"Nothing for you to worry on. Tell me, what are your plans today, lady wife?"

"I promised to walk through the gardens with the children and your sister. She said it's a formidable hike to see all the gardens around the property."

"Perhaps I will join you."

Charlotte came farther into the room. "I'd like that." She shyly ducked her head. "That is to say . . . your company would be greatly appreciated."

Tristan stood from his seat and came around his desk to stand in front of his wife. "You flatter me. Perhaps I'll use the time to steal you away for a kiss. One taste was simply not enough this morning."

Her eyes widened as she assessed him. A smile slowly tilted up her lips as she released her breath.

"Only if you can catch me to accomplish such a feat." She came forward, gave him a rather chaste kiss on the lips, and practically ran out of the room with a laugh.

She was an invariable tease.

Tristan suddenly felt like a bull ready to charge. He loved the type of challenge his wife had just presented to him. Today, he'd enjoy the company of his family and wife. Tomorrow he'd have word from Hayden so there was no sense worrying about what was to come of the challenge just yet. He tucked the letter from Ponsley into a drawer before heading up to his room to ready for their walk. Once ready, he knocked on the adjoining bedchamber door.

"You can come in," his wife called.

He ate up the sight of her when he stepped inside. She was breathtaking in her off-white dress with embroidered sprigs of yellow and green flowers. She wore a silk moiré bonnet in ivory with a chocolate-brown ribbon tied at the side of her jaw.

He offered her his arm. "Shall we?"

She gave him a shy smile and slipped her arm through his.

"I am only taking your arm with great confidence that

you'll give me the full history of this house and the lands."

"Your wish is my command. And I am as proficient in the history of Hailey Court as my sister."

"Then we'll have a grand day."

"Indeed," he said, brushing his thumb over the side of her face as he led her out of their room, and down the stairs to the front anteroom.

"Let us join the morning air, then," Tristan said to his sister and children. Hobbs opened the doors to the ballroom—which had direct access to the gardens.

Ronnie and Rowan ran ahead of them when they saw a turtle climb into the hedges, a trail of muddied water left in its wake.

"Can we bring him down to the lake, Papa?" Rowan asked excitedly.

"Please do. We can't have Mr. Welch pruning the flowers only to find a turtle snapping at his fingers." Welch being their gardener.

Ronnie giggled at the very idea. Hopefully she was in better spirits today. Charlotte broke off from his company, but didn't escape far before he grabbed her hand and pulled her back to his side.

"Where precisely do you think you're wandering off to without me? I'm to be your tour guide, at your request."

She rolled her eyes.

"Is that a challenge?" he asked in jest.

"For such a charming man, you can be dreadfully barbaric at times."

"I'm still new to the idea that you belong to me."

Charlotte laughed at him. "I belong wholly to myself, Tristan. You cannot cage a canary indefinitely, for they lose their will to sing."

"Then I'll remind myself every now and again to open the cage door."

"You will leave it open, Lord Marquess. This is not a negotiation," she said, in good spirit.

"There will come a time when you will enjoy nothing more than being locked away with me—and with no one to interrupt us." He gave her a sly wink.

"But that day is not today. I have a new family I must learn all about."

"You've already won over Rowan."

"Have I truly? I'm probably the mother figure he's longed for, but not truly a mother. Not yet."

Tristan let her go so she could walk ahead and catch up to Ronnie, who straggled behind her brother to gather daisies from the garden. Charlotte pulled some, too, breaking them close to the root. He watched her talk to Ronnie with a kind smile and a friendly twinkle in her eyes.

It was in that moment he knew he'd made the right decision to marry her—regardless of the circumstances that brought them together—and that this was the right decision for his family. The children would grow to adore her just as he had since first meeting her.

"What has you grinning like a fool?" Bea asked quietly next to him.

"Life." He took his sister's arm and walked with her, silent for a spell as they took in the scenery and the fresh air. "Life has a funny way of unfolding sometimes."

"Will you be spouting poetry soon?"

"Don't tempt me, even if only to torture you for the rest of the afternoon."

His sister gave him a look that said *I dare you*. He only shook his head.

"She has put you in a good mood. You were always meant to have a wife, and I daresay . . . a much larger family."

"Do you think? I find the idea preposterous."

"You're too hard on yourself. You've been a wonderful father since the moment Ronnie came into your life."

"No less than you've been a mother to them both. Which reminds me that we need to discuss Rowan."

Bea's smile slipped. "This is not the time or the place for such a conversation."

"You're right, of course. But I want you to think about what we'll discuss." Namely, revealing the true parentage of Rowan to both the child and to Charlotte.

The world was a cruel place, but he'd not shelter his children from the truths that would shape their lives—he could try his damndest to protect them, but he couldn't shelter them all their lives.

"The letter you received earlier, it had you worried."

"I'm not free to discuss the details with you before having a conversation with my wife."

"How quickly your loyalties shift."

He looked askance at his sister. "My loyalties have never shifted, nor will they shift. My life for the past ten years has revolved around you and the children. You, sister, cannot turn your back on what you deem to be an outsider simply because she's known us for so short a time."

"I don't want to argue," Bea said.

"Then stop looking for reasons to be contrary." He left his sister on the old stone path and walked toward Charlotte and his children.

Charlotte smiled as he approached. "Your son was showing me how far the turtle's head stretches out.

Look—" She held out a daisy she'd plucked from the garden. She gave a squeal of delight and released the flower just as the turtle's mouth snapped onto the tasty morsel.

"Even slimy reptiles find you endearing," he said. She gave him a droll look. "Run up to the lake, children, you don't want the turtle's shell to dry out."

"Can't we keep him, Papa?" Ronnie asked, batting her long lashes.

"All creatures of the wild must stay in their ecosystem; it would upset the balance to remove him." When her mouth fell on a pout, he added, "They eat insects and slugs, would you mind feeding those to him?"

"I don't mind," Rowan piped in.

Tristan ruffled his son's hair. "And what if this turtle has a friend in the lake? Surely you want to send him off so his friend isn't alone too long." With that reasoning, the children looked at each other, and then ran toward the lake.

"Well argued, my lord." Charlotte stared after the children, her hands folded behind her back and the long-stemmed daisies stretching out on either side of her.

"Will we be making daisy laurels over luncheon?"

She looked at him with a wry grin. "Only if you help."

"I am a king at making laurels."

Charlotte laughed. "You are a surprising man."

"I'm glad you are amused by the many facets of my character."

Chapter 19

A certain duke has made his intentions clear to this writer. Does he not realize his devotion to a particular woman has been noticed?
                    —*The Mayfair Chronicles,* August 1846

Tristan had been told that a rider was coming up to the property five minutes ago, so he awaited the arrival of his friend in the drive.

"Hayden." Tristan greeted his friend warmly as he dismounted from his bay horse.

"It didn't make sense to respond to your letter, so I headed straight here." Hayden removed his riding gloves and handed them over to the footman standing close by. "Have you had any further word or instruction?"

Tristan shook his head. "Nothing. I've yet to respond to him. Surely we can come to another agreement."

Hayden patted Tristan's shoulder as he turned them both in the direction of the house. "Were you given a location in the letter?"

"He doesn't want me back in London. The rags will

find out before long that something is brewing. And the last thing we need is to be discovered."

"If there was another way, I would have found it. But your honor is at stake here. You cannot refuse the challenge."

"And I cannot hurt Charlotte's father." The thought of dueling had been eating him up on the inside since yesterday. He didn't like it one bit.

"Then don't hurt him. You can always aim wide and miss your target."

"And do you think he'll be so kind as to do the same?" Tristan ran his hand through his hair, frustrated by the whole situation.

"Perhaps if you give him a few days, he'll decide against widowing his daughter."

Tristan led Hayden into the library and they sat across from each other in deep leather chairs.

Hayden sat forward with his elbows on his knees. "Now that I'm here as your second, we could formulate a response to Ponsley's need for satisfaction."

Tristan couldn't calmly sit down and discuss this like it was a normal day-to-day affair. He went to the sideboard and poured out two drams of brandy.

"I'd prefer to forget the whole sordid business and walk away intact and alive."

"Why would you worry about walking away alive from anything?" Charlotte asked from the door. He hadn't heard her enter the library.

Hayden stood from the chair and bowed.

"I'm sorry," Charlotte said. "I didn't mean to interrupt, Your Grace." She held a book out toward Tristan, her gaze narrowed on him. "I came to return this and was about to make my presence known when I overheard the last part of your conversation."

"I was attending to business matters in here," Tristan said. He hated to be found out this way. He had planned on telling his wife about the duel, but not until the logistics had been thought through.

"Life and death business. You know what the funniest thing is when you marry?" There was no missing the anger that slowly rose in her voice.

Tristan was calm when he responded. "I know you'll enlighten us."

"It seems that I now have a vested interest in your livelihood." Her gaze snapped to his. "Now tell me what has happened."

Hayden cleared his throat, drawing Charlotte's attention his way. "If you'll excuse me, my lady. I'll pay my respects to Bea and the children while you two discuss this privately."

Charlotte didn't even bid the duke farewell. Instead, she crossed her arms over her midsection and glared at Tristan.

"Well?" she said, irritated.

He drank the shot of his liquor and poured a healthier dose—he'd need it to tell Charlotte the truth. "Your father has called me out."

"As in he wishes you to duel at dawn?" Charlotte's tone held laughter, as though she thought he jested.

"Quite."

Her mouth dropped open. "Do gentlemen still engage in such barbaric acts?"

"Some do. I am not generally the type to do so."

"And neither is my father," she said, unbelieving.

"I wish that were the case, but sadly, it is not." He came toward her, took the book from her loose fingers to toss it in the direction of the chairs, and handed her the glass of brandy. "Take a sip. It'll calm your nerves."

She drank it down greedily.

"I don't understand how this is happening," she said in disbelief.

"I wanted to show you the letter, but haven't had the opportunity to do so before now."

"A moment ago, it didn't sound like you had any intention of telling me about this."

"What would you have me do, Charlotte?" He drank in the sight of his wife worried about him. It was testament to how much she did care about him and about their marriage.

"I'm your wife, doesn't that mean I'm entitled to know whether there is a threat against you?"

"I was hoping your father would have a change in heart." He caressed the side of her face, needing desperately to cement the feel of her in his heart.

"Ignore his summons," she blurted out.

He sighed, wishing that were possible. "You know I can't."

"You won't hurt my father, will you?" she asked in a small voice.

He pulled her into his arms and tucked her head under his chin. "I wouldn't dream of it, even if the old blighter might deserve it for the way he's treated you—or have you forgotten?"

She shook her head. "He's my father. I love him, Tristan. What will you do?"

"I have to respond. I will choose the place, and I suppose he'll choose the weapon."

"Can't you simply respond with a no?"

He put Charlotte at arm's length. "As preferable as that is, no, I cannot. That's why Hayden is here. Your father would only hurt your name more if I ignored his challenge. He'd run both our names through the mud for cowardice and lack of honor."

"Oh, Tristan." Charlotte placed her hands on either side of his face and gave him a sad look. Tears filled her eyes. "I can't lose you when I've only just found you."

He smiled in an attempt to make light of the situation. "You have so little faith in me, wife."

"I don't. You won't hurt my father?"

"I promise I won't. But I doubt he'll return that favor."

"Who would put this idea in his head?"

"I can think of only one person," he said darkly.

"I must be there, Tristan." She reached for him, but he stepped away. "I can talk sense into my father."

"You will be far removed from everything." He caressed her cheek. "Hayden will be with me."

"He's not your wife." Her tone was stern.

He pulled her in close again, his arms around her hips, hands over her rear, their pelvises lined up as she fisted her hands in his sleeves. He pressed his forehead to hers. "It won't happen today, so we've time yet to get to know each other, fall in love, do all the things a man and a woman do when they are smitten with each other."

Her fists squeezed tighter as if he were a lifeline she refused to release. "I'll not let you change the topic so easily. I will continue to persuade you that this isn't the right choice."

"It might not be what you want to hear, but it has to be done."

"How will I know you fare well?" The worry was palpable in her tone.

"Just believe it and it'll be true." He kissed her lightly on the mouth. "I love the feel of you in my arms, Char."

"I love being in your arms. If that's taken away from us . . ."

His hold tightened around her "I'll not leave this life lightly. You and the children are everything to me."

He wanted to retire for the remainder of the day, lock him and his wife in their room, and do what had yet to be done since they had married. But Hayden had only just arrived so he would have to settle for a few stolen kisses.

"I have to make sure Hayden is settled in," he said as his lips brushed across hers again.

"He'll be with Bea now." Her voice was husky, desire overcoming her just as it was overpowering him. "I don't want you to go yet."

"You're right. Bea can handle him for the time being. I'm sure Rowan and Ronnie are showing him the mass of treasures they've gathered since arriving here."

"Their rocks?"

He nodded—Ronnie had convinced Rowan to collect any sort of sparkling granite rock since they'd been home in Birmingham. They had a box full of useless rocks, but it was an amusement that was easily entertained. "And that damn turtle I saw in the garden again this morning, chomping down on a strawberry left for him by one of the children."

Charlotte's eyes lit up with amusement. "I would bet my finest frock that it was Rowan."

He smiled down at his wife. The door wasn't locked, but it was unlikely that they would be disturbed, since the children would be occupied with Hayden, as would his sister.

"I think you're right on that count. You've taken a quick liking to them."

"It's hard not to when they are so much like their father."

"I'll take that as a compliment." He walked her backward, toward the sofa situated between the two leather chairs that faced the fireplace.

Their steps were slow, like they were dancing. One of his hands was on her waist, hers resting above his cravat and moving higher to his face. They stared into each other's eyes. Good Lord, he wanted her here and now.

It was like a dance of seduction. Charlotte wanted to repeat everything that had happened the night before their wedding. Right now. Was it the fact that his life was on the line that frightened her and made her seek comfort in an intimacy that could only be shared between a husband and wife?

Really, she couldn't believe she was contemplating this at only eleven in the morning. But the things he'd said and hinted at. Could it be that he more than liked her? Could it be that he was indeed falling in love with her?

The thought of anyone hurting her husband made her heart leap right into her throat. She couldn't lose him when she'd only just found him. Did that mean she'd fallen in love with him? Certainly it must when she couldn't bear thinking of a life without him.

"Tristan," she whispered as his mouth pecked gently at hers again.

"I want you, Char. God, don't say no." He kissed her again as her back hit the top edge of the sofa. "I need you."

The way he said that made her melt from the inside out. She didn't doubt his need for even a second because it matched hers.

"I need you, too." She kissed him more fiercely this

time, slipping her tongue between his lips. Her hands moved higher, one at his neck, the other tangled in his unruly hair.

His arms came tightly around her, and he nearly lifted her from the ground. Her skirts inched up, and the heated air around them touched her shins. She pushed his coat from his shoulders, but the material stopped at his elbows.

His mouth savaged hers, their teeth clanking together in their need to be closer. Her body felt like it was on fire. Her breasts felt heavy and ached for his touch, her stomach was full of butterflies flitting to and fro, and the most private part of her pulsed deep inside, needing him to stroke her desire to full life.

"I'm going to take you here," he said as his mouth tore away from hers.

His teeth nibbled a path over her jaw and neck, lighting a fire beneath her skin that could only be vanquished with his touch. He edged them around the sofa, and then they were both falling over the arm, the cushions softening the impact of their fall.

The press of his body atop hers sent a thrill of desire through her whole body. She had craved his touch. It was time they stopped dancing around each other and embraced what they both wanted.

"I want you inside me again, Tristan." She pulled at his cravat, wanting to feel the heat of his skin.

He leaned over her, his weight on his hands and braced on either side of her shoulders. "You're sure?" His expression was somber, serious.

In demonstration of how much she truly needed him, she lowered her hands to her thighs and pulled up her skirts.

"I've never been more sure."

His hands tangled in her hair, and his eyes closed as he pressed his forehead to hers. He lifted his lower body from hers as she hiked the intrusive material of her dress right up and over her hips. He groaned as his hardness met her center.

"We should go to our room," he said.

It was a sound suggestion, but not one she was willing to listen to.

She needed him now.

Needed to know that what they'd shared less than a week ago had really happened. To know that he needed her as much as she needed him even if it was only on the physical plane right now. No, there was a visceral connection that called them, each to the other. Intimacy was what would seal the bridge between their feelings and their desires.

They both needed this.

"I've wanted you every moment of every day," she admitted. She'd just not known how to tell him that.

An animalistic groan emerged from him as he pressed her legs wide and rocked himself right into her center. "Tell me again you need me now." His voice was hoarse.

"I do," she moaned, tossing her head back, sinking into the sensation of his body against hers. She loved the feeling of him atop her. "I need you, Tristan."

"I will give you whatever you wish for."

His promise was like sweet nectar on her tongue, and she licked at his chin before pulling at his lips and sucking his tongue into her mouth.

His hands moved between their bodies and released the buttons on his trousers. Then his fingers were slicking between the folds of her femininity. Tristan bit playfully at her earlobe, tonguing the earring fastened there, and then his teeth nibbled a sweet erotic path over her neck, and over the vein that pulsed sharply in tune with her heart.

Sweat beaded at her brow as Tristan ran his free hand over her bodice and cupped her breasts through the material separating them—tonight it would come off, and they could be skin to skin finally. His other hand was moving in a hot rhythmic fashion over the bud of pleasure between her legs. His movements didn't cease until her breathing grew ragged and hitched.

He chose that moment—the moment before she hit that final precipice of pleasure—to pull his hand away and bury himself deep between her thighs. He cupped her chin and kissed her as he filled her body over and over again. Their actions were hasty . . . desperate.

She clutched at him, wanting him to take her harder and faster, wanting it to never end as their breaths mingled and their bodies slapped and pounded together in crushing need.

"We should never have waited," he said on a deep, hard thrust that moved her an inch up the sofa. She clasped her thighs around his hips and rubbed her hands over his back, trying to pull his shirt from his trousers.

"Had I known it would be like this . . ."

"It can be more." He cupped one breast through her dress again. "It can be so much more," he hissed out before biting gently at the tip of her material-covered breast.

She arched up against him as he thrust deeper inside her, his pace more frantic now. Grasping his head in her hands, she held him close to her breast, never wanting him to stop what he was doing to her body. She swore he made it hum in perfect accord to his.

One of his hands moved lower and she felt the flick of his thumb against the bud of pleasure between her thighs.

He moved in time with his thrusts, and she felt her body tighten, building up to that final explosion of pleasure.

He covered her mouth with his when she hit that final apex. He kept kissing her, slowing the motion of his pelvis, as she rode out the exquisite feeling. When she grew cognizant of her surroundings, her gaze snapped to his. There was a hunger visible so deep in his blue eyes that her breath caught in her lungs.

"Put your hands above your head," he demanded.

She could do no more than comply. She'd do anything he asked of her right now.

He tangled his fingers through hers, holding her hands where he'd asked her to place them. His other hand moved to the small of her back and he tilted her pelvis in such a way that he sank deeper inside her, causing a moan to press past her lips and her eyes to slip closed again.

"Look at me," he said.

The small ring of crisp blue in his eyes ensnared hers. He grinned down at her as his hips thrust at a steady rhythm that brought her to the point of ecstasy once again. He met his end with a groan just as she exploded around him. Breathing heavily, he collapsed on top of her.

Charlotte tangled her fingers through his hair and closed her eyes. Getting up now would be an ordeal. She should have taken him up on his offer to retire to their bedchamber. But such a thing was not possible when they had a duke visiting them. She hadn't an ounce of energy to pull herself together and go back to her daily duties. Lounging about seemed ideal.

Tristan stirred above her and lifted his weight away—she missed him immediately. His grin was charming as he fixed her skirts, pulling them back down around her shins. He stood in front of her, tucking himself away and fixing his clothes as best he could. He looked rumpled and as though he'd just come out of a nap. She wondered if she looked much the same.

"Let's leave direction for Hayden and go to our room."

She sat up and smoothed her hair back with her hands. "You know we can't."

"It's our house; we can do precisely as we please."

She put out her hand for Tristan to take. He helped her to her feet, but dropped to his knees to fix the wrinkles in her skirts and rubbed his hands along her calves in the process.

He buried his face in her lap and pulled her tight against his body. She rested her hands on his strong shoulders for a moment, feeling the strength that held on to her.

She had to believe her father would not hurt him.

"That was but a taste of what it will be between us," he said.

She brushed her fingers through his hair, loving the silky feel of it. "We have the night to ourselves. It was reckless to do this in here. Anyone could have happened upon us."

"But they didn't." He made his way to his feet and soundly kissed her on the mouth.

"I would like to meet your friend, especially since you expect me to entrust your safekeeping to him." She searched his eyes, seeing his good humor lurking in wait, ready to tease her for the sudden recloaking of her modesty.

She realized then that the desperation to have him had stemmed from the worry that her father might actually cause him harm. For what reason did men play such foolish and dangerous games? If Tristan thought she wouldn't interfere with what her father planned, he had another think coming. And on the heels of the realization, she knew she had fallen in love with him.

Without a doubt, her heart would shatter if she lost him. She'd send a letter to her father and beg him to call off the duel. Certainly she had some say in this. She'd been the one to disobey her father's direct wishes, not Tristan. If anyone was to blame, it was she. But really, her father should ask himself where everything had gone wrong. Had he listened to her pleading against marrying Mr. Warren, none of this would have come to pass.

Tristan wasn't sure what exactly had brought on his reckless need to have his wife in the library, but he was glad for it. Perhaps that would break the last of the barriers erected between them. Perhaps now they would stop dancing around their feelings and learn more about each other.

"Shall we head out to the garden, then?" Tristan asked some time later. They'd had to go up to their room, not to extend their morning tryst but to straighten out their clothes properly. Charlotte had also had to take down her hair and repin it.

"Is my hair at least presentable?" Charlotte patted away a few stray pieces at the back of her head as she looked in the vanity mirror. Tristan stood behind her, barely containing his need to carry her over to their bed and demonstrate how to disarray it further.

"You look flushed and lovely." He took her hand, had her stand, and pulled her against his body so he could properly kiss her again.

"I cannot go out there looking *flushed*. What would your sister and friend think?"

"That our marriage is not only in name," he teased.

He led her out of their bedchamber and headed toward the back garden.

She shoved at him. "You're being impossible and far too smug."

He grasped her hips and brought her closer to him as they walked. "It's your fault. And you look perfectly fine. No one will be the wiser. Besides, Hayden expected a row between us, I'm sure, not a morning interlude."

"Then perhaps I should act cross," she suggested.

"Don't even think it. I like it when we are in perfect agreement."

"Yet I do not agree with you or my father dueling," she said. "I know better than anyone that my father has a steady aim."

"And you can rest assured that I do not—at least not while facing your father."

"He's quite angry." She worried her lower lip. "I wouldn't put it past him to aim true."

And how dare her father try to rip away everything that was perfect in her life. Tristan couldn't imagine a life without Charlotte . . . not now. Looking back to their earlier friendship, it surprised him that he'd waited so long to wed her; she'd always been the perfect woman for him. What he should have done was elope with her the very first time he'd mentioned marriage.

Hayden and Bea sat on an old stone bench as the children waded into a shallow part of the lake, fishing nets streaming through the water as they caught tadpoles and minnows.

"Hayden," Tristan called out to his friend as they approached. "I'd like for you to meet my marchioness, Lady Charlotte."

Hayden stood and bowed. "It's a pleasure to meet the

woman who finally caught up with this rapscallion." Hayden slapped Tristan on the back of his shoulder as he said this.

"It's a pleasure to finally make your acquaintance. I'm surprised we haven't been introduced before now." She took the duke's hand. "Will you walk with me a moment?" she asked him.

"Certainly," Hayden said. Tristan gave her a dark look. What was she about?

His wife went off on the arm of the duke, and Tristan raised his brows as he sat next to Bea, facing the lake and the children.

"Why is Hayden here?" his sister asked, suspicion filling her voice.

"Ponsley has requested a duel."

His sister laughed. "You cannot be serious."

"That's exactly what Charlotte said when I told her."

"Why would he wish to harm the man who married his daughter?"

"Maybe he still plans to marry her off to Warren."

"You and I both know that Warren won't have her now. He's always preferred a woman with a pristine reputation," Bea said sourly.

Tristan took her hand in his. "He doesn't deserve you, Bea. He never has."

"I wish I could believe that. Instead, I feel as though I've failed somehow in life."

"Never think that. The only person who failed is Warren." He put his arm around his sister's shoulders and pulled her against his side. She rested her head briefly on his shoulder. "Charlotte's father has always stood against me, Leo, and Hayden in Parliament matters. His actions don't surprise me in the least."

"Will you travel back to London?"

"No, I don't want the duel written about in the rags. And I don't want to hear any whispers about Town that there is some tension between the Castleigh and Ponsley households."

"So where will you do it then?"

"Here, most likely."

Bea placed her hand on his forearm. "You have to stop this—it's foolish to duel with someone. What of the children if you're hurt?"

"I won't be hurt. Surely Ponsley is only doing this to save face amongst his peers. He'll not widow his daughter." He had to believe that, because anything else . . . There could be no other outcome than for them both to walk away without injury.

"I hope you're right," Bea said.

So did he.

"Are you his second?" Charlotte asked the duke, unable to look at him or give away how much this was tearing her up on the inside.

"I am."

His hand was reassuring where it rested over her hand as they walked around the edge of the lake.

"I don't want anything to happen to him."

"I've already arranged for a physician I trust to be on hand." The duke seemed calm about the whole situation.

"That's not reassuring." Charlotte looked off into the distance, fighting back the tears that came with the weight of what her husband had told her.

The duke looked at her, drawing her gaze to his. His dark brown eyes were assessing but calm. "Do you love him?" he asked.

"I—" She closed her mouth. "Everything has happened so fast that my feelings are a jumbled mess."

"That sounds a lot like love to me," he said matter-of-factly. She didn't doubt it for a minute. But she'd not share her feelings with the duke before sharing them with her husband.

"You love someone, then?" she asked.

His chest puffed out a little. "I do. She'll not have me, but that doesn't change my devotion to her."

Charlotte suddenly felt sad for the duke. Who could this woman be to capture a man regarded so highly above everyone else? Truth be told, she couldn't believe they walked arm in arm, sharing a conversation. There was no one with more pull in society than the man currently on her arm.

"You know you could stop the duel," she pointed out.

"I've set a few things in motion to aid Tristan. But I cannot outright prevent a debt of honor from taking place."

She stopped walking and turned to face her husband's friend. His expression was kind, and when she looked at him, she knew he was a man of his word, one she could trust implicitly. "All that matters to me is that he's spared any harm."

"I will do my best to bring Tristan back home to you and to his children."

"That's all I ask." She took his hands in hers and squeezed them. "Thank you."

Chapter 20

*The infamous Marquess of C—— has taken up his
sword in defense of his new bride. You would be shocked
to know who stood on the opposite side. Though I hear
rapiers are passé and the preference these days is something much more deadly.*
                    —*The Mayfair Chronicles,* August 1846

Tristan had been forced to leave the house at four in the
morning—otherwise, he might have had to face not only
his sister, but his wife on where he was going so early in
the day. Both women knew the duel was to happen; they
just didn't know *when.* And he'd been right to keep that
information from them. He did not want his wife to watch
him being shot at by her father of all people.

A physician had come in tow with Ponsley and
Warren—though it was Tristan's understanding that
Hayden had requested this man's presence. He was tall
and older than Tristan by a good two decades. He had
graying hair and a chestnut beard clipped close to his face.
He wore a suit in brown herringbone twill and a tall bea-

ver hat. The doctor stood next to a folding table, his hands tucked behind his back as he awaited the *proceedings*.

A wooden case sat open on top of the wooden table, the black dueling pistols displayed neatly inside. Gilt decorated the nozzles, and the handles were carved wood—the set looked as old as Ponsley and hopefully was in good working order.

The cock had yet to crow this morning, and a thick fog blanketed the ground around them. It was a perfectly macabre setting for what was to transpire.

"The rules, gentlemen, are simple," Warren said. "The field of honor was given to you, Castleigh. Ponsley will choose his pistol first."

"Let's be sure there is no funny business," Hayden interjected. "The pistols came with you, so Castleigh has every right to choose his firearm first."

Warren looked at Ponsley with a droll expression. "Do you have a preference?"

"Let him have his pick." Ponsley crossed his arms over his midsection. "Castleigh, you've been a thorn in my side since your father died. It's about time I plucked the nuisance free."

Tristan was sick to death of the delay. He wanted this over with. He took the pistol closest to him and handed it to Hayden, who would load it for him.

"We've agreed on first blood, not death," Hayden reminded everyone present.

Though that wasn't a problem for Tristan in the least. It was a shame his wife wouldn't forgive him if he *accidentally* grazed Ponsley. Such was life.

He had avoided marriage like the plague, and then when he finally took the plunge, he wanted nothing more than to please his wife.

"Why are you even here, Warren?" Tristan asked. "You don't honestly expect me to believe you of all people have been wronged where Ponsley's daughter is concerned."

"My business is my own," Warren sneered and looked at Tristan as if he were the lowest form of life.

"If it's your own, then why do you stand here for his honor?" Tristan nearly spat the words at his foe.

"She was to be *my* wife."

"I've saved her a great deal of misery. I should be lauded and congratulated for my good sense in marrying her." Tristan fixed his gloves and nodded to Hayden when the pistol was loaded. "You don't deserve her."

Warren came forward like a barreling bull, rage clear in his eyes as he locked his gaze on Tristan. Hayden stepped forward, grabbing Warren's arm in a viselike grip. "Stand aside and mete this out as was predetermined."

Warren shook Hayden off and made his way back to Ponsley's side, all the while glaring at Tristan. They spoke too low for him to hear as Warren went about his task of loading Ponsley's weapon.

"This is a bloody joke," Tristan hissed at Hayden.

"Just see it to the end, and all will be fine."

He wished he was as sure as Hayden, but he wasn't. "Let's finish this, then. I can't stand the build-up."

Hayden turned to the challenger. "Are you ready?"

Ponsley nodded.

They put their backs together and stood in the center of the field, which was ten minutes on horseback to Hailey Court, should *he* need to be rushed there in the event Ponsley didn't spare him any injury.

Tristan closed his eyes and breathed in deep. "It's

pointless to have to come to this point," he said to his father-in-law.

"You're no more than a cur and you need to be put in your rightful place."

"If you want to hurl insults, you should remember that my rank and my title stretch a great deal farther back than yours. Wouldn't that make me the better man?"

"Don't flatter yourself, Castleigh."

"I'm not. But if I'm a cur, I'm not sure what that makes you. A mongrel, perhaps."

"Can you be so sure you aren't a mongrel, considering you mother's history?"

"That's a low blow, even for you."

"You should have left well enough alone. I had my daughter's future set out."

"To benefit you, no doubt." Tristan couldn't keep the scorn from his voice. "She was never a good fit for Warren—and should you ever want a story of male sluts, perhaps you should ask him why exactly I loathe him so much."

"That's rich coming from a man that cats about Town, creating bastards at every turn."

"Only two," he corrected the earl. Even though there was just his daughter, he was not willing to give away his sister's secrets to this man, or any man for that matter.

"Shut your mouth and take your paces," the old man spat out. "I'd like to be home before nightfall."

Tristan supposed he couldn't talk all day and delay what was inevitable. It was a great shame that Ponsley couldn't be sweet-talked out of the duel—perhaps if he survived this he could brush up on his skills of persuasion. With a heavy sigh, Tristan counted his twenty paces and turned to face Ponsley.

"First blood. So if he hits me, we're done here?" he called over to Hayden.

Hayden nodded. "But you will have to take aim and shoot at the same time."

"Bloody hell," Tristan cursed. He'd look like a bloody coward aiming wide.

Reluctantly, he brought up the pistol and closed one eye to measure the distance. It was tempting to miss Ponsley altogether and put a bullet through Mr. Warren, but then he'd just have to explain why the blighter was being cared for under his roof when they arrived back to the house, doctor and bleeding man in tow. Tristan suspected his sister wouldn't be too appreciative of the gesture either.

Ponsley did the same, his arm raised, and his hand steady as he rested his finger on the trigger. "Hayden, if I should perhaps be maimed beyond saving . . ."

"Don't even think it," Hayden said. "And I hear riders; this needs to be finished or we'll be discovered."

"We're on my land."

"The women?" Hayden asked.

"Shit." Now there was a stronger urgency to finish this—before anyone could interfere. "Are you ready, Ponsley?" Tristan called to his opponent.

"As ready as I'll ever be."

Both seconds moved out of the range of the pistols, standing on either side of the doctor. The hooves of horses running at full gait grew louder. Tristan pinched his eyes closed, gave a quick prayer to the Almighty Lord, and squeezed the trigger. Smoke came up from the pistol and filled his nostrils just as a bite of pain lanced his side.

He looked at Ponsley, whose pistol was still pointed toward Tristan, lowering marginally as four horses came into the clearing. Tristan brushed his hand over his side. It was slick to the touch.

Raising his hand to his line of vision, he saw the tell-tale signs that Ponsley's aim was indeed true and collapsed to his knees.

"Damn that bastard," he muttered, though he wasn't sure the words actually made it past his lips as the pistol fell from his limp hand.

It was the realization that Tristan wasn't lying next to her, keeping her warm, that had Charlotte jumping out of bed before the sun rose for the day. She'd gone straight to Bea's room, and they'd dressed quickly as the servants were ordered to ready horses. They had taken a footman and the stablehand around the property in search of her husband and the duke.

Bea said that there were four possible places on the thirty-acre property that would work as a dueling field— all far enough from the house that the children would be unlikely to hear pistols going off or the ring of steel. The first two places had been nothing but empty fields.

As they came upon a lea and saw the dueling field, the unmistakable reports of two pistols going off gave flight to the birds perched in the trees around them.

"No!" she shouted and pulled back on the horse's reins.

She was too late.

Her horse reared up and neighed. She held the reins tight and once the horse was on all fours again, she jumped off, twisting her ankle in mud as she hit the ground hard. But she didn't care. Tristan fell to his knees and she knew . . . she knew that a bullet had found him while her father stood with a smug expression of satisfaction on his face. She picked herself up from the mud with the help of one of the staff that accompanied them, all pain forgotten in her need to be by her husband's side.

She ran as fast as she could to Tristan. Tears streamed down her face, sobs wrenched from her throat. She thought she might have shouted something, but the only thing she could hear was her blood pounding and ringing in her ears as she ran. Faster, faster, but not fast enough.

It felt like an eternity before she reached Tristan's side, sliding on her knees in the muck and mud. She caught him around the waist as he fell to his side, a stupid smile tilting his mouth up when he saw her.

"Don't you dare do this to me," she cried, touching his face, ready to smack him if he so much as closed his eyes.

"Don't cry, Char." His voice was so calm and steady, but the color was quickly draining from his face. "Oh, love. I'm sorry." He reached for her face, running his knuckles along her cheek before his dead weight took them both down to the ground.

"Tristan!"

Taking his shoulders in both her hands, she shook him.

When he did not wake, she started pulling off his clothes; she had to find his injury.

"You cannot leave me when we've only just fallen in love. You told me no harm would come to you." She ripped his coat as she pulled it back over his shoulders, but it got stuck midway off.

She turned to Hayden, tears blurring her vision. "Help me!"

Bea was next to her in the mud. "Here, let me help." She pushed her brother to his side and pulled his frock coat the rest of the way off his arm. "Can you see where he's injured?"

His left arm was clean, but a dark stain of red bloomed

at his side. She wasn't sure where her strength came from, but she ripped his shirt open from the center down and spread the material wide. She moved slowly and carefully, feeling around where she thought he'd been shot.

A man she did not know knelt next to her with a white cloth in hand. He pressed it to Tristan's side, dabbing away enough blood to see the wound caused by the bullet her father had so callously put there. The man leaned over and prodded at the raw wound.

"It's no more than a grazing," the man said to her in a calm, even voice. "Bullet only skidded across his ribs."

Despite the good news, Charlotte was still worried, but her sobs were less of fear and more from her relief that her husband wasn't seriously injured. "Why isn't he awake?" she asked, still not fully convinced of the doctor's prognosis.

"Could be the shock," he said.

"The blood," Bea said, taking Charlotte by the shoulders, urging her to her feet, and moving her away from Tristan. "Let the doctor look him over. We'll be back at the house soon enough—you can fuss over him there."

She felt numb and let Bea pull her into a comforting hug before she turned and looked her sister-in-law in the eye.

"He is going to be fine," Bea said, her voice surprisingly steady. "The best thing we can do right now is get him home and comfortably situated before the children are awake. They need not know of the ill-conceived vagaries of men."

Charlotte nodded. Bea was right. "How long will it take to bring the carriage around?"

"Not more than fifteen minutes," Bea said. "I've already asked the stablehand to have it hitched and brought immediately."

Charlotte looked around her; light was finally stretching across the sky and dissipating the fog that lingered on the ground. The ground seemed so cold and lifeless where her husband lay. The doctor had a listening device stuck in his ear and pressed to Tristan's bared chest, right where his heart was.

Turning, she saw the duke discussing something with her father and Mr. Warren. They were responsible for this. She'd nearly been widowed . . . and for what reason? There was no reason good enough to take away the man she loved.

"Charlotte," Bea said, sternly drawing her attention away from the men she needed to have words with. "Have you heard a word I said?"

She shook her head and moved out of Bea's reach. "My father," she said.

Rage unlike anything she'd ever felt in all her life took hold of her. She fisted her hands at her sides and barreled toward her father and ex-fiancé.

"What did you think to accomplish?" Her voice was low and surprisingly calm.

"You don't belong on the field of a duel," Warren said carelessly, drawing all her focus on him.

Charlotte pointed her finger at him, stepping threateningly closer as she glared at him. "You will never tell me what to do. Your worth as a decent man was called into question with this little charade."

Mr. Warren only cocked his brow at her and crossed his arms over his chest. "I was not the one to call out your *husband*."

"She's right, Adrian," Bea hissed and came up to stand next to Charlotte. There was solidarity in numbers. "You have no honor so you could never have called a challenge to begin with. Yet here you stand as though to prove something."

"I ought to put you in your place, Beatrice." Warren flicked his eyes over Bea in a cold manner. "You've no right to talk to me as you are. There are things I know."

"And you've no right to step foot on my property without a proper invitation. You can hurl as many insults my way as you wish. They no longer have the leverage they once did, because I know you. I know the *real* you. And you'd do well to hide yourself away from the truth of your vile nature, lest the world find out what sort of man you really are. Leave," she demanded in so low a voice that even Charlotte was afraid of the wrath that might befall the man should he disobey her.

What was their past that they addressed each other familiarly? It was a question for another time, for the carriage came around and her focus returned to her husband. First, she needed to have a few words with her father.

"Your Grace," Charlotte said, reaching for the duke's arm. "Will you help my husband into the carriage?"

"Of course."

"And you, Father. Was all this," she waved her hand around the field, "for your honor? Have you been so wronged because of a decision I made?"

"You knew your place and your duty, daughter."

"I begged for an alternative to marrying him, even a delay in the nuptials. Perhaps your pride and your grand love for politics got in the way of seeing just how much Warren disregarded me and how miserable life with him would have been for me."

"You know nothing of how life works."

"Oh, but I do. I loved you unconditionally as a child, Father, as any doting daughter would. No longer. You have betrayed me—your only child. You wanted to take away the one thing I cherished most in my life. I don't think I can ever forgive you for this."

"You're acting like a child. You don't know what you're saying." His expression seemed wounded. Did he have regrets? She hoped he did.

"You would have married me to your dear friend Mr. Warren. I hope you have found your honor, because if not, it will be me on the other end of the field for your next duel." She pounded her fist against her heart. "And you taught me well as a child—my aim is always true."

"You speak blasphemy to your own flesh and blood."

With a heavy heart, she said, "My only loyalty now is to my husband and his family. You have brought this outcome onto yourself. Ask yourself, Father, what is honor without love?"

With that parting comment, she turned on her heel, grabbed up Bea's hand, and made her way to the carriage. Tristan's eyes were open, but he was not lucid.

"Wife," he whispered as his eyes slipped closed once more.

She took his hand and remained quiet for the rest of the trip home.

Charlotte sat on the edge of the bed, tucking and retucking the sheets around her husband's prone form. The doctor had given him something to keep him asleep while they cleaned out the wound at his side—which wasn't nearly as bad as she'd originally thought.

She hadn't been able to leave his side all morning. Bea

had gone down to amuse the children. They'd been told that their father had taken ill and that they must let him rest for the remainder of the day.

"What am I going to do with you?"

She sighed, and took his hand in hers. He squeezed it back. Her gaze flicked up to his open eyes. "How much damage? I thought I was a dead man when my hand came away soaked with blood."

She gave him a wry grin. "It's good that you are awake."

"How can I not be with a lovely angel watching over me?"

"Still charming even when injured, I see." Though she was pleased by his good spirits. Surely that meant he was on the mend.

"I'm sorry I couldn't give you the details."

"But you didn't escape me for long," she said sternly.

"Do you think we can start our life now without worry of reprisal from our hasty marriage?" he asked, pushing himself up into a sitting position, cringing while he did so. She helped him, leaning forward to grab more pillows and shoving them behind his back so he was better propped up.

"Come here." He motioned with his head toward the empty spot next to him. "Sit with me for a while."

She scooted up the bed and sat next to him, thigh-to-thigh, hip-to-hip. She rested her head on his shoulder and let out a deep breath. "I thought I'd lost you."

"I told you I would be fine."

"I think my father very much wanted you dead. I'm not sure why he didn't put the bullet right through you."

"Because he loves you, Char."

She snorted at that. "I'm not so sure about that at the moment."

"I know it. How could he not? Besides, I don't know a more lovable woman than you."

She raised her head and stared at him. "So did we fall in love before you dueled?"

He tangled his fingers with hers. "I'm sure it was long before that."

"But we didn't know each other. I'm not sure we know each other very well even after all that we've been through."

"Don't be so sure of that. I know what's in your heart."

"I don't know whether I should kiss you or smack you for daring to lose what we've built in our newfound marriage."

"I'll take a kiss any day."

She smiled and pressed her forehead to his. His eyes were closed, and he hissed in a pained breath as he turned to face her.

"I wouldn't want to hurt you, my Lord Marquess," she said tenderly.

"Pain is good every now and again. I'll take the pain if it means I get you all to myself in the middle of the afternoon."

"And what would Bea and the children think?"

"That I'm in love with my wife and that I have an insatiable need to spend every waking moment with her." His hands cupped either side of her face. "And how do you feel?"

"Don't you know?"

"I'd like to hear it from your lips before I claim them."

"I nearly died inside as I watched you fall to your knees, bleeding into the cold ground. I thought I was too late." The thought that he'd almost been taken from her brought a fresh deluge of tears.

"I promised you I would be all right."

Tristan gently kissed her tears away.

"Promise me you'll never scare me like that again? You've made me fall in love with you and to lose you . . ."

"I'll always be here for you, Char."

"Do you promise?"

"I promise."

"Good. Because now you can kiss me."

The touch of his mouth was soft and persuading. She sank into the feel of him, careful not to touch his injured side as he slipped his tongue into her mouth and nibbled at her lips.

"I love you, Charlotte. There was a moment on the field where my last thoughts were not only of the children but of you. I couldn't bear losing you when I'd just found you."

"And I love you," she said as she kissed him again.